Murderous Justice

Plucked from the dole queue by the surprise offer of a job, journalist Alan 'Archie' Archibold suddenly finds himself working for a television station reinvestigating a murder. Was the innocuous Terry Frampton really guilty of the grotesque killing for which he was convicted? Or has there been an appalling miscarriage of justice?

Working under the directions of his eccentric boss George Stredwick, Archie starts a search which leads him from the breathtaking heights of the Yorkshire moors to the low-life backstreets of the Midlands.

It is a search that throws up a confusing array of new suspects, and draws him into the passion and violence of their lives.

And it is a search that almost costs him his own life too.

STEVE HAYWOOD

Murderous Justice

THE CRIME CLUB
An Imprint of HarperCollins *Publishers*

First published in Great Britain in 1991
by The Crime Club, an imprint of
HarperCollins Publishers, 77–85 Fulham Palace Road,
Hammersmith, London W6 8JB

9 8 7 6 5 4 3 2 1

Steve Haywood asserts the moral right to be identified
as the author of this work.

A catalogue record for this book is
available from the British Library

ISBN 0 00 232365 6

Photoset in Linotron Baskerville by
Rowland Phototypesetting Ltd
Bury St Edmunds, Suffolk
Printed and bound in Great Britain by
HarperCollins Book Manufacturing, Glasgow

Plundering unashamedly from Malcolm Brad-
bury, I feel compelled to emphasize that
'Archie' Archibold does not exist, nor does
George Stredwick, or Rita Brassington, or
Maureen Paton, or any of the other sundry
characters who appear in this book.

Not only do they not exist, but as far as I
know, no one remotely like them exists either.

Nor is there a television station that broad-
casts a programme called *Verdict Unsafe*, and if
there was, it certainly wouldn't consider
broadcasting a programme about a man called
Bill Alexander who never worked for the
Water Board and certainly never got murdered nine years ago in Yorkshire.

The rest, as Malcolm says, is true.

Even down to Squiffy the cat, who sits here
at my feet as I write, and to whom I dedicate
this book.

CHAPTER 1

That morning Alan Archibold had woken to a wet Wearside Wednesday, a Wednesday not in substance promising to be much different from the previous Wednesday, or the Wednesday before that, or, indeed, the intervening days between. He pulled the duvet over his head, and curled himself into a warm ball.

June had been up for an hour already, clattering noisily around their small rented flat, Radio Four's *Today* programme on full volume. She was never her best in the mornings. She'd been worse since he'd been out of work and she'd been reluctantly cast in the role of breadwinner.

'For the last time, Archie, are you getting up?' she shouted.

From the resonance of her voice he could tell she was serious. It angered her to go to work with him still in bed. It angered him too, but with a different sort of anger, an anger at the futility of his life recently. There wasn't much to get up for, that's what it came down to.

He heard her again, in the room now, her voice more comforting. 'Come on, love, there's a letter downstairs. It looks interesting. You never know, it might be something promising.'

He received this news without enthusiasm. The trouble was that he'd heard it all before. She'd used the same trick six or seven months ago, and had got him out of bed in excited anticipation that maybe one of his countless, carefully constructed job applications might have brought a positive response. But there'd been nothing but disappointment, and her taunting threat that if he was going to develop into such a slob then she couldn't be blamed for doing what she could to halt his slide into total degeneracy.

The strategy wouldn't work now, though. June wasn't to know, for it had become part of a personal, secret life that he spoke very little about, but the truth was he hadn't written a job application since October; it just didn't seem worth it any more. Even when the applications he'd sent had led to interviews, there was always that single embarrassing topic from the past guaranteed to return to haunt him.

'There's just one other thing I think we need to discuss, Mr Archibold . . .'

(That was how they always introduced it. He knew what came next.)

'We notice you're unable to provide a reference from your previous employer. Is there any reason for that . . . ?'

No, no reason at all, he thought to himself bitterly, curling himself into the bed, except the bastards sacked me.

(And how can you ever explain how that sort of thing happens? What are you supposed to do, take a bold approach? Be direct?)

I was sacked because I discovered that the council's planning boss was being employed on the quiet by a local building firm which was doing council work . . .

What can you say after that, though? You wonder if the complacent sods believe you. And if they believe you, do they really care? Does anyone really care any more about this sort of petty provincial corruption?

In his bed Archie felt himself secure. Could anyone blame him for not wanting to get up? He used to be a journalist once, a good journalist, even though he did say it himself, but journalism was just a job, and without a job he felt without purpose. That was what embittered him most, more even than the injustice he felt at why he'd lost the job.

'But, Mr Archibold, you sold the story to another paper. Wasn't that an unethical course for a journalist to take?'

Unethical my arse, Archie thought, curling himself even deeper into his bed. What's ethics got to do with it? My own paper didn't want the story, they were too afraid of a legal action to use it. So I gave it to the *Observer*. OK, I got money for it, but I didn't do it for the money. And I didn't do it because I was fighting some crusade for a better bloody world either. I did it just to get the story published, that was all.

'Christ!' Archie suddenly sat up in bed. June, sitting at the dressing-table, was applying the final touches to her make-up. She looked over her shoulder, startled at this uncharacteristic burst of energy.

'What day is it, June? Oh my God! What time is it? It's my signing-on day. I should have been there half an hour ago . . .'

And so, on this most unpromising of wet Wearside Wednesday mornings, Alan Archibold, former journalist, threw on a pair of jeans and, without even bothering to comb his hair, dashed to the end of the road where he caught a bus to Bishop Auckland and the grim single-storey prefabricated hut which was a district office of the Department of Employment.

It was almost one o'clock before he arrived back. Because he'd arrived late for his appointment they'd kept him waiting around half the morning. Finally, once he'd got away, he discovered that in his haste to leave home he'd forgotten to ask June for money, so that with just 8p in his pocket he'd had to walk the four miles back to the flat, rain soaking through his clothes because he'd been in such a rush he hadn't taken a coat with him either.

He made himself a cup of tea when he got in, measuring out the last of yesterday's milk carefully, knowing that without money it would have to last him the whole day.

Then he noticed the letter.

The surprise he felt was as much because there *was* a letter at all, as because the franking mark announced it to be from a major television company. He turned it over in his hands a few times as if uncertain of its genuine existence. So June hadn't been lying. This time there really had been something in the post.

When he finally plucked up the courage to rip it open, it was disappointingly brief. Beneath the logo of the television company were just seven words, an indecipherable signature, and a telephone extension number.

The words read, *'Ring me. It'll be worth your while.'*

9

He got through to the extension at his first attempt. 'Excuse me, I don't know if you can help. I got a letter this morning, but I can't make out the signature . . .'

'Is that Archie Archibold?' asked a brusque voice on the other end of the line.

'Well, Alan Archibold, actually. Everyone calls me Archie . . .'

'Yes, I know. Where the hell have you been all morning? I was expecting you to ring before now. I've been waiting. Don't you want to work for me?'

Archie was rarely one to be lost for words, but at that moment he was dumbfounded. Was this someone's idea of a joke? Was this all a hoax? He looked again at the letter. If it was a hoax, then it was a wonderfully contrived one. The headed notepaper could conceivably have been faked, but there was surely no possibility of the franking mark on the envelope being a forgery?

'My name's George Stredwick,' the voice barked. 'I'm boss of a programme you may have heard of called *Verdict Unsafe*. When can you start work?'

Again Alan Archibold found himself speechless.

'A programme you may have heard of'—the tone of proud understatement in the voice was unmistakable. How could any journalist worth the name not have heard of *Verdict Unsafe*? The programme had been running intermittently for some twenty years and had become a byword for television investigative reporting. It re-examined court cases where it felt there had been a miscarriage of justice. Over the years it had won so many awards that now there was even an award for investigative television named after it.

Archie had even heard of Stredwick, an old newsman who'd worked for *Picture Post* in his youth and had since kicked around every Fleet Street paper and TV current affairs programme worth the name. The man was a towering personality in the world of television, but—unusually for such a public industry—he was virtually unknown outside it. But then he had a reputation for courting publicity about as much as he did popularity, which is to say he wasn't much interested in either. He was notorious for the way he treated his staff, as well. The meticulous quality of his research might be renowned, but it was rumoured that he had no sense of time and would expect people under him to work as he did: round the clock, weekends, high days and holidays, without concession to any private or social life. It was said he was thoughtless, self-absorbed, obsessive, manic, even mad. But the people who said these things of him, and even those who'd suffered at his hands, admitted too that he was a genius, a journalist of unrivalled intuition, accuracy and skill, a television producer of unique imagination and vision.

Again it crossed Archie's mind that this whole thing— the letter, the telephone call, the apparent offer of a job— could be a hoax. But he couldn't countenance that now; he couldn't afford to allow himself to even consider that possibility. If it was a hoax, then he had been hoaxed, and hoaxed cruelly. For the fact was that over endless months of enforced idleness during which it had sometimes seemed he'd never work again, he'd desperately craved a job, any job. That this job, of all jobs, was apparently being offered him, seemed not just a wildly improbable break, a chance of a lifetime, but on another level it was a lifeline, a chance to salvage something of a self-respect he'd felt eroding in the embittered indolence of which June justly accused him.

One other thing troubled Archie. 'If you're serious, you have to know that I can't offer you any references from my last employer.'

'I *am* serious. £26,000 a year serious,' said Stredwick. 'And I know about your last job. Do the same for me and you'll be worth every penny.'

And so, on that wet Wearside Wednesday, a Wednesday that had not in substance promised to be much different from any other Wednesday, Alan Archibold made a decision that changed his life.

'OK then,' he said, 'when do you want to interview me?'

Stredwick grunted exasperatedly. 'What the hell do I want to interview you for? I've found out everything I want to know about you already. I'll arrange for a contract to be

11

sent. And if you're not doing anything today you could get to Yorkshire, there's something there I'd like you to look into. Get there as soon as you can, I'll get a car delivered. And some petty cash. Five hundred should do to be getting on with. I'll show you how to fill in an expenses form sometime . . .'

And so, incredibly, preposterously, later that day Archie had found himself speeding across the windswept Yorkshire moors in a brand new, pure white Astra GT with less than 200 miles on the clock, a four-speaker stereo in the dashboard and his pockets bulging with wads of twenty-pound notes.

All he'd had from Stredwick was some general instruction to base himself in the Dales, near Rainsford—'some nice hotel in the country somewhere'. It was long past midnight when Archie had stumbled across this crumbling pile. It had been in darkness but for a small coach lamp left burning on an outside wall, highlighting the building's gothic bay windows and casting strange shadows over the wet, dark granite of which it seemed to be built.

Archie had very little idea of where he was except that an hour or so before he'd passed through Ilkley where the drizzling rain that had accompanied him from home suddenly blew into a squally storm, beating against his windscreen so hard he could scarcely see the road ahead. He had soon found himself lost and had driven across open, windlashed moorland and through what seemed a maze of narrow, stone-walled lanes, the eerie grey outline of flocks of huddled sheep the only sign of life.

The single light of the hotel on the bare ridge of a hill stood out like a beacon on the landscape, and Archie had driven towards it, hoping at least for a house where he might ask directions. It had been a surprise and a relief to discover the light was a hotel, but the place was locked up for the night and at first it seemed unlikely he'd be able to wake anyone.

In the event, the building burst into light before he could even knock. A face appeared, scrutinizing him from the recess of one of the windows. Soon someone was fiddling with the door. Whoever it was—the hotel manager surely?—spent what seemed an eternity unfastening catches and chains, and turning all manner of locks. The place seemed to be secured like a bank vault.

'Mr Archibold,' he said eventually, throwing open the heavy door. 'Come on in, it's a wild night out there. I was expecting you earlier.'

Archie stood frozen on the threshold.

Mr Archibold? How did this man know his name? And how could anyone be expecting him when he hadn't known where he was going to stay himself until now? Archie was not superstitious, but the manner of this welcome and the strangeness of this solitary building could easily have alarmed him.

'Come on in, come on in. You'll be soaked to the skin,' the manager went on, shepherding Archie into a large balustraded reception foyer, as vast and chilled as a baronial hall. 'I'm sorry your journey's taken you so long, but we'll soon have you comfortable. I've turned up the heating in your room and there's a bottle of Lagavulin on your bedside table.'

Once again Archie recoiled. Lagavulin? How could anyone have known his penchant for Lagavulin Islay malt? Was there something he wasn't understanding here? Was someone playing a game with him?

'Oh, and one other thing,' the manager went on. 'A package has arrived for you. From London, I believe. I was told to make sure you had it as soon as you arrived. If you'll take a seat for a moment, I'll fetch it for you—'

Archie cut in before he could leave. 'Has Mr Stredwick arranged all this?' he asked. 'Mr Stredwick—from the television company?' he added, seeing a puzzled look on the manager's face.

The manager shook his head. 'Mr Stredwick? I don't think I know a Mr Stredwick,' he said carefully. 'I knew you were coming weeks ago. All arranged and confirmed by letter, room paid for in advance. Now, if you'll excuse me, I'll get you that package. I was asked to make sure you had it tonight.'

13

And he marched off, leaving Archie alone to listen to the wind that had blown up outside with a fresh abrupt violence, screeching across the moors and licking at the hotel with its icy tongue.

CHAPTER 2

The next morning Archie began to examine the package he'd received. He ripped off its brown paper wrapping to discover half a dozen large case files bound together roughly with twine. They contained sheaves of police statements, witness depositions and court transcripts. He flicked through them unenthusiastically. The material cetainly wasn't the thing to inspire him this early on any morning, let alone this particular morning when he'd slept, it seemed, so briefly, disturbed by a thunderous dawn chorus which had woken him at the sort of unearthly hour that, at home, was often the sort of time he was thinking of turning in for the night.

With the files was a short note over Stredwick's indecipherable signature:

'*Take a few notes on this lot. Have a look round. I'll ring sometime.*'

The abrupt tone of the note added to his general irascibility and he threw it aside petulantly, took a shower and made his way to breakfast.

His room, like all the others in the Shornewan Hotel, led on to an open gallery overlooking the reception hall. Last night the building had seemed unsettling—threatening even. Today, bathed in the thin sunlight of a late March morning, it seemed merely incongruous: proudly Victorian, but the worst type of Victorian: ponderous, ornate and over-embellished. Archie leaned for a moment against the intricate wrought-iron banister of the gallery. Below him, the staircase fell away in an extravagant sweep of veined russet marble. Clearly, money had been no object when the place had been built, but despite the cash shovelled into it,

14

its only characteristic of any merit was its location. Here at least the architect had resisted any temptation to impose himself too heavily on the designs of God. The building afforded a spectacular view which it turned to account by a series of large, gothic-arched windows set into spacious bays the size of rooms.

On three sides, these windows looked out on to a vast expanse of moorland rising away in the distance. But it was on the fourth side that the view was most impressive, for beyond an outcrop of granite rock the land dropped away over an escarpment beneath which the whole county could be seen as if from an aeroplane.

'It's the highest point for miles. There used to be a beacon point near the rocks in Elizabethan times. Before that, there was supposed to have been a temple: dawn sacrifices, vestal virgins, that sort of thing.'

Archie swung round. Behind him was the hotel manager he'd met last night.

'Peter Webber,' he said, introducing himself. 'If you want breakfast, we'll be serving until eleven.'

Archie picked up a local paper from reception and made his way to the dining-room where York ham and scrambled eggs didn't do much for his mood. Nor did the newspaper. He'd only bought it for something to read, but apart from a front page story of a local girl who'd been raped on the moor, there was nothing resembling real news in it. Eventually, he went back to his room and tried unsuccessfully to get interested in Stredwick's files. But the more he read of them, the more the story they told bored him. The problem was that his discipline for work was rusty, his concentration jaded; there was too much temptation to stare out of his window across the moors.

From what he could make of it, there'd been a murder one January nine years before, the victim a twenty-eight-year-old man called Bill Alexander. Most of the witness statements seemed to concern another man called Terry Frampton, however. Archie leafed through the files, where he'd seen a series of trial transcripts. From these it became clear that Frampton had been tried for the murder. From other documents, it was clear too that he'd been convicted of it, and sentenced to life imprisonment.

Frampton and Alexander, it seemed, had once been friends. They'd worked as labourers with the West Riding Water Board and the week of the murder they'd been working together, as they usually did, operating as a team from a Water Board van.

In court it was claimed there'd been an argument between them over a woman, which had started that morning in a local café and culminated in Frampton smashing Alexander's skull to a pulp. The weapon had been one of those long, T-shaped water keys used by plumbers to control the flow of mains water. Afterwards, according to the prosecution, Frampton had attempted to hide the body and it hadn't come to light until a walker stumbled across it a week or so later.

Frampton was the obvious suspect. For a start he had been the last one to see Alexander alive. It hadn't taken the police long to tie up their case against him, and, as far as Archie could see, that case was about as open and shut as you could get. Hardly the ideal subject-matter for *Verdict Unsafe*. For the life of him, Archie couldn't see why Stredwick was so interested in it.

Archie was thinking about getting himself a sandwich for lunch when his eye was caught by the words 'Shornewan Hotel' in one of the statements he'd been reading. The statement had been made by the walker who had found the body, a man with the unlikely name of Jeremy Germaine de Groot.

'I was crossing the moors close to the Shornewan Hotel where I was staying. At first I thought it was a bundle of old rags someone had thrown away. Then I thought it might be a tramp . . .'

Well, at least Archie now knew why he'd finished up at this particular hotel, however it had happened. And as he read on, the story increasingly excited his curiosity.

The killing had been particularly bloody. In one of the files, Archie had come across an envelope of crime photographs. Most of them were routine shots of unidentified locations, some were police photographs of Frampton. But

16

in the middle of the pile, when he was least expecting it, he turned up two pictures of Alexander's corpse. The first was a long shot of the body, taken from perhaps thirty feet away and showing, as the improbable Jeremy Germaine de Groot had suggested, a sight that could have been a pile of rags or a tramp asleep near a wall. The only unusual element of the scene was the water key—the murder weapon— which lay casually discarded on the ground nearby.

As a photograph of a murder, the first picture was inconclusive; the second was less ambiguous, though. It was a close-up of Alexander's stoved head, the edge of his splintered skullbone clearly visible like a halo around his distorted features. Archie was horrified by the picture. It wasn't just that Alexander's head had been crushed like a boiled egg—that much he could have stomached. What he found totally hideous was the face—or what remained of it—for though it was unclear from the grainy black and white police print, it somehow seemed that the face had been flailed, ripped apart by a series of deep gouges like the clawmarks of a wild animal.

It was late afternoon before Archie thought about eating again. By that time the notebook in which he'd started idly doodling as he'd been reading, was almost filled with a frantic scrawl. The more he discovered about the case, the more it now engaged him. There was so much about it that seemed to be contradictory, so much that was said that seemed to be untrue or at the least unconvincing.

Take that woman that Alexander and Frampton were supposed to have been arguing about. What was her name? Archie shuffled through the files. Rita Brassington, of course. Her name conjured up images of a brazen blonde with glossy red lipstick. Now, what was it she'd said during her evidence?

'*No, sir, it is not my practice to be walking out with more than one man at a time . . .*'

As a denial that she was involved with the two men, it sounded so stilted, so . . . so false. Even allowing for a certain nervousness at the court formalities, Archie couldn't for the life of him believe that this was the sort of language

17

anyone telling the truth would ever use. Besides, what was that other comment he'd found in one of the other files he'd read? Again he searched through the papers until he'd found a statement made by one of Rita Brassington's friends, a woman called Maureen Paton who described one evening when she had been in a pub and Alexander had walked in.

'I noticed him particularly because I knew he was seeing Rita. I thought he was good-looking. It is accurate to say that I found him an attractive man . . .'

As Archie ran his eye down the statement a picture sprang vividly to mind, but it wasn't the picture of a woman in a pub. It was of a woman and a policeman sitting in some grim, ill-lit room in a police station somewhere. Maureen Paton was chain-smoking, she was nervous, sullen and intimidated. Or perhaps she was garrulous, so flattered to be the centre of attention that she was talking excitedly, saying anything that happened to come into her head, casually agreeing to every proposition put to her. As she talked, in his mind's eye Archie could see the policeman interviewing her, and picture him encouraging her from time to time, coaxing her to say more than she wanted while he struggled in a desperate shortened longhand to capture on paper at least the general drift of what she was saying.

No, this might be Maureen Paton's statement, but it was no more Maureen Paton talking than it had been Rita Brassington's true voice in court.

Archie read on, still searching for that elusive detail of the statement which had been playing on his mind.

Eventually he found what he was looking for: it was towards the end of the statement. Maureen Paton had played her meeting with the murdered man for its last ounce of drama. Now she was being questioned more generally about her relationship with Rita, and the constable interviewing her had meticulously recorded everything he was able to in the stilted style that included as many of his questions as Maureen's answers:

'We were friends. We met each other first through work and began

to socialize regularly. Rita used to confide her problems to me. At that time she had a lot of problems with boyfriends. I cannot remember the details, but she had two or three men in tow. There used to be a lot of rows . . .'

So she *was* going with more than one man at once, thought Archie with a sense of triumph. So why had she lied in court? And why hadn't she been challenged? Did the defence barrister just miss the point? Did everyone miss it?

No, there was too much that didn't add up in the case, too much that was confused about it. At the moment he couldn't put his finger on what he felt was wrong, but that there *was* something wrong he was certain. Just reading the case had left him with an uncomfortable sense of disquiet that couldn't be explained away by a few contradictions in the statements of witnesses, even ones as obvious as he'd found. The trial, he somehow felt, had only served to confuse the truth, not clarify it.

It was after two in the morning when, exhausted, Archie swept the files from his bed and turned in for the night. He was asleep when the telephone on his bedside table woke him.

It was Stredwick. No introductions. No formalities.

'Have you worked out yet why we can be so certain that the truth of this murder hasn't come out fully?'

'I'm sorry,' Archie mumbled, though God knows why he should have been the one apologizing. 'I was asleep . . . I'm still a bit dozy . . .'

'Yes, but have you worked it out?' Stredwick barked.

Archie reached over beyond the telephone to the Lagavulin bottle and poured himself a slug. Was this man deranged? Did he expect his people ever to sleep?

'I thought some of the discrepancies in the witness statements were interesting . . .' Archie began to explain about Rita Brassington and Maureen Paton, but Stredwick cut him off sharply.

'Is that what you've been wasting your time on today? Good God, son, forget all that. You ought to have been looking at the forensic evidence. Haven't you sussed yet why it's likely the truth of this murder hasn't come out so far? Heavens, son, its literally staring you in the face. Haven't you got eyes in your head?

'Look,' Stredwick went on, his voice only slightly less frenetic. 'You're new to this game and there's a lot you've got to learn. Forget all your university degrees and all your bloody newspaper training. Look at this case through the eyes of ordinary people. What's odd about this death? What's strange about it? What's horrific and appalling yet fascinating too?'

Archie thought of the close-up photograph of Alexander. The stoved head. The flailed face. He took a gulp of his whisky. 'The manner of the death,' he said eventually.

'Right,' said Stredwick. 'The manner of the death. Look at the post-mortem report. He was hit just once with the stop tap, it killed him immediately, he could hardly have known what hit him. But afterwards—after he was dead—someone set upon him with their bare hands . . .'

'Like an animal,' Archie interjected.

'Exactly. Like an animal, ripping and tearing at the flesh of his face.'

Stredwick paused for a moment. 'You're new to this game, son,' he said again, 'you've a lot to learn. But take my word for it, there are a hundred reasons why someone might kill—believe me, there's no shortage of motives for murder. But there's only one reason why, after someone has killed, they'd fall on their victim clawing at them with their bare hands.'

'Hate,' Archie said softly. 'You'd have to hate someone to do that.'

'You're learning,' said Stredwick. 'But get off to sleep now. It's late. You've a busy day tomorrow. Look at those police pictures again—the ones of Frampton. Think about what I've been saying.'

The conversation was over as abruptly as it had started.

Left holding the receiver on a dead line, Archie felt at first bewildered and then consumed with rage. Perhaps it was this feeling Stredwick was watching him, and somehow directing him. What the hell did he mean ringing so late at night and third-degreeing him like some schoolkid caught smoking behind the bike shed? What did he mean tossing questions at him like some end-of-term exam? Why couldn't the man explain himself like any normal human being? Why did he have to be so secretive and conspiratorial?

Archie dragged himself out of bed and poured another whisky. Sod the man, he was impossible. What could the police pictures of Frampton tell him anyway? Archie angrily searched the floor where he'd thrown the files. Where were those bloody pictures?

He found them almost immediately, and still kneeling on the floor, stared at them for a long, long time.

The pictures had obviously been taken in a police station. In one, Archie could even make out the corner of a poster, stuck on the wall behind. Frampton was staring directly into the camera. He was unshaven and his face was sullen. He looked frightened too, trepidation visible in his sleepless eyes. It wasn't surprising. By the time the photographs had been taken, he'd probably been interrogated for hours. Probably threatened too, no doubt, if not actually slapped around a bit. In the photograph he sat as stiff as a board, his back straight, his hands resting before him like a pianist's resting on a keyboard.

And like a pianist's, his fingers were long and thin, delicate and suprisingly graceful except that . . .

'Oh, shit!' Archie said eventually. 'Just like he said. Staring me in the face.'

Frampton bit his nails.

CHAPTER 3

Archie was sitting over another mound of York ham in the hotel breakfast-room, cursing himself for his impetuous stupidity. Half an hour before—without giving himself any chance to consider the implications of what he was doing, he had barged into Webber's office, determined to clear up the mystery of his arrival once and for all.

'I don't want to seem impertinent, but would you mind letting me have a look at the letter you got reserving my room?'

The hotel manager had been caught unawares. He'd been sitting at his desk in his pyjamas and a worn velvet dressing-gown, working on an ancient manual calculator. And he was clearly in no better temper in the mornings than Archie.

'I'm sorry,' he'd said stiffly. 'I didn't hear you knock.'

His tone of voice alone had been enough to confound Archie, who had stood totally nonplussed for a moment or two.

'I'm sorry . . . it's something that's been worrying me. The thing is, I didn't know myself that . . . oh, it doesn't matter, but do you mind if I see the letter?'

Webber had walked over to a battered filing cabinet and pulled open a drawer. 'You'll excuse me for not being dressed more formally,' he said. 'I don't officially begin work until after the cleaners get in.'

Archie had read the letter impatiently. 'There's nothing to say where it came from. Didn't you think that odd?'

'The instructions were clear enough, the room was paid for . . .'

'A cheque?'

'Cash. Well, a postal order.'

Archie handed back the letter. 'The thing is—' he'd begun. But then he checked himself, realizing that any explanation would involve disclosing the purpose of his stay. If the hotel was central to the investigation of Alexander's murder, then that could be unwise.

'The thing is—' Archie started again. 'The thing is that—I wasn't given clear instructions to come to *this* hotel, just to—to go to a hotel in the country near Rainsford. It was just luck I arrived here at all. It was very inefficient—of my secretary, I mean. But I didn't want to say anything to her until—until I'd seen what she'd sent you.'

Webber had sat down again in front of his calculator. 'Yes,' he said after a while. 'You'd certainly have arrived here earlier if you'd been given more specific directions.

But assuming you wanted to stay in the country, you'd have arrived here sooner or later. This is the only hotel for miles around.'

Archie had gone to breakfast cursing himself for his own stupidity and cursing Stredwick for having devised such a pathetic adolescent game for—for what?—as some sort of test? Stredwick obviously knew the Shornewan; he must have known that it was the only hotel Archie could have stumbled across. Was Stredwick so conceited he thought he could mystify anyone for long by such a simple trick? Archie felt ridiculous for not having seen the obvious sooner.

Then he remembered the Lagavulin.

And he remembered too what Webber had said on his first night, about how the reservation for the room had been arranged 'weeks ago'. How the hell had Stredwick known weeks before that he was going to take the job? And how had he arranged the whisky? He must have telephoned, it was the only thing that could explain it; Webber must have been lying when he'd denied knowing Stredwick. It was the only explanation. Archie was damned if he was going to let Stredwick get the better of him on this one. All the same, it did confuse him.

The question of Frampton's nails confused him too. As soon as he'd woken that morning Archie had checked through the files and discovered that during the trial Frampton's barrister had brought a local forensic expert— a Dr Alec Remus—to court to testify that the lacerations on Alexander's face had been caused by fingernails. The prosecution hadn't seemed to challenge the testimony. So why had the jury apparently overlooked the point? Was it just that all the other evidence against Frampton added up to such a strong case against him?

Stredwick had urged him to look at the forensic evidence, and so after breakfast Archie felt at liberty to ring Remus's office in Rainsford and arrange an appointment for later in the day.

'Yes, the case is one I remember very well,' Remus said, pushing back his chair and taking a file of notes from his desk drawer. He was an old man, very old, and his movements, though slow, were meticulously precise. 'It sticks in my mind. You see, some time before, I'd been involved in another case involving one of the main witnesses at the trial. Now, what was the woman's name—that woman that Frampton and Alexander were supposed to have been arguing about?'

'Rita Brassington?'

'Yes, it could have been her, the name rings a bell. I really can't be sure. Whoever it was, though, it was a nasty incident, very nasty indeed. She'd been punched and kicked about pretty badly, almost blinded, I seem to remember. The police were on the verge of charging someone, I understand, except she didn't want to cooperate. It's not worth it for them then, you see. Juries aren't going to convict on serious assault charges without the testimony of a victim.'

'Juries are odd,' Archie said. 'I really can't understand how the one in this case overlooked your testimony about the fingernails.'

Remus looked at Archie quizzically and smiled. 'My dear boy, juries are constantly convicting against the evidence. And acquitting too. It's a great strength in the system. They use their common sense, you see. Common sense can often shed light on matters which science merely obscures.'

'That seems an odd line for a man of science,' Archie remarked. 'Surely science can only clarify matters. In this case you testified that the marks on Alexander's face were caused by fingernails. You were certain of it; that should have helped the jury.'

Remus raised his eyebrows. 'No, I wasn't "certain",' he said carefully, 'if by that you mean incontrovertibly sure. You amateurs always expect too much from forensic science. It comes of a surfeit of American police films. What I said was that in my opinion, on the balance of probability, those lacerations were caused by fingernails. Equally, if you ask me, I think it likely they were caused around the time of his death, shortly after he'd actually died, to be more precise. But I can't be certain. It was only my opinion.'

'But if he *was* scratched, then he couldn't have been scratched by Frampton. It does seem to suggest Frampton might be innocent.'

'That, if I might say so, is a somewhat stark way of summarizing matters,' Remus replied. 'It assumes that the person who killed Alexander was also the person who caused those lacerations. I would prefer to approach the options more openly. Guilt and innocence have nothing to do with analytic fact. To me a fact is just a fact: the interpretation I leave to others.'

Archie was unprepared for Remus's calm indifference to the implications of what he did. It somehow irritated him. Wasn't he concerned that there might have been a miscarriage of justice?

'My dear boy,' said Remus, smiling again. 'We are surrounded by miscarriages of justice. It's a miscarriage of justice that you and I are overfed while half the world starves. But the world isn't perfect and neither is the legal system. Most of the time, I suspect, that system gets it about right, and when it doesn't . . . well, you mustn't become too jaundiced by the occasional slip-up. And you mustn't become so intolerably earnest about mistakes you discover. Everyone makes mistakes, you know . . .'

When Archie finally left Remus's office he slipped a tape of Beethoven's Ninth Symphony into the car cassette and turned the volume to full blast. There was something about the ridiculously riotous enthusiasm of the music that made him feel less indignant at Remus's cynical precision. Now at least Archie was certain about what he was going to do. Stredwick might think he was wasting his time with witnesses but there were things Archie wanted to understand, things he was already beginning to suspect Stredwick didn't want him to know.

A couple of days ago he'd never even heard of Rita Brassington; now there was something about her that was beginning to obsess him.

Finding her was not difficult and only involved a brief telephone call to her mother, who was still in the same

25

house she'd lived in at the time of the trial when Rita was living with her. Rita Brassington had now married and become Rita Archery. Her home was on a monotonously modern estate outside Leeds. There were no hedges or fences to any of the front gardens, and only the cars parked in the individual driveways delineated one house from another. Outside Rita's was a newish-looking red Fiesta.

It wasn't what Archie had expected of the former Rita Brassington, but then Rita herself wasn't what Archie had expected either. Far from the tarty, peroxide blonde he had imagined her to be, she was a delicately featured brunette with wide brown eyes, strangely hard and determined, yet vulnerable and trusting too.

She had two children, a baby girl and a boy about eight or nine years old. It seemed to be his birthday. A line of cards stood along the mantelshelf. The floor was strewn with wrapping paper and large toy trucks.

'I'm sorry to bring it all up again,' Archie said. 'But we need to know more about the background to events. We need to know more about Alexander and Frampton, what sort of people they were.'

Rita drew herself up in her chair. She seemed uncertain why she had invited this man into her house and why, having invited him, she was considering talking to him. It was clear that she'd rather not have been reminded of this period of her life.

'I was surprised Terry Frampton had it in him,' she said after a while. 'Frankly, I wouldn't have thought he'd have had the guts for that sort of thing. He wasn't a violent man, you see—exactly the opposite, if anything. He was a bit of a coward when it came down to it.'

She got up and walked to a carry-cot in the corner of the room where her daughter lay asleep. For a moment or two she stood absently rearranging the tiny eiderdown that covered it. 'You know, we had some good times together, me and Terry. I don't like to think of him rotting away in prison for years and years. He was too much under Bill Alexander's thumb, that was his problem. If Bill wanted to go out drinking then so did Terry; if Bill got a new car then

Terry wanted one too. You know, Terry had a good job in the offices up at Walter Foreman's until Bill persuaded him to jack it in for the Water Board. He was a fool to himself, Terry.'

'You ... you knew Bill Alexander ... you knew him well, didn't you?' Archie asked uncertainly. 'I mean, there was supposed to have been some argument between them about you, wasn't there?'

Rita laughed. 'That was ridiculous. No one ever believed that, did they?'

'The jury must have believed it. They found Frampton guilty. There had to be some motive for the killing. You knew Alexander, what other motive could anyone have had for smashing in his head?'

Although it was Rita herself who'd first mentioned Alexander, Archie saw her flinch slightly at the question. 'My husband's going to be back soon,' she said. 'I'd rather he didn't find you here. He knows about my involvement in the case, of course, but I don't think he'd like me talking about it.'

She jumped up abruptly and disappeared into the adjoining kitchen where earlier Archie had glimpsed her son bent over some board game laid out on the table.

Archie heard her say something to him and he heard the child's shrill, defiant reply. Again Rita said something, her voice becoming increasingly louder and sterner until it echoed around the house. He heard the sound of a sharp slap. The child began screaming and then bawling in choked, breathless sobs. There was another slap, louder than the first.

'I will not have this disobedience, Gary, now do what I tell you and clear up that mess or you'll be off to bed straightaway.'

The tone of her voice was chilling. She was obviously a woman used to getting her own way in the home, and probably, Archie suspected, outside it too; not the sort of person you'd want to cross lightly. And she wasn't unintelligent either; if anything, there was something about her that struck Archie as too shrewd for her own good. What could she have meant then by doubting that anyone had believed there'd been an argument between Frampton and Alexander?

'I really don't think I can help you,' she said, returning to the room as if nothing had happened. 'I don't want to be rude, but I really think it would be better if you went . . .'

'Please,' Archie said. 'I'm sorry to press you on what must be a very distressing memory, but I need to know more about Alexander . . . about what sort of a person he was . . .'

'I don't really think I can help you,' she said again. 'I really didn't know him that well.'

Archie could see this exchange was getting him nowhere; despite his best endeavours, he sensed he was up against a brick wall. Appraising the options open to him, be decided to go for broke.

'But I thought he beat you up once. What was that about?'

The question certainly stopped her in her tracks. Part of her seemed puzzled at the idea that anyone might ever have beaten her up, but nevertheless her eyes betrayed a truth she couldn't mask.

'What an extraordinary idea,' she said eventually. 'You seem to know a good deal about Bill Alexander already. I really don't see what I can add. Yes, he was an unpleasant man, if that's what you mean. And that's putting it mildly. The truth is he was an animal, Mr Archibold, but you probably know that already, and if you don't you soon will. For what it's worth, I think he got what was coming to him. If someone hadn't murdered him when they did, then he was the sort who'd have been murdered sooner or later anyway. I know half a dozen people who'd have happily seen Bill Alexander dead, me included . . .'

'Because of the beating he gave you?'

Rita walked over to the door and opened it with an unmistakable determination. 'You really must go now,' she said. 'My husband will be back from work soon. He wouldn't be at all happy at finding you here.'

28

On the front porch, more in hope than anticipation, he gave her his hotel telephone number.

'Just one last thing, though,' he said. 'Just one thing that intrigues me. You said just now about "someone" murdering Alexander. Terry Frampton murdered him, didn't he? He was convicted for it.'

She had been looking up the street, apparently anxious at the imminent arrival of her husband, edgy to get Archie away from the house. Now she just looked at him blankly, incredulity etched across her face. 'You surely don't believe he committed that murder,' she said. 'You wouldn't be here otherwise, would you?'

'But do *you* believe it?'

'Good Lord, no,' she laughed. 'But I've a pretty shrewd idea who did,' she added, almost as an afterthought.

CHAPTER 4

Back at the hotel, Archie was feeling a sense of accomplishment at the day's events. He was, at least, beginning to feel that he was earning his wages. The meeting with Rita had left him elated; it may not have been the substance of what she'd said that pleased him, but she was a difficult interviewee, and hadn't he at least got her to talk when it was clear she'd rather have seen the back of him? Hadn't he at least established a relationship with her? And now, who was to know where it might lead?

Lying on his bed, a celebratory glass of whisky to hand, he repressed his first inclination to crow to Stredwick. If Stredwick could ring at all hours of the day and night, then so could Archie. He'd telephone Stredwick later. Instead he called June at home.

'Are you coming back for the weekend?' she asked him immediately.

'It's just not going to be possible. I've told you about Stredwick—he's obsessed. I could be up here for weeks yet. Look, perhaps you ought to start forwarding my mail . . .'

'What? To Yorkshire? You can't be serious?'

The upshot was an argument, a brief and bitter altercation during which Archie almost slammed down the phone in frustration.

'June, you've been bickering at me for months to get a bloody job and now I've got one, you start complaining. A couple of weeks ago you were belly-aching about me getting under your feet. What am I supposed to do to please you?'

'I didn't expect you to go gallivanting off to all corners of the country, did I? I expected that you'd get a . . . a normal job, a job where at least you came home at night.'

'Oh, I'm sorry,' Archie said sarcastically. 'I do apologize. I'll ring Stredwick and tell him he can stuff his job and his twenty-six grand a year. I'll tell him I want a "normal" job where I can earn half as much and get bored shitless writing puff pieces about local companies winning export orders to bloody Hong Kong or some other such place.'

June went silent. 'That's not what I mean, Archie. It's just that . . . that . . . well, for Christ's sake, it's been a bit of a shock. One morning I'm kicking you out of bed; the next you're holed up in the middle of Yorkshire somewhere. It's . . . well, it's hard to suddenly have to re-adjust to living alone again. Oh, damn it,' she snapped. 'It's not like that, you know it isn't. I've got my own life and my own friends, and I can be happy on my own. But I'm not on my own, am I? You're not here—physically, I mean. Yet we're still supposed to be living together, aren't we? It's neither one thing nor the other.'

'June, it's only been a few days.'

'I know that, but—but when two people live together, it doesn't matter how independent they try to be, they start to depend on each other,' she said falteringly, struggling for what she wanted to say. 'If one of them isn't there anymore, what's supposed to hold them together?'

'What's that supposed to mean?' said Archie suspiciously. 'I'm not sure I know what you're talking about.'

'No, you wouldn't, would you? This case is likely to go on a lot longer, Archie, and afterwards there'll be another one, and another, and another after that. I'm worried about what it's going to mean to us. I'm worried about what it's going to mean to *me* . . .'

It was Archie's turn to go silent. Already he was regretting calling her at all. Perhaps he ought to have written, perhaps just dropped her a postcard. If they'd been talking face to face, rather than down this piece of plastic, at least he could have held her and reassured her, at least he could have taken her to bed and confided in her his own worries about the job and what it was likely to do to their relationship.

It was Friday, he'd almost forgotten. Friday was the night they stretched their budget for an evening out, a trip to the Classic sometimes, or maybe to the Bella Vista in town where you could take your own plonk and drink yourself silly over a cheap paella. It was the Bella Vista where they'd first met, Archie out of his mind drunk at the paper's annual Christmas bash, June out for a night with the girls from the Housing Department. He'd finished the night dancing an unlikely Flamenco on the table with Alistair from advertising rapping out a castanet rhythm on a pair of spoons until Archie had got his feet tangled in the tablecloth and had gone diving headlong into her lap.

'I've heard of throwing yourself at someone, but this is ridiculous,' she'd said.

'Share a bottle of vino with me, darling,' he'd replied. 'Then let's make mad, passionate love . . .'

They hadn't, of course. She wouldn't. People might throw themselves at her, but even in those days of safe sex, June wasn't the sort to commit herself to anything without due and serious consideration.

'You know, you're such a chauvinist,' she'd told him a week or so later. 'Hasn't anyone told you that girls become women at eighteen, and that even then most of them don't take kindly to being called "darling"?'

'You're so serious,' he'd said. 'Life's for having fun.'

But it had soon become serious, and soon it wasn't even fun. In the words of the song, he got it bad and it wasn't good. Yes, she had her own friends and her own life but even in those early days her ability to lose herself in both

31

without him was irksome. He became unaccountably jealous at her independent self-reliance, her ability to be involved with him, but uninvolved too. Having once got her into bed, he wanted to possess her and own her, and be with her all the time. It had shocked him to discover he was in love; love was like a disease, like cancer or MS which always struck someone else, never you.

But having made the discovery and declared it to her one summer Sunday as they'd sat in a country pub sheltering from the rain, he set about giving it some effect. He would have married her straightaway except that June was never one to do anything without balancing all the pros and cons with the same sort of care she might take preparing a report for her Director. So he'd gone for second best and set his stall at getting her to live with him—under the mistaken apprehension that somehow this might be easier.

She'd kept him on tenterhooks for more than a year, sometimes interested, most times sceptical that it would ever work, that they could ever spend more than a month together without her beginning to feel closeted and over-committed. When, finally, and still reluctantly, she'd agreed, he felt like a character from the final pages of Jane Austen who sees life stretching before her as one long happy ending and so many dreamy romantic days. That night he'd rung all his friends to tell them the news. He'd even rung his mother.

Now, at the drop of a hat, he'd left her for £26,000 a year and a flashy white Astra. And the awful thing was, he wouldn't have had it any differently.

Hell, it was Friday night, Friday night and they might still have been at the Bella Vista debating whether the budget would extend to an ice-cream and a couple of coffees. Instead he was at a four-star hotel drinking expensive malt on a full stomach of king prawns and best Scotch beef. He might have enjoyed it more with her, but even so, he felt no guilt at how quickly he'd adapted to his changed circumstances.

'What are you going to do, then?' she continued stridently. 'Are you going to try and get back soon?'

'I'll talk to Stredwick.'

'And after that? Am I supposed to sit around crocheting in the hopes I get to see you a couple of times a year? I'm not going to have it, you know. I've got my own needs . . . my own plans . . .'

'So what are you going to do, then? Have an affair to keep yourself occupied?' Archie said, striking out angrily.

'Who would I be planning to have an affair with?'

'That guy Simon at work you're always drinking with. Or Jim Moran—you see enough of him as it is . . .'

'Archie, I'm not having this, they're friends. I don't have to justify myself to you. You're acting like a child. Don't you think I've got better things to do than think about men all the time?'

And she hung up.

Archie poured himself another drink and rang Stredwick. He was expecting, indeed savouring, the prospect of getting his boss out of bed. In the event Stredwick answered almost immediately and in the background Archie could hear what he took to be the burr of a computer printing. The bastard had evidently still been working.

'It's me,' Archie said, determined to be no more forthcoming with Stredwick than Stredwick was with him.

For his part, if Stredwick noticed any discourtesy, he didn't betray it. 'So you've been to see Remus, have you? Odd old stick, isn't he? Quite brilliant, though. He gave me one of my first big stories years ago. What did he say?'

Archie began to recount the conversation from his notebook, but before he'd got very far he was interrupted by what seemed to be a curious interference on the line, a noise like a shrill crackle punctuated by explosive popping. It was a moment or two before he could identify it.

Stredwick, it seemed, was chuckling.

'So the old bugger gave you the standard lecture, did he? Well, I never . . . he did the same to me twenty years ago now, no . . . it was nearer twenty-five. He must have liked you, though. He doesn't usually bother unless he does.'

Archie went on to his meeting with Rita, and as abruptly as a sailboat tacking to the wind, Stredwick's mood changed. For a full five minutes he ranted deliriously. Archie wasn't only dangerously idiotic, he was wilfully destructive, naïve and arrogant, he had set the investigation back months, he had destroyed years of work.

'For heaven's sake, son,' he said without pausing, his voice still hysterical. 'You're twenty-six years old, you can't spend the whole of your life acting like a headstrong sixteen-year-old. You've got to think a bit more about the implications of what you're doing.'

'Don't you think it possible Rita might get us some-where?' Archie said, a tone of defiance in his voice. 'It seems to me she's given us the best lead we've got on this case. She obviously knows something.'

From the other end of the line came a sound like an animal shrieking, and for a brief instant Archie thought Stredwick might be the second person that night to put down the phone on him.

But when Stredwick spoke next his tone was more composed, his voice now barely rising above a whisper. 'Look, Archie, you're a good journalist—an excellent jour-nalist—but you must be more rational in your thinking: is it likely that Brassington genuinely knows anything that she hasn't already told the police? They're not idiots, you know. They may be careless sometimes, sometimes they may be less than efficient. Occasionally they're corrupt. But they're not stupid, not by a long chalk. If there's anything at all in what she has to say, then you can rest assured the police have already looked into it closely, and probably already discounted it as irrelevant.'

Archie was far from convinced, but he had to concede that there was at least some sense in what Stredwick was arguing. If Rita had told him what she did—a journalist who'd just knocked on her door—then she surely must have told the authorities.

'There are elements of this case that seriously worry me,' Stredwick went on. 'The geography of the case, for a start. It troubles me that Frampton might be innocent. I don't know any answers yet, son, but take my word from one who's been in the game longer than you: this early the trick

34

isn't to have answers, but to have the right questions. If you can ask the right questions, then eventually you'll get your answers. At the moment there are four questions that are concerning me.

'First of all, what is it Frampton and Alexander were arguing about the day of the murder? What Rita said to you doesn't surprise me—that story about an argument over her never rang true. It was too much of a cliché. I mean, just use your common sense. Alexander was far too strong a character to argue with a wimp like Frampton. Yet we know from that woman in the café in Rainsford—what was her name—Jennifer Rochford, wasn't it?—we know from her testimony in court that there *was* some fracas the morning of the murder—'

'And the hotel manager, don't forget him,' Archie interrupted. 'What was his name?—Carrington, wasn't it? Didn't he say he'd seen them arguing later that day? Didn't he say one of them threw a punch at the other? They were almost fighting then. And they were almost fighting in the café too, surely?' Archie said. 'There were some chairs knocked over.'

'There was *a* chair knocked over—that's very different. But it's intriguing, I agree, because whatever the fracas was about it got them both very agitated. That strikes me as unusual too. We know Frampton was under Alexander's thumb and that he wasn't the sort of person to confront him on anything. So what was getting them both so upset on this occasion?'

Stredwick fell silent for a moment. 'More important, it seems to me, is to discover why Alexander's body wasn't discovered earlier. That's always struck me as being odd. The walker who discovered the body—Jeremy Germaine de Groot—'

'An extraordinary name.'

'Absolutely. It was extraordinary too that he was on a walking holiday. A walking holiday!—at the beginning of January, just after New Year! Can you believe that?'

'But he didn't arrive at the hotel here until after the murder. Are you suggesting he might be involved and that

35

maybe the murder didn't happen on the day we think?'

'There you go again,' Stredwick said, a tired weariness creeping into his voice. 'You must get out of this habit of always trying to find a murderer, and making every poor bugger involved in the case a suspect. No, I'm not suggesting that at all. There's no question that Alexander was dead by the time de Groot arrived at the hotel. What interests me about him is why he didn't discover the body earlier. I want you to get your boots on and look around the place, because it seems to me from the map that if de Groot was walking like he claimed to be, then it would have been almost impossible to avoid stumbling over the body earlier than he did. It just doesn't add up. The other thing that doesn't add up is what Frampton and Alexander were doing the week they were working together.'

Archie reached across his bed to one of his files. 'They were repairing a burst water main, weren't they? Wasn't it supposed to have frozen up or something?'

'Was it?' Stredwick said. 'Are you sure? Because I've read through the files more times than I care to remember, and the only thing I can be sure of is that at the beginning of the week of the murder the hotel had reported that it didn't have any water supply. It's true that Frampton and Alexander *told* their foreman back at the office that it was a burst, and that they were having problems repairing it. But we've only got their word to go on. Nobody came out and checked. It may have just been a burst, but if so, I'm intrigued it took four whole days to repair it.'

'I don't have a problem with that,' Archie said. 'The Water Board foreman—what was his name—Percy Elliot, wasn't it?—he said that Frampton and Alexander were a couple of lazy sods. It strikes me they were just swinging the lead and making the most of a cushy job.'

'Exactly,' Stredwick cried jubilantly. 'Exactly my point. So why did they finish the job on *Thursday* night? They'd strung it out for four days, why not make a full week of it? I want you to visit Percy Elliot and see if he can clear this one up. I find it odd. No one seemed to be supervising them; they could have just disappeared. But they didn't.

36

Instead, Frampton went into the office the next day as if nothing had happened. Of course, there could be one simple explanation for that . . .'

'That he'd murdered Alexander?'

'We should never overlook the possibility,' said Stredwick.

Archie jotted a few lines down in his notebook. 'You said their were four questions: the argument, the discovery of the body, and the burst pipe. What's the fourth?' he asked.

'The fourth?'

'The fourth question you want answering,' Archie said.

Stredwick chuckled again. 'Oh yes. The fourth question. I thought you might have guessed. I want to know now who Rita Brassington suspects might have committed the murder?'

Archie felt suddenly jubilant. 'So you think there might be something in what she says after all?'

'I think what she told you was . . . very interesting,' Stredwick said. 'But not for any of the reasons you think.'

CHAPTER 5

Archie woke up in an unusually good mood. With the sun streaming through his window, the prospect of a stroll on the moors cheered him no end. Since it was a Saturday he'd determined on a leisurely breakfast, and then maybe a drink or two later in the day in front of an open fire in some country pub.

But it wasn't to be. Before he'd even finished shaving it had started pouring with rain.

He went down to breakfast his usual irritable self.

The breakfast-room was busier than he'd seen it, and seemed full of corpulent middle-aged couples with American accents and baggy pastel-coloured slacks; even at this time of the year the Shornewan was a popular stopping-off spot for tourists.

Webber was helping out as a fill-in waiter. 'Out walking today, are we?' he said, pushing another mound of York ham Archie's way. After their set-to the previous morning the atmosphere beween them was strained, and it seemed to Archie that Webber had determined on a strategy of facetiousness. Archie was almost certain now that he was one of Stredwick's men; he was equally certain he didn't like him. The novelty of the York ham was wearing a bit thin too; Archie would just as soon have made do with a couple of greasy sausages.

'Walking? Whatever makes you think that?' he said. 'It's hardly the weather for walking, is it?'

Webber winked knowingly. 'Oh, I don't know. Round here people go walking at the most extraordinary times of the year. If I were you though, I'd get a decent pair of boots.'

Archie glanced down at his feet and the worn pair of trainers he was wearing. On the question of footwear at least, Webber had to be taken seriously, and so after break-fast Archie drove into Rainsford where he braved the Satur-day crowds to find a shop with the intimidating name of *Outdoor Pursuits*. Archie, whose idea of an outdoor pursuit was a game of long alley skittles in a pub yard, soon found himself pressured into buying not just the boots, but an expensive anorak, a one-inch Ordnance Survey map and even a compass.

Later that afternoon though, despite the professional attire, he found himself suddenly and hopelessly lost. How it had happened he wasn't altogether sure. He'd been sen-sible enough not to venture out until the rain had stopped, and careful then not to stray too far from a footpath marked clearly on his map. But he'd walked no more than a couple of hundred yards from the forecourt of the hotel before the footpath had petered out in a sodden bed of heather, and the rain had set in again, throwing up a grey mist that made it difficult to see more than a car's length ahead. A bitter wind had blown up too, ripping into his anorak and stinging his face raw. He was soon soaked to the skin, and soon wishing he'd worn his trainers after all: the new boots had started chafing him so cruelly that he could feel his feet swelling with every step.

He really ought to have turned back there and then, but having started out, he was reluctant to give up so easily. His plan was simply to follow the route de Groot must have taken the morning he discovered Alexander's body, as Stredwick had asked him. It surely wouldn't be a long trek. Besides, at this time of the year he couldn't count on the weather being much better any other day.

And so he had pressed on, limping across a rough gorge and a stretch of bog until eventually, to his surprise (for the map said he ought to have been somewhere entirely different) he found himself at the Shornewan rocks where the moor suddenly fell away impressively in a sheer drop. The rocks were the outcrop of granite which Webber said had once been a pagan temple. No doubt on warm summer Sundays the place was a magnet for day trippers and ice-cream vans, but on an afternoon like this it had different attractions and a particular grandeur of its own. Archie had only ever seen the rocks from the hotel, where they looked unremarkable; close to, they were incomparably more impressive, for on their far side, where the moor dropped towards Rainsford, they jutted outwards to a spectacular cliff face which, even through the mist, Archie could see curved around in a graceful sweep to form a naturally enclosed amphitheatre.

Having arrived at the rocks, however inadvertently, it seemed churlish not to explore further and he climbed down the inside of the cliff wall, to end up in the enclosed well of the granite.

Inside, it was sheltered from the wind and clear of the moorland mist which poured over its edges like a vast ethereal waterfall. Archie stared around him entranced. From inside, the rocks looked even more like an amphitheatre, an enormous amphitheatre, eerily quiet but for the discordant howl of the wind above. The place had a timeless quality about it, as if it were a landscape from a different age. But there was something sinister about it too, something uncomfortably malign. Archie trusted Webber's history about as much as he trusted everything else about the man, but he could easily imagine how the place might have been used for ritual worship and sacrifice. In places the cliff even seemed to form a series of steps, like banks of seats laid out for spectators.

By this time Archie had started enjoying the whole adventure hugely, and he might have explored further except that as the afternoon progressed, the need to find the spot where Alexander's body had been discovered was becoming more pressing if he were still to have time to make that country pub as he'd planned.

He climbed back up the cliff face, and guiding himself by the map, set out once again across the moor. A couple of hours later he was still wandering about, nowhere near his destination and totally lost again. The map was proving worse than useless. Geography had never been his stongest subject at school: the truth was he didn't seem to be able to read the damn thing. What was more troubling was that the weather seemed to be worsening by the minute. The wind was blowing up more strongly, and the rain had turned into pelting hail.

His plans for an afternoon in the pub had long since been abandoned; indeed, the way things were going, he was beginning to think he'd be lucky to get back to the Shornewan before closing time. In the back of his mind too was the niggling doubt that if things didn't look up soon he'd be lucky to get back at all. Archie wasn't the sort of person to panic, but all the same he was too intelligent not to recognize the precariousness of his situation. The new boots had become agonizingly painful, and the earlier chill he'd felt had turned into a gnawing cold that from time to time racked him with fits of uncontrollable shivering.

Eventually he dropped down behind a convenient pile of rocks where he could shelter from the wind and take stock of the situation, his niggling doubt now developing into serious concern. It was still light, thank God, and even in these overcast conditions likely to stay that way for a while yet. And he had a compass. It occurred to him that what he needed to do was to set a course in the general direction of the road and stick to it regardless.

But what was the general direction of the road? Some half an hour before, he'd heard what he'd taken to be the sound of a lorry grating at its gears, but was he sure enough to risk himself to it? Could it have been the wind? Or a trick of the moors—he seemed to remember hearing stories about how sounds distorted in open places? For the first time Archie felt genuinely frightened.

He loosened his boots and pulled his anorak around him. Should he just stay put? Wasn't that what they advised you to do in this situation? Perhaps he ought to try and knock together a basic shelter of some sort? The idea seemed somehow absurd, for despite the time he'd spent lurching about lost, he felt he couldn't be too far from the hotel. But how far, that was the question? A hundred yards or a mile? Either way, in these conditions, he was uncertain he had the strength for it. He was beginning to feel lightheaded and ravenously hungry. And—curious this—he was beginning to feel sleepy too, desperately sleepy.

It was perhaps in an attempt to counteract this, to force himself to think clearly, that he began to focus more closely on his immediate surroundings. As he did, it gradually dawned on him where he was. At first it was just that the spot felt familiar, but then he rifled through his anorak pocket for the police photographs which he'd brought with him. They confirmed that the rocks where he was sheltered were actually what remained of a wall. On one of the photographs he could clearly identify the very stone against which he was leaning, the black and white photograph showing it as a dull grey, darkened on its top by what seemed to be . . . a bloodstain.

Archie sprang to his feet. It was bad enough to be lost on a deserted moor in filthy weather without sitting in exactly the same spot that some poor bastard had been found with his skull smashed to splinters. All the same, the stone fascinated him. Looking at it, it was almost as if the bloodstain was still there. Surely not? Impossible! Archie crouched down and examined it in more detail, comparing

41

it with the photograph. Inexplicable though it was, closer inspection only confirmed his first impression. It seemed—incredibly—that after nine years the bloodstain—Alexander's bloodstain—was still there, its awful pattern exactly the same. Archie automatically ran his fingers over it, but then suddenly pulled them away, gripped by horror.

It was bizarre enough that the bloodstain had somehow survived.

But it still seemed to be wet!

Without a thought to where he was going, Archie turned on his heels in panic and fled into the enveloping mist. He couldn't have guessed how far he'd run before, eventually, he slowed down. He couldn't have said how long after that he spent stumbling around trying to find his bearings, heading for the road and finding it wasn't the road, heading back in the other direction and finding that led nowhere too. It was becoming darker now, much darker. And it seemed colder too, if that were possible. At length he dropped down to the ground, too exhausted to take another step.

The running had drained him of energy. His legs had become unaccountably weak, and every breath he took seemed to strain his lungs.

The softness of the moor as he lay on the ground seemed seductively comfortable too, almost like a bed. And he felt so inexplicably tired again.

If only he could sleep—just for a minute or two, that was all—perhaps he might find the strength to go on. It was a risk, he knew, but it needn't be a real sleep, not a deep sleep. He only needed a brief nap, no more.

He closed his eyes cautiously, by way of an experiment almost . . .

Close by, a man laughed, a thin unpleasant laugh resonant with a note of triumph.

CHAPTER 6

Stredwick had been sitting at his telephone for the best part of a day, and he'd have kept on sitting there for as long again, and longer, except that on his last call he'd discovered what he'd been searching for. Now he leaned back, picked up his cat Squiffy, and sipped a cup of coffee that had gone cold on him an hour before. By rights he ought to have felt some sense of satisfaction at what he'd achieved, but at fifty-seven he was getting too old for this work. These triumphs of discovery that had so stimulated him years before he now took for granted, so that if they didn't materialize he blamed not circumstances, but himself, doubting talents that he'd once scarcely been aware he possessed.

Perhaps it was time for a change, he thought wearily as he emptied a can of Whiskas into one bowl, and the remnants of a packet of cornflakes into another. It was four o'clock on a wet London Sunday. The rain was driving against the window of his small Kennington bed-sit, and the cornflakes and the catfood had cleared his larder. Perhaps he'd pick up a take-away later. Perhaps he wouldn't bother.

Yes, it was time for a change, but how often had he said that to himself over the years? At his age, what option was open to him apart from retirement? But what would he do with himself? How could he afford it? He'd never been careful enough with money, that had always been his problem. He'd been a sucker for a sob story from friends, and too much of a soft touch for wives who only ever seemed to stay with him for long enough to get maintenance. Money had never interested him, that's what it came down to. But then nothing had interested him except his work and now even his enthusiasm for that was waning. Or he was waning. It amounted to the same thing.

He took the cornflakes back to his desk and ate them,

ritualistically flicking through a pile of Sunday papers. He couldn't decide which left a worse taste in his mouth. He'd worked for this paper once as a young man—1953 was it, 1954? It had never been the world's greatest newspaper, but at least it *had* been a newspaper then: something that told you what was happening in the world. Now it seemed full of interminable extracts from military memoirs, or autobiographies of minor literary figures. And this magazine that came with it was like a comic, full of special offers for mattresses they called beds, or worse, interviews with arty, creative types who seemed to spend so much time socializing it was a wonder they ever found time to do much else.

They'd tried to interview him often enough in his time but he'd never been even tempted by the idea. It was bad enough his friends or people at work interrogating him about his personal life, let alone a journalist prying into his failed marriages, or wanting to know why he didn't have a bigger home, or why he kept the one he'd got like an untidy library with piles of newspapers and files scattered over the floor.

'You mean you don't even own your own place?' people said incredulously when they discovered he didn't. 'Do you have somewhere in the country instead? Go on, tell us, George. We won't give your secrets away.'

Most of all people seemed fascinated with his cat.

'It's just a cat,' Stredwick would say, impatient with them. '*Felis domesticus*. Nothing special.'

'But it's—it's spastic.'

'It's not spastic,' he'd snap angrily, as much offended at their terminology as their triviality. 'It suffers from a sort of feline cerebral palsy.'

'But it can't walk properly,' they'd say somewhat obviously, since the only way the creature could move was by dint of limping like some war veteran.

'It's just a bit unsteady on its feet, that's all.' Stredwick would say defensively. 'It used to belong to my mother. It's very affectionate, though . . .'

George Stredwick had never thought his life sufficiently

interesting for others to show such curiosity in it, and he certainly didn't think the way he lived materially different from anyone else who worked for a living. But he was the sort of person to whom rumour clung, and around whom mythologies grew. He was a recluse who shunned publicity to live a lonely existence with a disabled cat in a South London slum. He was eccentric, obsessive, infatuated with his job. From time to time he'd hear what was being said about him, and he'd be deeply troubled. He couldn't see himself as that sort of person, and it perplexed him that anyone else might. It was like waking up to find he was carrying a birthmark across his face that he'd never noticed before.

What did they mean by 'eccentric' anyhow? Did they mean he lived his life the way he wanted? Well, yes, that was true. But what was so unusual about that? Was it so unusual that he valued what he did, and because he valued it, he was willing to commit himself to get the results he wanted? Hell, what did they think journalism was but commitment? There certainly wasn't anything about it that was glamorous, or that would warrant a trite story about him next to some piece on a New York fashion designer or whoever. You might have thought he was some media personality, and the cat some sort of bedroom poodle, the way they talked.

He just couldn't understand what was so unusual about the cat, and what was so obsessive about how he worked. The way he'd just traced this man, de Groot, for instance. It was clear to anyone that the name wasn't common, so all it had involved was a few hours scouring telephone directories to find the numbers of every de Groot in the country and ringing them, one by one. OK, so the name hadn't been as unusual as he'd anticipated, but it wasn't as if it had been Smith. He hadn't had to make more than forty calls before he'd found him. Well, perhaps he hadn't exactly found *him*, but he'd found his aunt, which was next best thing, and she'd given him an address. After that, because de Groot wasn't on the phone, and because it was a Sunday, it was just a matter of ringing a local councillor in

45

Lewisham where de Groot lived, and persuading her to go through the electoral register to give him the names of people who lived in adjoining flats. Sure enough, one of them was on the phone and they didn't need much convincing to get Jeremy Germaine out of the bath.

What was so obsessive about that? He'd needed to find de Groot. Now he'd found him. He had a job to do. He'd done it.

The trouble with young people today was that they were too cynical, Stredwick thought, they didn't value what they did. He'd felt that about reporters who'd tried to interview him, and he was beginning to think it about Archibold, who so far had been a painful disappointment to him. But how could he have known? Before employing him Stredwick had done all the checks, from old school to bank balance, but things like cynicism never showed up in files.

The cornflake bowl ended on top of a pile of similar bowls next to a computer. Stredwick reached over to a heap of books leaning against a wall, extracting a battered A-Z. Lewisham? Along the Old Kent Road, wasn't it? De Groot's flat seemed to be near the river, closer to Greenwich than Lewisham.

Perhaps he was judging Archibold too harshly, though. The lad was naïve, it was true, but there was nothing wrong with naïvety, especially if it was coupled to curiosity. After all, wasn't that why he'd been employed? Stredwick picked up the phone again and dialled. Yes, perhaps he was being too harsh on Archibold. The lad showed promise, if only he could demonstrate some real commitment, if only he could stop treating the work as just a production line job. But he had a sort of obdurate professionalism about him which lacked any sense of mission. It led him to see only what he wanted to. He hadn't even registered that broad hint about the geography of the case, for instance. Stredwick idly wondered how the lad would react when it finally struck him that he'd been totally set up.

His call was eventually answered. It was the Shornewan Hotel. The female voice on the other end of the line was nervously deferential.

'No, I'm afraid Mr Archibold's still not back yet, Mr Stredwick. But the message you left is waiting for him; I'll make sure he gets it. Like I said before, no one's seen him since breakfast yesterday.'

'And you're sure he didn't come in last night? You're certain about that?'

'Yes, absolutely certain. We checked his room; his bed hadn't been slept in.'

'And Mr Webber?'

'Not back either, Mr Stredwick. But we've had a telephone call from him. He's tied up on something, but I'll pass on your message as soon as he returns.'

The most difficult part of finding de Groot turned out to be finding his flat. He lived in a rabbit warren of a council estate adjacent to the deserted mudflats of Deptford Creek. De Groot himself, whose name suggested an estate agent, or an accountant, or at least something in the City, appeared to be a dissolute drop-out in his mid-forties. He lived alone in a couple of squalid rooms where plates coagulated with week-old food littered the floor, and where half a dozen mangy cats wandered around.

'Of course, it's not my real name,' he explained, his voice a peculiar cocktail of the Surrey suburbs and a Peckham market stall. 'No, my proper name's Clements. But I used to play with a band—de Groot, Driver and the Southside Boys. I was Germaine de Groot. I rather liked the name. Kept it ever since.'

'But your aunt . . .' Stredwick started.

'She's not really my aunt. She used to be my nanny. I took the name of the band from her in the first place. Of course, I don't play any more. Well, not seriously, at least. I've got a chain of video shops now; I let other people do the work.' He laughed. 'That's what you call the enterprise culture.'

He must have seen a look of amused curiosity on Stredwick's face, for he went on, without pause, as if he were explaining some simple point to a child.

'Yeah, I'm a thrusting entrepreneur, I suppose, except

I'm not thrusting enough. Perhaps at my age I ought to be more ambitious, move somewhere else, perhaps. But really, I had enough of that sort of shit as a kid. Who needs it? I don't want the hassle. Besides, I've got good friends in Deptford . . .'

He'd been idly stroking one of the cats fawning around him as he lounged on the floor. But now he pushed it away brusquely.

'What do you want anyway?' he asked abruptly. 'I'm telling you straight, if one of the tribe's croaked, you can piss off before you start. I'm just not interested in their fucking money, they should know that by now.'

'It's nothing to do with your family,' Stredwick said. 'It's to do with an innocent man in prison for a crime he may not have committed . . .'

After Stredwick had finished explaining, de Groot slowly rolled himself a cigarette. 'Of course, I'd like to help,' he said eventually. 'But I don't see what I can do. I told the police everything I knew, and I gave evidence in court.'

'What was that like?'

'Court? Some heavy scene, I can tell you. Mopsie—my mother, that is—she was all for getting me a brief. She was convinced I'd end up in the dock. Can you believe that? All I'd done was stumble across a stiff on the moors, and she wanted to bring in a QC.'

Stredwick smiled. 'A strange thing to be doing at that time of the year, though, wasn't it?'

'Walking on the moors, you mean? Yeah, the police asked me about that too. But I'd had a lousy Christmas that year—I thought it'd be a bit of a crack. Get away from things, you know, have a break. It was a crazy idea, crazy. I didn't know what I was letting myself in for.'

Again he began to toy with one of the cats. 'Do you know the moors around Rainsford? Take my word for it, in January that place is like the Arctic. Cold isn't the word! I nearly got frostbite walking from the car to that bloody hotel. What's it called again—something to do with sheep-shearing . . .'

'The Shornewan.'

'Yeah, that was it: a weird place—the hotel, the moors, those rocks nearby, the whole scene—weird, very weird. It used to be a pagan temple once, did you know that?— sacrificial victims, the whole scene.' De Groot shuddered. 'Horrible, really, isn't it? You're still supposed to be able to hear the victims screaming sometimes; they're supposed to haunt the place. Funny how these ghosts always come back to haunt places they were killed. You'd have thought after their experiences of the world, they'd have had enough of it.'

'So what did you do with yourself all week?' Stredwick asked. 'Did you spend much time in the hotel?'

'Are you joking? I'd have been warmer on the moors, believe me. That week was a bloody disaster from start to finish. The hotel was freezing, and for the first couple of days there wasn't even any running water in the place. It was a horror story. I should have left, except I'd nowhere else to go. No, I spent most of my time drinking in pubs in Rainsford. At least that way I avoided exposure.'

'And walking?'

'Eventually, on my last day,' de Groot agreed. 'I think it surprised the guy running the place—what was his name?—Carrington, wasn't it? He'd gone out of his way to warn me it could be dangerous that time of the year but . . . well, I'd gone to Yorkshire intending to do some walking—I couldn't go back to London without setting foot on the moors, could I? Good job I did, looking back on it. I know the body wasn't far from the hotel, but if I hadn't found it, it could have been there until summer.'

He got to his feet and disappeared from the room, returning a short while later carrying a tray on which were two stained cups filled with a pungent, pale liquid. He pushed one towards Stredwick. 'It's camomile, I'm afraid. I don't drink caffeine.'

Stredwick wet his lips politely. 'So who was at the hotel while you were there?'

'Apart from me and Carrington, you mean? Well, there was Carrington's wife. And there was a girl there . . . well,

49

a young woman. A receptionist, waitress. Julie, I think her name was . . .'

'Julie Taylor. Yes, she worked there. I know about her. Anyone else?'

'It's difficult . . . it was a long time ago. I remember a German family staying one night . . .'

'I mean when you first arrived, were there any other guests then?'

De Groot shook his head firmly. 'No, no one. I remember that clearly. I had the place totally to myself.'

It was late when Stredwick eventually left.

'Would you mind if I asked you a personal question?' he said as he was getting up to go. 'I mean—I know it may sound a little odd, but has—has anyone ever described you as eccentric?'

'You mean because of the cats?'

'Nothing wrong with cats,' said Stredwick. 'I've got a cat.'

De Groot nodded absently. 'Funny you should ask that, though. My bloody family always describe me as eccentric. It makes me furious . . .'

Walking to his car, there was a fresh, more optimistic air about Stredwick, a new confidence in his step. He'd liked de Groot, but more importantly the meeting with him had been useful, useful in a way that was entirely unexpected. There was a lot of work to be done yet, Stredwick thought, smiling to himself because now, at least, he felt more like doing it.

Of one thing, though, he was certain: he'd better not say anything about Yorkshire weather to Archibold. The lad wasn't stupid and if, God forbid, he should draw too many implications from the meteorological, he might start asking some uncomfortable questions. Then the whole thing might be blown before it even got started.

CHAPTER 7

He pulled himself up on to one elbow. His head was leaden, his limbs aching. He seemed to be lying in bed; someone— was it Webber?—seemed to be standing over him.

'What in hell's name happened?' Archie asked eventually as the room around him fell into shape and the figure over him took on a clearer form.

'They kept you overnight in hospital. You—you overdid it a bit,' Webber said. 'God!' he suddenly exploded. 'I blame myself. You're just an idiot; I should have known better. I should have stopped you going out in those conditions. It can turn dangerous so bloody quickly.'

'I seem to remember hearing you,' said Archie. 'You seemed to be laughing. It was you who found me, wasn't it? You were looking for me, I suppose?'

'I'd expected you back earlier. I know how the weather can turn. You learn a lot about the moors: you have to, when you live on them.'

'I kept losing all sense of reality,' Archie explained later on the phone to Stredwick. 'There didn't seem to be anything I could do to prevent it. I couldn't think clearly, I was just stumbling about all over the place.'

'Exposure. Typical symptoms. It's the chill factor. I investigated a case a couple of years ago that hinged on it.'

Stredwick's tone was so disparaging and unsympathetic that Archie found himself doctoring his account of the day. The truth was, he'd only subsequently become aware of how dangerous his position had been, and he felt sheepish at his own stupidity. His memory of the blood on the rock, for instance. The stickiness of it on his fingers was even now so intensely vivid that he'd begun to realize how near he must have been to delirium, nearer to collapse than Stredwick could have realized. Archie carefully avoided mentioning the topic.

51

'I suppose I must have just panicked,' he admitted eventually. 'By then I was totally confused. I'd forgotten how close to the hotel Alexander's body had been dumped.'

'Yes, de Groot made the same point,' said Stredwick. 'It was a revelation to me. But I didn't have to play heroics on the moor to discover it . . .'

Archie slammed his Beethoven into the car cassette and drove to Leeds faster than was either legally or physically safe. Christ, Stredwick infuriated him! There was absolutely nothing you could do to satisfy the man, including, it seemed, virtually killing yourself in the cause of duty. That snide dig about heroics had been totally out of order. Did Stredwick somehow imagine he'd planned to get himself lost, that he schemed to get himself into hospital? The man was so unbearably patronizing. While Archie had been stumbling about Yorkshire in near-Arctic conditions, Stredwick had been sipping camomile tea in South London. Blast him! He'd not even mentioned his plans to see de Groot! Damn him! Weren't there supposed to be two of them involved in this? How could Archie get a complete picture of the case if he wasn't told what was going on? How could he feel a part of a team if Stredwick persisted in acting so secretively?

Stredwick hadn't even been forthcoming about what de Groot had said. What was more, he'd made no pretence at being forthcoming.

'Leave that side of things to me,' he'd said. 'You just find out about the water. Frampton and Alexander were supposed to have repaired the burst, but according to de Groot the hotel water wasn't connected until a couple of days after he arrived. Find out why. Go and see Percy Elliot.'

And when Archie had wanted to know why de Groot hadn't discovered the body earlier Stredwick had just exploded with that extraordinary chuckling of his, mumbling incomprehensibly about areas of high pressure and isobars. Isobars, for Christ sake, isobars! How could anyone work with a man like this . . . ?

*

52

The West Riding Water Board offices where Percy Elliot worked were set among horticultural nurseries in a Georgian house in one of the more attractive suburbs of Leeds. Around the house were clutches of massive greenhouses where groups of men worked, slowly moving along rows of pots filled with cuttings. Beyond them, rising in a gentle slope, stretched the formal lawns of a park, its borders bare and empty at this time of the year.

'Sit yoursen' down, lad,' Elliot said. 'Park your arse. We don't stand on ceremony here.'

His office was as bare as the park. It was lined with clinical metal shelves stacked with files, and on one wall was a commercial calendar sporting a glossy picture of a tractor displayed in the manner of a pin-up. Elliot himself was a small, florid man in his late fifties. His voice was gruff and accusatory, and his accent less Yorkshire than Derbyshire, or at least that bit of Derbyshire near the border where the coal seams underground are no respecters of the county boundaries above.

'No, there'd been a burst, all right,' he said. 'No question. If everything had been straightfor'd, the job ought to have took a couple of days, maybe three allowing for the weather. It's a sight harder to dig when t'ground's frozen.'

'Who had responsibility for monitoring how long jobs took?'

'Me. Officially. But I'd best part of a dozen gangs on't road then. I couldn't keep track on 'em all. Most of the time I had to take what the lads told me at face value.'

'Frampton and Alexander didn't finish the water main until the Thursday, though? That's what you said to the police, wasn't it?'

Elliot folded his arms and surveyed Archie critically. 'What are you getting at, lad?' he asked, an unmistakable suspicion in his voice.

Archie suddenly felt uncomfortable. 'It's just that we've traced a guest who was staying at the hotel the week after the murder. He said there was no water for a couple of days after he arrived. Yet you told the police Frampton and

53

Alexander finished repairing the burst on Thursday.'

'No, lad,' Elliot said brusquely, in the same tone he might have used to some recalcitrant employee caught fiddling his time-sheet. 'No, that's not what I said, and you better get this right. What I said to the police, and it's in my statement, was that the job was finished *by* Thursday. Now there's a world of difference between those two things, lad, you think on it.'

For the life of him, much as Archie did think about it, the subtle difference escaped him. There was no chance at that stage of clarifying what Elliot was getting at, though, for by now the Water Board man was warming to his theme, and was waxing passionate on the topic of his former charges.

'That pair were a couple of nasty bastards,' he said bitterly, 'And lazy too, take my word for it. Alexander were the worst. Thieving? I've never known a man like it. In the three years he were working here we lost more stock than a little. But could anyone catch him at it? Could they hell! He was clever, that one, sly as a fox.'

A look of distaste crossed Elliot's face. 'Well, he's dead now, and I were taught always to have respect for t'dead. But the fact is, I was glad to see the back of him, even though . . .' he faltered, 'even though I partly blame myself for his death . . .

'Don't get me wrong,' he went on, suddenly unfolding his arms and prodding aggressively at Archie with his finger. 'I'm not soft-headed or owt like that, but I should have sacked him years before. Leastways, I should never have let him work with his mate Frampton. With those two together there were bound to be mischief of some sort, as sure as day follows night.'

'So why didn't you get rid of them?' Archie asked.

Elliot said nothing for a few moments. He glared at Archie angrily, but the anger he was feeling was actually at himself. It was as if he was struggling inside with something, something that evidently disturbed him, and something, equally evidently, that he was reluctant to disclose lightly.

Then his eyes dropped, and he shook his head sadly. 'I'll be honest with you, lad,' he said eventually. 'If you want to know t'truth, I were frit of Alexander. Frightened,' he explained. 'Everyone were frit of Alexander, even his mates, even Terry Frampton. Alexander put the fear of God into people, you see. If you'd ever met him, you'd know what I was on about. He were nasty, nasty to the core. If you upset him, he were the sort to get one of his mates from Chapeltown to put a brick through your window.'

For a long while he was silent. When his eyes met Archie's again his voice was quiet, almost a whisper.

'Look, I'm telling you this just so you know and because . . . because it's been preying on my mind over the years. But I'm telling you straight—I don't want any of this getting on t'telly. If it does, I'll just deny everything. It's a thing I need to get straight wi' mesen, but it's nowt I'm proud of.'

Again, he went silent, his head sinking into his hands.

'I didn't want trouble, that's all,' he said at length. 'Fact is, I weren't up to t'job, and I knew it. The wife had a dicky heart, you see, and we had a couple of lads at home. The last thing I wanted was trouble wi' bloody Alexander. But I blame mesen all the same . . .'

Archie fiddled self-consciously with his notebook. All this was engaging stuff, but this father-confessor role wasn't getting him very far.

'Forgive me,' he said eventually, 'but I don't see what this has to do with the job being finished by the Thursday.'

Elliot's eyes flashed and his hand suddenly crashed down on the table. 'I'll spell it out for you if you can't see it,' he shouted. 'That job *was* finished Thursday night, it's true. But it might have been finished Wednesday. Or Tuesday, for that matter. For all I know they might have been skiving the whole bloody week, because I weren't to know any different, and they certainly wouldn't have said owt.' He trailed off. 'They could do what they wanted wi' me, that pair, that was t'problem. They could wrap me around their little fingers because they knew I hadn't got t'bloody guts to stand up to 'em . . .

'It makes me ashamed of mesen, even now,' he went on after a while. 'That's the reason I sent another gang up to the hotel, straight after. Because although that pair of bastards had spent four days there I couldn't be sure, even then, that t'job had been done proper.'

'But I don't understand,' Archie said. 'Frampton clocked on for work the next day, didn't he?'

'Oh, aye. Frampton clocked on, as cocky as buggery considering that the day before he'd just smashed in his mate's head.'

'So he must have told you the job was finished? You wouldn't have seen him otherwise, would you? He'd have gone straight to the Shornewan?'

'That's right,' said Elliot. 'He *did* tell me t'job were done. But before the morning were out I'd had two or three calls from t'owner up there, Mr Carrington. He were pestering me telling me there was no water.'

Archie scribbled a few lines in his notebook. 'Well then, it must follow that Frampton was lying, and the job hadn't been done. But you just said—'

'I know what I just said,' Elliot interrupted. 'I said the job had been done by Thursday. It had been done. Taff Owen and his gang spent the best part of the weekend on double time, digging up the road. And when they found t'pipe where the burst had happened, it *had* been repaired—clean as a whistle.'

Again, Archie scribbled in his notebook, becoming more puzzled as the apparent illogicality of what he was being told began to dawn on him.

'Let's get this right,' he said. 'You're saying to me that you sent Frampton and Alexander out to repair the burst on the Monday, and that on the Friday when he came into the depot Frampton told you that the job was finished—'

'Aye, that's right,' said Elliot, 'except that I kept getting calls from the Shornewan saying there was no water coming through the taps—'

'So you sent two men up there to check—'

'Right again,' said Elliot. 'And they found the burst *had* been repaired.'

Archie chewed on the end of his pen. 'So why—why was there no water at the Shornewan, then?' he asked eventually.

Even Percy Elliot couldn't suppress a smile. 'Because no bugger had turned t'stop tap,' he said. 'After the job were finished, it were left off.'

It had turned dark by the time Archie left, and the rain had begun to blow up in a penetrating drizzle which cast a pall over the town. Archie turned up the volume of his Beethoven, but even at full blast the 'Ode to Joy' failed to dispel the unrelenting grimness of this overcast Yorkshire evening. He'd begun to dislike Yorkshire intensely. Or maybe it wasn't Yorkshire he disliked, but the work he was doing, and maybe not even the work, but the lives he had to probe to do the work effectively. Archie had found Elliot a sad character, burdened by a weakness that must have plagued him over the years, and which had now materialized in the shape of a TV researcher raking up the past. Oh, it was easy enough to see what had happened, easy to see how things had developed as the possibility of losing his job loomed fearfully to threaten Elliot's sick wife and family.

What could he have said at the time? Was he supposed to have admitted that despite being the man in charge, he had so little control over Frampton and Alexander that he'd absolutely no idea of what they were doing that week? Was he supposed to have admitted that to the police and, by implication, to his employers? So he'd decided to be careful in what he'd said. Of course, he hadn't lied. Men like Elliot, blunt men, honest men—they didn't lie. By the same token, though, they didn't always tell the truth, or at least not the whole truth.

'The job were finished by Thursday night, Officer.' Archie could hear him saying it.

What an inspiration that terminology had proved to be, what a careful formulation of words. The job *had* been done *by* Thursday night, and never had a man protected himself better by such an apparently irrelevant preposition.

The implications of what he'd disclosed were intriguing, though. Surely the police had made the same assumption as Archie by concluding that if the job were finished by the Thursday, then it must follow that Alexander and Frampton were working on it right up until the day of the murder. But now he knew that the job might have been finished days before, and Alexander and Frampton needn't have been at the hotel at all for large parts of the week. They might have been anywhere. After all, they had a van at their disposal, they were mobile. What implications might this have had for the original investigation into the murder? What implications might it still have in terms of Frampton's guilt?

Another thing that intrigued Archie about that van was how, without it, Alexander planned to get back home the day he was murdered. In court, Frampton didn't deny that after the two of them had finished working at the Shorne-wan, he, Frampton, had taken the van. But he was adamant that when he left, Alexander was alive.

'Bill told me he'd got some business to do,' Frampton had said from the witness-box. 'So I just left him to it.'

It was clear from the transcripts that this was a vulnerable point in his defence. Frampton had never been able to explain satisfactorily what this 'business' of Alexander's was, and in cross-examination he came over too guarded; indeed, reading through the transcripts even Archie couldn't help thinking that he was hiding something. Counsel for the prosecution had made a meal of it.

'You mean to say, Mr Frampton, that you were willing to leave him without transport on the edge of the moors?'

'Yeah. He said he had this business to do.'

'Did you offer to wait for him until he'd completed this— this "business"? Did you even inquire what this "business" was?'

'It was nothing to do with me.'

'Nothing to do with you? Mr Frampton, I put it to you that the reason you didn't offer to give Alexander a lift, was because at the stage you drove away from the Shornewan Hotel, he was already dead. I put it to you that you'd killed him, and concealed the body in an attempt to hide your guilt. Indeed, Mr Frampton, I put it to you that this whole preposterous story of Alexander having "business" is an attempt to hide that guilt.'

'No,' Frampton had replied flatly. 'That's not true.'

But what then had been the truth, Archie wondered? Why had Alexander stayed at the Shornewan, and why had Frampton left him there? The simplest explanation by far was that he committed the murder, but this explanation seemed unsatisfactory to Archie. He had a shrewd idea now of what sort of a man Alexander was, of the fear he could engender in others. No, if Frampton was telling the truth, then the only reason he'd have left the hotel without Alexander was because Alexander had wanted him to go. So what then was this 'business' that kept Alexander? And how much did Frampton know about it? And why, if he knew something, had he denied it in court?

It was like Stredwick said, the trick at this stage was not to have any answers, but to have the right questions. Archie at least felt he was asking them, and for the first time since leaving Wearside he began to feel he might be on to something.

The difficulty was, he had no idea what.

CHAPTER 8

Rita Brassington stood on her doorstep until the white Astra had disappeared down the street. Then she turned on her heel and went back into the house, locking the door behind her.

For a long while she sat almost motionless, tracing the outline of the embossed pattern on her armchair with one of her long fingernails. Outside, the light was fading, but Rita had lost track of time and noticed neither the gloom descending on the room nor, later, as a streetlamp outside the window burst into light, the harsh glare that caught her face as if in a stage spotlight.

He would be back, she knew that for sure. If she didn't contact him like he'd asked, it could only be a matter of days before he came knocking at her door again. Only this time he would be more persistent, this time he'd be less polite. She'd only encouraged him, she knew. If only she'd not burst out like that at the end, if only she'd not tried to defend herself when it wasn't clear a defence was necessary. After what she had said, he'd be bound to come back. It had been foolish, stupid. And stupid too to have mentioned her husband. She ought to have kept her mouth shut— God knows, she'd had enough practice lying in the past. It was common knowledge on the estate that Brian had left her; the television researcher wouldn't have to nose around much to rumble that. He'd already been nosing around, that was clear from what he'd said. The lie could only alert his suspicions.

Of course, she could refuse to talk to him, but that hadn't worked after Terry's trial, had it? The reporters then had camped on the doorstep, interrogating her every time she came outside so that for a week both she and her mother had felt prisoners in their own home. There was no way she would willingly suffer that indignity a second time.

But what was the alternative? The more she considered her options, the more limited they seemed, so that eventually, in trying to find her way out of the labyrinth the problem posed, she found all exits but one closed to her, like a trap from which there was no escape except to the huntsman's hands.

If it had been down to her, she'd have just brazened it out. Oh, she felt confident enough to do that; she'd lived with this long enough for the skills to have become second nature to her. But it wasn't just down to her, was it? There had to be another player off stage; how otherwise had he discovered about the assault? What other explanation was there? Without that there'd have been nothing to worry about, and certainly nothing to be afraid of. Rita Brassington was not an unintelligent woman, and realizing how far things had gone already, she realized too how far they might go. It was like watching the first gently tumbling rock of an avalanche.

She'd have to talk to him again, there was no question of it. There still might be time to avoid getting swept away. But how in God's name had he found out about the assault? There could only be one person, surely, who'd have mentioned that. Yes, she'd have to talk to him again so as not to arouse his suspicions further. But she'd have to be better prepared next time. And if the worst came to the worst? Well, a lot of water had passed under the bridge. Terry's imprisonment would be an embarrassment to them, surely? And as for Bill Alexander? Well, there'd be a tidy justice there, that no one could be blind to, least of all blind Justice herself. It might only mean probation. She had a couple of kids: at worst it could only be a year or two in prison. But even so, it was a terrifying prospect. She wasn't going to take the risk if there was any way of avoiding it.

She was disturbed in her thoughts by a crash from the kitchen, and leaping to her feet she discovered Gary standing against the sink, his clothes dripping with water and the smashed remnants of a china serving bowl around his feet.

The child's eyes were bright with fear. 'I was playing boats,' he said, fighting back his tears. 'I didn't mean it. It was an accident. Honest, it was just an accident.'

He stood paralysed with terror while Rita kicked at the fragments of broken china with her feet.

'Come here,' she said finally, her voice cold with disdain.

'I didn't mean it, honest. Honest, Mum, it was an accident . . .'

'Come here,' she said again. She could hear the quivering anger in her voice and feel the tension of the last few hours rising uncontrollably to the surface. 'Come here,' she screamed. 'Straightaway.'

The child sidled towards her, his face contorted into the soundless beginnings of a howl.

She looked down on him, scarcely able to hide her distaste. He was such a ridiculously clumsy child, always breaking something. She'd once hoped it was just a phase,

61

but instead, as he'd got older he'd become worse, growing into a great unco-ordinated creature, with long gangling limbs over which he seemed to exercise only the most marginal control. Watching him sometimes—as he played in the garden, or at nights when she looked in on him asleep in his bed—she was horrified by the passion of her feelings towards him, horrified by the way she could look at him, not as a mother, but as she imagined others must see him, graceless and gauche.

This deep aversion she felt could scarcely be contained when it came upon her. Sometimes she was struck by such repulsion it verged on hatred, a hatred so consuming that if ever she were to express it, she feared it might explode into unpredictable violence. She had such potential for violence, she knew. Yet she had such reserves of love as well.

For there were other times—when he came to her, hurt after a fall perhaps, trusting and dependent, or when he arrived home from school, tearful at some minor, childhood crisis—she could find herself overwhelmed by his vulnerability and by the intensity of her own vehement emotion. He was her child, after all, he was her son. Nothing would ever change that.

He flinched slightly as she lifted her hand to him, but once in her arms, he held on to her with the same desperate fervour that she clung to him, until they were both sobbing uncontrollably, each overwhelmed by the other's tears.

'It was an accident. Honest,' he kept repeating while she comforted him, stroking his soft hair, and chanting her own lament like an anguished mantra.

'I don't know what to do, Gary. I'm frightened. What can I do . . . ?'

George Stredwick had had a wretched morning wrestling with plumbing at the British Library in Bloomsbury. This was partly the result of the previous day's cornflakes and camomile which together had conspired to reduce his insides to an onerous liquid. However, in those brief periods when he hadn't been called upon to use the library's notoriously malodorous facilities, he'd put his nose to better use, immersing it in various technical tomes which, while they didn't help too much in directly furthering his understanding of the case, at least went some way towards explaining why the antiquated Victorian sewers of England were fast becoming inadequate to deal with twentieth-century demands.

It wasn't that he was hoping to prove anything by his reading; but then he wasn't after firm evidence, rather searching for some explanation of the inexplicable conundrum on which Percy Elliot had failed to cast light during his interview with Archibold. Why exactly had the stopcock at the Shornewan been left off after the burst water main had been repaired?

In a series of intermittent bouts Stredwick managed to trawl through Thomas Parkinson's *Water Supply and Sewage Systems*; *Handbook to Statutory Regulations* and Frederick Ross's riveting classic, *Civic Freshwater Supplies in High Altitude Areas*. Not having any technical background in hydraulics, they left him for the most part totally confused, but eventually enough understanding of the subject penetrated for him at least to be able to come up with some theory of what might have happened.

OK, perhaps the idea didn't amount to very much, perhaps to no more than one explanation in many of what could have occurred, just a suspicion, really. But suspicion could be the beginning of understanding: the whole issue could be irrelevant, but Stredwick's professional meticulousness wouldn't allow him to leave any stone unturned, not at any rate when there were so many unresolved questions left hanging as intriguing possibilities.

No, he knew this had to be taken to some sort of conclusion. Archie had already discovered too much about Alexander's character, and though part of Stredwick cursed him for clouding what should have been a straightforward investigation, another part of him couldn't help but admire the lad for having stumbled so instinctively into the very area that had been throwing up so many moral dilemmas. But it disquieted Stredwick, he didn't mind admitting it.

He was disquieted too by the Controller who rang him soon after he got home.

'Malcolm,' said Stredwick, 'I think before you start I ought to tell you that you've caught me at a bad time, a very bad time indeed.'

The Controller sounded sceptical. 'The trouble with you, George, is that there's never a good time. This really can't wait any longer. I've got Features barking at me from one side and the boys from Scheduling barking at me from the other. Are you actually intending to make a programme for us this season?'

'Yes, of course I am. But can't this wait half an hour or so? I'll ring you back later. I'm a bit . . . a bit tied up at the moment.'

'No chance. Now I've got you on the phone, George, I want to get this one settled. I was ringing you last night until all hours. Didn't you get a message on your . . . your thingamy?'

The Controller was prone to lose words like this on occasion. For a professional communicator, it sometimes seemed to Stredwick that, in his vocabulary at least, he was singularly ill-equipped to communicate to anyone.

The two of them had worked together for years; in fact, the Controller had once worked under Stredwick as a company trainee just down from Oxford. Despite occasional difficulties, the two had established a solid working relationship based on an understanding of each other's strengths and limitations. Malcolm, even as a young man, couldn't have made a decent television programme to save his life, but he was an administrator of consummate skill who'd salvaged Stredwick's career more than once when the professional knives were out.

'I must know a few more details,' he went on. 'I've an offers meeting in ten days, and if we don't bid for the spot, Features will be in there like a shot. You're leaving yourself very tight, George, very tight indeed . . .'

'Look, I know all this. But couldn't we just talk about it another time?'

'Another time? Another time? George, when I wangled

it for you to get into this department we agreed you'd keep me in touch with everything you were doing. That favour cost me a lot of friends, George. I'm not having you reneging on your word and turning into some lone cowboy responsible to nothing and no one. Now what about this Yorkshire thingy? Is it going to make?'

Stredwick mumbled something or another.

'Good. Good. That's good news, George. Problem is, Finance tell me you're already wildly over budget. This new man you've taken on isn't helping either. You're already about ten per cent over on research, and the chances of you coming in on target are ... George? ... George?' he broke off suddenly. 'George, are you still there?'

'Of course I'm still here. Where the hell else would I be?'

'OK, no need to get tetchy. I just thought I heard ... well, it doesn't matter. Have you got the file? There are a few above-the-line costs I need to query ...'

'Malcolm, are you sure this couldn't wait half an hour?'

'No it can't. Have you got the file?'

'No.'

The Controller went quiet. Stredwick could picture him sitting at his expensive mahogany desk in his panelled fifth-floor office. By this time he was probably chewing at a pencil—if he'd been able to find one among the debris of computer terminals, printers and Fax machines that littered the room. He'd always chewed at things when he felt stressed, and he'd kept the habit despite his promotions.

'George, I sense you're not being altogether cooperative,' he said eventually. 'Have you got the file with you?'

'It's not that I don't have it,' Stredwick said, mustering as much dignity as he could command. 'The problem is, I don't have it here, at this particular moment. You see, Malcolm, I'm sitting on the toilet. And, I might add—if you don't find the topic too distasteful—that I'm in some considerable discomfort ...'

Stredwick could have sworn he heard muffled sniggering on the other end of the line. 'You mean ... you mean you actually have a telephone in the ... the thingamy?'

'The bathroom, yes,' said Stredwick. 'I sometimes find it convenient. Now, can we talk later? I'll ring you back.'

But he never did, for soon afterwards he received another call that threw him more than anything that had happened that day. It was from Rita Brassington. She'd rung the office to check that Archie was who he claimed to be. They'd given her Stredwick's home number.

'Yes, he works for me,' Stredwick reassured her. 'I should be talking to him sometime today,' he added casually, so as not to over-alert her to his curiosity. 'I'll get him to come round. You'll be in, will you?'

Immediately she'd gone he was dialling the Shornewan. It was imperative to get Archie to her as soon as possible in case she changed her mind. That she'd followed up Archie's visit at all surprised Stredwick, and he was not certain yet that he understood her motivation. Of course, she could be totally irrelevant to the investigation, but now she'd rung back, somehow Stredwick couldn't believe it. Sometimes even the apparently irrelevant had a relevance of its own, once the jigsaw began to take shape.

Of one thing, though, he was absolutely certain: the interview had to be handled carefully. Archie had better not blow this one, Stredwick thought as he waited for someone to answer the phone at the hotel. He'll have to get it right first time, he won't get a second shot.

It wasn't that he didn't trust Archie. Far from it. The lad was beginning to show an admirable instinct for the some of the basics of the job—even if his understanding of its complexities sometimes left a lot to be desired.

His decision to barge in on Brassington, for a start—that might yet come up trumps.

No, it wasn't that Stredwick didn't trust either Archie's instincts or his professionalism. But he still had some reservations about his judgement. The blood on the rock where Alexander's body had been discovered, for instance. It wasn't in the least important, but Archie wasn't to know that. Stredwick was disappointed he hadn't at least commented on it. Surely he couldn't have missed it?

Why, Stredwick himself had gone clambering over the

moors not a couple of months before. The blood had been there then, as fresh as if the murder had just been committed. It surely hadn't just disappeared?

CHAPTER 9

Archie sat poring over the papers in front of a plate of untouched York ham, his face set in a grim frown. The morning's news was dominated by accounts of two further rapes, both of which had happened within miles of where he was now sitting. The ferocity of the attacks alone would have guaranteed coverage in the national newspapers, but their proximity in location, and the fact that that location was Yorkshire, ensured them additional prominence. As yet, the police hadn't connected the two incidents, let alone connected them with the previous rape, but already the tabloids were talking ominously of an 'epidemic' of attacks, and hinting at the existence of a 'second Ripper'.

Archie finished his coffee and was about to leave when Webber flung a package on to the table without a word of explanation. It turned out to be from June, the mail he'd asked her to forward: an uninspiring pile of bank statements and circulars. He searched for any letter from her, but found nothing, not even a note. It was confirmation, if he needed it, that she'd taken umbrage with him since she'd hung up during their conversation a couple of nights before. Since then she'd made no attempt to contact him, and he'd not been able to contact her either, so that she didn't even know about his episode on the moor. He'd telephoned her half a dozen times the previous evening, and when he hadn't reached her, again, earlier this morning before the time she normally left for work. The phone had remained suspiciously unanswered.

He tried her once more before he left the hotel, dialling her office number, but instead of June he found himself talking to Rosemary who sat at an adjacent desk. Rosemary was one of the friends June had been with in the Bella Vista the night they'd first met. She'd been around a lot since then too. Too much for Archie's liking; he'd never been keen on her.

'Archie. How are you? How's the new job?' she said with altogether too much bonhomie to be natural. 'June's, um . . . June's out for the minute. No . . . I've no idea at all where she is. I'll leave a message for when she gets back.'

Frankly, Archie had never trusted Rosemary further than he could spit. He didn't trust her now, and suspected that June was probably sitting opposite with her nose in the air, or more probably, knowing June, making V-signs at the telephone to the general merriment of the whole office.

She'd probably gone out for the night, and stayed over somewhere—most likely with Rosemary. She was probably avoiding him to make a point, unless, of course . . . Archie dismissed the notion from his mind. He hadn't really been serious when he'd mentioned her having an affair. June was right, did he think she had nothing better to think about than men. An affair? June? It was probably what she wanted him to think now. He wasn't going to get involved in these sorts of games.

There is on the outskirts of Rainsford, along the dales road close to the river, a small terrace of about a dozen ugly Victorian cottages, the remnants of what had once been an industrial settlement. The cottages are unusual only in being positioned where they are. In Manchester or Birmingham or any of the East Midlands towns, similar buildings compose most of the back streets and are singularly unremarkable; but in this part of picturesque Yorkshire their grimy nineteenth-century functionalism stands out like a sore on the landscape.

It was in an end cottage of the terrace, now a ramshackle transport café, that Archie found himself later in the day. Following Stredwick's plan of action, he'd set out to discover what he could of the argument that Alexander and Frampton were supposed to have had the morning of the murder, and he'd spent the day tracing Jennifer Rochford, the woman who'd testified to it in court.

The transport café where she now worked was closing when Archie arrived, and a woman with a bucket was emptying ashtrays and smearing the formica tabletops with a grubby rag. The place smelt of bacon fat and cabbage water.

'I'm looking for a woman called Jenny who works here,' Archie said. 'Jenny Rochford.'

The woman put down her bucket. 'And who might you be, then? You're not one of Frank's mates, are you?'

She seemed to find Archie's explanation that he was a television researcher wildly amusing. She burst into a hoarse laugh, like a turkey cackle.

''Ere, Jenny,' she shouted. 'There's a bloke for you sez he's from the telly. 'E's going to make you famous. Jenny, are you deaf? Come 'ere quick.'

Jenny Rochford arrived from the kitchen wearing a pair of rubber gloves and with a tea-towel slung over her shoulder. Even in her work clothes she was a handsome woman, with broad shoulders and strong features. Though Archie knew from the date of birth on her statement to the police that she was nearly fifty, she could have passed for ten years younger.

'I wonder could we talk?' he asked. 'Somewhere private, perhaps?'

He took her outside to the Astra where she sat staring stiffly at the windscreen as he explained what he was doing.

'Why are you lot so convinced this bloke Frampton's innocent?' she asked when he'd finished.

'We're not convinced,' Archie said. 'We're just trying to get at the truth.'

Archie explained to her about the scratches on Alexander's face, and about Frampton's fingernails. She became more interested, if no less sceptical.

'But that don't prove nothing,' she said.

'I'm not claiming that it does. It's intriguing though, isn't it? How would you feel if Frampton was your family? Your brother perhaps? Wouldn't you just want every stone

69

to be turned? How would you feel if he was your husband?'

Jenny Rochford laughed. 'If he was my old man, I'd tell 'em to throw away the bleedin' key. Anyhow, why should I get involved? We have enough trouble with the law here already, without me going upsetting 'em.'

'But you are involved already. You gave evidence at the trial.'

She looked at him sharply. 'I'm not going on that bleedin' telly, making a spectacle of meself.'

'I'm not asking you to go on the television,' Archie said. He tossed aside his notebook. 'Look, I won't even write down what you say, if it makes you feel any better. I just want you to tell me what happened that morning.'

For a long time, she said nothing. Archie could feel her debating with herself whether to speak, always a difficult decision for people faced with a journalist for the first time in their lives. But it was difficult for the journalist too. With some people, it was best just to sit out the wait in a silence that sometimes became unbearably tense. With others, it was better to ask some irrelevant question in the hopes of striking up a conversation from which information might emerge more naturally.

'Does this place make any money?' Archie asked eventually, judging Rochford would respond better to the chatty approach. 'You can't get much trade on a road like this, can you?'

'You'd be surprised,' she said, her eyes flashing into life. 'It may be a bit quiet this time of day, but you get here about six or seven in the morning when the HGVs are going south. You can't hear yourself think, it's so busy . . .'

They talked for twenty minutes, maybe half an hour. Archie lost all track of time, aware only that she was beginning to relax with him, and that in relaxing she was becoming less suspicious of him. Eventually he offered to drive her home, and they stopped off at a pub on the way.

'You'll get me tipsy,' she said after Archie had fetched her a third vodka and orange. 'I can't afford to get into this drinking habit.'

70

Archie, by this time, was beginning to enjoy her company. He was drinking whisky and she'd had him in hysterics at her apparently inexhaustible fund of garrulous stories about her various and sundry husbands.

'He were good to me, that one,' she said, 'but when I found those knickers in my bag, honest to God, I wished the ground had opened up and swallowed me whole . . .'

He was enjoying himself, yes, but at the same time he was watching and waiting as patiently as any fisherman. He knew the hook had been swallowed; now it was just a question of landing his catch. Eventually, in the natural way experience told him it would happen, the conversation turned to the café in the town centre where she'd once worked, and then to events on the morning of Alexander's murder.

'Oh, they were coming in regular that week—the pair of them. It were a wonder they got any work done. That bloke that got himself murdered—Alexander, were that his name?—he were a right good-looker. You couldn't help but notice him.' She laughed. 'A shame he got himself killed. I could have done with the likes of him at home. With a bloke like that to warm your feet on in bed you'd know you were safe from burglars. 'Ere, let me get the next one. I'm not so poor I can't stand me shout.'

'Had they been arguing much that week, then?' Archie asked when she came back from the bar.

She pushed a whisky towards him. 'Arguing? They hadn't been arguing at all. And they weren't really arguing that morning either. I told the police. It were more a tiff than an argument.'

'A tiff?'

'Aye, yer know, a tiff—a bit of a squabble. Well, not really a squabble. It were over too quickly. One second they were sat talking to each other, and the next they were fighting to get outside.'

'To get outside?' asked Archie. 'What for?'

''Ere, you ask a lot of questions, don't you? How should I know? All I do know is that they sent a table flying, well, a couple of chairs. And they nearly knocked over a girl

71

walking by on the pavement, I remember that much. I suppose once they got outside they knocked seven shades of shit out of each other. I don't know.'

'Didn't you look? Weren't you interested?'

'I didn't have time to look, did I? It were the middle of the breakfast rush. I had customers to see to. As long as they were out of my way I didn't care what they were doing to each other.'

Archie took a slow sip of his drink.

'Didn't you get *any* idea of what it was about, then? Were they shouting? Anything like that?'

'It weren't like that,' said Jenny, shaking her head. 'Like I told you, one second they were just . . . like, looking at each other . . . and the next they were all over each other to get out the door.'

'To start fighting?'

'Perhaps,' she said uncertainly. 'That's what I thought, any road. Like I said, I didn't see what they did outside. I'd got customers to feed.'

'Of course.' Archie nodded. 'Did anyone else see anything?'

Jenny sat for a few moments thoughtfully, idly tracing patterns on the table with her fingers where it had become dampened from the drink.

'Not that I know,' she said eventually, shaking her head. 'Bert were there, but she didn't see owt. The police talked to her.'

'Her?'

'Her name were Bertha—everyone called her Bert. She were manageress. There were another girl there too—a student—Jan, I think she was called. She were only temporary though, just doing a holiday job. She were out the back, any road. She couldn't have seen owt.'

Archie picked up his glass and swilled the remains of his drink around. For some moments he said nothing, then, looking her straight in the face and summoning as much in the way of a smile as he could muster without showing his scepticism, he said, 'Jenny, don't think I'm being rude, or that I'm trying to get you to say something that you don't want, but can you be *absolutely* certain they were arguing at all?'

She looked back at him, returning the smile, with only the merest trace of caution in her lively eyes.

'To be honest, Archie,' she said in her direct way. 'Now I've thought about it again, I can't . . .'

CHAPTER 10

The moment she opened the door it was obvious to Archie that Rita Brassington was dressed to create a certain impression. Her hair, which had been lank and unkempt at his last visit, had been washed and now fell in soft waves around her neck. She wore make-up, low-heeled sensible shoes, and a simple three-quarter-length dress in brown needlecord. Archie was struck by the air of characterless respectability which emanated from her. She might have been giving evidence in court.

'It's good of you to see me again,' he said flatly. 'I hope I'm not causing you too much inconvenience.'

She led him inside and sat facing him, perching on the edge of a dining chair with her knees pressed together primly and her hands resting, lightly clasped, in her lap. 'Tell me, Mr Archibold,' she said without any further formalities, 'do you genuinely enjoy this kind of work? Forgive me for asking. Idle curiosity on my part, but I just wondered if you needed training or qualifications for it.' She smiled. 'You don't strike me as the sort who'd naturally enjoy prying into people's lives . . .'

Archie was caught unprepared. Stredwick had warned him this might be an awkward interview, but he hadn't anticipated anything of this sort. 'I'm a journalist,' he managed to stutter eventually. 'I've got a job to do.'

Rita had been staring him out, unperturbed at any embarrassment she might be causing him, indeed almost welcoming signs of it. Now she threw her head back in an extravagant laugh. 'Of course,' she said. 'You've got a job

73

to do. You know, Mr Archibold, I had a lot of dealings with journalists at the time of Terry's trial. They had their jobs to do too,' she added acidly.

'It was a big case,' Archie said. 'People were bound to be interested in it.'

Again Rita fixed him in her gaze. 'A big case, Mr Archibold? What do you mean, a big case? A lot of corpses littering Yorkshire, were there? The death of a gangland leader, perhaps? No, it wasn't a big case at all, and you're not so stupid you believe that. It was a grubby bit of provincial thuggery, of no interest to anyone or anything—except for one aspect.

'Sex.' She spat out the word as if she were clearing something distasteful from her throat. 'Sex. That's all it was, Mr Archibold. The rumour was that there might be a . . . a love triangle—is that what you people call it? How old-fashioned you can be sometimes, how coy. They thought I might have been sleeping with Bill and Terry at the same time, so they arrived in their droves like flies to a cesspit.'

She ran her tongue across her lips. 'For that, Mr Archibold—for that, and just for that, me and my mother were under siege for the best part of a week. I mean, you read about it all the time, don't you? But you still can't believe it when it happens to you. They were literally going through the dustbins, can you believe that? It made me sick, and frankly—' she smiled at him again—'so do you. Now, what do you want to know. Let's get this over with.'

Archie took out his notebook, deliberately leafing through the pages to allow him time to marshal his thoughts. Even so passionately indignant, something in Rita's tone had struck altogether too false a note. Perhaps she was just a little too belligerent, her view of him as a journalist too pat by half? Or perhaps it was just that the outburst was too practised, too rehearsed.

'Look, I'm sorry if this is upsetting you,' he said. 'I don't mean to pry any more than I have to, but if Terry's innocent, there are more important issues at stake. I was hoping you'd feel differently . . .'

'Differently?' she snapped, her voice quaking with anger.

'How would you feel if someone came knocking at your door raking up a past you'd rather forget? Mr Archibold, I've got nothing against you personally, I hope you understand that. For all I know, you may be kind to your cat and your mother may love you dearly. But as far as I'm concerned, the sooner you get out of my life, the better. Come on, let's get this over with,' she said again. 'What do you want to know?'

Archie took out his pencil. 'OK, tell me more about Terry Frampton.'

'A nice man. We were friends.'

'What's he like?'

She shrugged her shoulders. 'Why don't you go and see him in prison if you're that interested? He's not dead, you know.'

Archie closed the notebook with a snap. 'Rita, you're going to have to make up your mind whether you want to talk or not. No one's forcing you. You were supposed to be a friend of Terry's, weren't you? It's him we're doing this for. He's the one stuck in prison for a murder he may not have committed. Believe it or not, we're trying to help him.'

She laughed cynically. 'The only person you're trying to help is yourself. I'm not stupid, you know. You're just like the rest of them: you're after a story. You may be a bit politer than the other pack, you may be a bit posher with all your talk of miscarriages of justice, but fundamentally you're just the same. If you really were trying to help Terry you'd just let this whole thing lie. It's nearly ten years ago now. No one cares any more . . .'

Archie felt himself suddenly irritated, even though he knew by responding this way he was rising to her bait. Who knows, she might be right about his motivation, but so what? The crusading Stredwick might view things differently, but Archie saw himself as a professional and he felt he'd a right to be judged by the criteria of professionalism, not by some set of ethical absolutes. She'd volunteered to talk, hadn't she? Did she imagine that her reluctance would make him just throw in the towel? Well, she'd have to think again, wouldn't she? Something—whatever it was—had

75

made her come back to him when there was no compulsion to ever see him again. Something—probably the same thing—was making her, he suspected, more gratuitously rude than came naturally to her.

Two could play at that game, though.

'What about Alexander, then? I can't go and see *him*, can I? Tell me what he was like. And tell me,' he said, 'tell me who you think killed him.'

'I've told you what he was like. He was an animal. That's all.'

'And who killed him?'

'Terry killed him. Look in the papers if you don't believe me.'

'OK,' Archie muttered to himself. 'If that's the way you want to play it.'

He took a deep breath. 'Fucking him, were you? Was he giving you one?'

For a second or two she sat open-mouthed, so that he knew he'd shocked her. Eventually her eyes narrowed hatefully. 'You're—you're disgusting,' she said slowly. 'I loathed Bill Alexander. He was repulsive . . .'

'It wasn't Bill Alexander I was talking about. I meant Terry Frampton. Weren't you screwing him?'

'You're despicable,' she screamed. 'You're just dirt. It was never like that with me and Terry.' Her hands, still resting on her lap, clutched at each other desperately and her eyes started to mist over with tears . . . 'It was never like that between us,' she said again. 'I—I loved Terry, I always did . . .'

The tears, once they started, came in great floods, contorting her features in such intense anguish it rocked her whole frame. She was like a tree-trunk that having weathered the storm for just so long, could bear its strains no longer and, choosing its moment, bowed and splintered in the wind.

'Let me make you a nice cup of tea,' said Archie. 'Then let's talk about it.'

The tea, when it arrived, didn't help at all. She sat alternately sobbing into her cup, or rubbing her eyes with tis-

76

sues, smearing her mascara around her eyes into grotesque black rings which only added to the general impression of her distorted face as some sort of primitive mask.

'Terry had it rough from when he was a kid, you see,' she explained eventually. 'I'm not trying to make excuses for him, don't get me wrong. He's always been in trouble with the law—but it's only been cars, a bit of thieving, that sort of thing. Nothing violent until he met Bill Alexander. He couldn't keep away from Bill, that was his trouble, and when he was with him he was . . . he was a different man. It was as if Bill had this control over him. It was like I said to you before: if Bill wanted something, Terry had to have it. It didn't matter whether he really wanted it or not. He just had to have it all the same. But it was more than that. It was almost as if Terry sometimes wanted—wanted to *be* Bill, as if he wanted to think like him . . . Do you remember that awful film years and years ago?' she asked suddenly. 'That chain saw film?'

'What? *The Texas Chain Saw Massacre?*'

'Yes, I think that's the one. Bill Alexander was really infatuated with it. He really got off on violence. Violence turned him on, it excited him. He could talk for hours and hours about fights he'd had, and how he'd smashed glasses into people's faces. He somehow used to think—I don't know—that it was some sort of joke. Anyway, he just kept going on about that film. He must have seen it a dozen times. He used to keep talking about what it must be like to cut at someone's flesh with a chain saw.'

'But what's this got to do with Terry?' Archie asked.

'It had everything to do with Terry, that's what I'm saying.' Rita's eyes began to mist over again. 'It was frightening. Terry's a meek man, soft, some might say. Violence frightened him as much as it attracted Bill. But he used to watch that film with Bill and—you could see it happening to him—he gradually began to talk like Bill. He started going on about chain saws day and night. Eventually, they decided they were going to borrow one. They were going to cut each other—'

'Each other!'

77

'Yes. Nothing serious. Or so Bill Alexander said. It was some sort of pact they'd made between them. It sounds unbelievable, doesn't it? But they were going to borrow this chain saw and slash a bit at each other's legs—just to see what it was like. I don't know, maybe it was all mouth. You could never tell with Bill Alexander, though . . .'

'They must have been winding you up, surely?' said Archie. 'What were they planning on doing afterwards, taking a stroll down to casualty to get themselves stitched up? They couldn't have been serious?'

Rita gave a dry laugh. 'Perhaps not. Who knows? Anyway, it never got that far, thank God. I put a stop to it as soon as I heard about it. But Bill Alexander was enough of a head case to have gone through with it, and he was mad enough to have sliced off Terry's leg just for the hell of it. But that's how Bill was, you see. And there was something in Bill that Terry felt he needed. I don't know . . . maybe Terry was just too gentle . . . maybe it worried him. Maybe he thought that to be a bloke—a proper bloke, you know what I mean—you had to be violent. Perhaps he was trying to learn from Bill Alexander. Does that make any sense?'

Archie was scribbling in his notebook, attempting to keep up with her in his rusty Teeline shorthand. Now, he paused and stretched his aching hand. 'I'm not sure it does,' he said. 'But one way or another you're hardly painting a picture of an archetypal murderer.'

'Oh, I don't know,' Rita said in such a casual way that at another time Archie might almost have missed it. 'Perhaps he did learn eventually. I was always telling him he had to get away from Bill Alexander. Well, now he has, hasn't he?'

'I couldn't make her out,' Archie said later on the phone to Stredwick. 'It was like talking to two different women. First of all she gives me all this crap about loving him, and then—bang!—he's the murderer! No question about it! No doubts in her mind. He killed Alexander, and why are we wasting our time bringing the whole case up again?'

For the previous couple of hours Stredwick had been

sitting at his computer, attempting to puzzle out the intricacies of a computer spreadsheet he'd bought that afternoon to sort out the programme finances. On one side of him lay the manual, already marked at various pages with odd scraps of newspaper he was using as bookmarks. On the other side, in a couple of dog-eared files, lay a pile of reciepts, order forms and costings. In buying the spreadsheet, Stredwick had harboured some spurious idea that all he would have to do would be transfer the contents of the files to the computer, and press a couple of buttons which would miraculously sort everything out. He was now learning painfully that before he could twist his mind around the finances, he needed to twist it around the spreadsheet first. This had proved no easy matter.

By the time Archie called, his head was such a bad-tempered confusion of keystrokes and codewords that the interruption came as an exquisite relief: against the perplexities of new technology, the complications of the Alexander murder were as a shaft of sunlight through a foggy morning.

'I mean, she was in tears within minutes,' Archie went on. 'But I couldn't help feeling that it was all a performance put on for my benefit. Oh, it was a good performance, I grant you, but it was too—too slick. And there were aspects of it that didn't quite gel.'

'Be more specific,' Stredwick demanded.

Archie poured himself a Lagavulin. 'It's difficult,' he struggled. 'She was upset, there's no doubt about that— but it was as if she couldn't work out what she was upset about. She was like a Lady Macbeth speaking the lines of a Juliet.'

'She's still denying there was any sort of argument between Frampton and Alexander over her?'

'Vehemently. And she was just as adamant that there'd never been any sort of relationship between her and Alexander. She said that was just an invention of the papers.'

'And this assault by Alexander? Did she admit he'd beaten her up?'

'Difficult again,' said Archie. 'She was aware we knew there'd been an assault—I let that one slip the first time

79

we met—she could hardly deny it, could she? But she wouldn't confirm it either. I must have brought up the subject half a dozen times. She seemed more worried about *how* we knew about it in the first place. She was convinced one of her friends had been talking about her, and that really seemed to upset her too. I was treated to another bout of the waterworks on that one.'

'Her friends? Did she mention any names?'

'No—not at that stage. She mentioned Maureen Paton at one point, but that was much later,' said Archie, flicking through his notebook. 'Maureen Paton was her friend from work, wasn't she? Rita seemed to be implying that Maureen was sweet on Bill Alexander—did we know that?'

'Some of us had worked it out a long time ago,' Stredwick said wearily. 'Why else would the police have spent time taking a statement from her? Did Rita say anything else about Maureen?'

Archie went through his notebook again. 'I got the impression there was some antagonism between them. I don't know . . . it's difficult . . . I might have been mistaken. Do you think it could be relevant?'

Stredwick gave one of his explosive laughs. 'I'm not sure,' he said. 'All the same, I'd have thought that your idiosyncratic mind might have found it intriguing. Maureen Paton and Rita Brassington were close friends once, weren't they? They obviously don't see much of each other now. Didn't you ask why they'd drifted apart?'

'No,' said Archie sheepishly. 'It didn't occur to me.'

After he'd put down the phone Stredwick worked at his spreadsheet for a couple of hours until he became aware from the cat's insistent fawning that it was feeding time. At first he tried to ignore the distraction, but interpreting his discouraging kicking as some form of game, the creature began clawing at his carpet slippers. Stredwick went into the kitchen, made himself a pilchard sandwich and turned the remainder of the can into the cat's bowl.

Anyone looking at the two of them as they ate might have come away with a totally false impression of the efficacy of pilchards to satisfy an appetite, either feline or human. The cat, by disposition as much as disability, was totally resistant to any food that resembled a living creature, however well disguised it might be by disparate sauces. It was bobbing its head into the bowl, and with no coordination whatsoever was attempting to strip the fish off its bone, an operation that left the kitchen floor like Immingham dock after the trawler fleets had landed.

Stredwick appeared to have problems himself and gave the impression that he had one of these same bones stuck in his teeth. He seemed to be rotating his mouth in an attempt to dislodge it without the inconvenience of removing his dentures. In fact—how wrong appearances can be—he was chuckling to himself, or as near chuckling as any man can get with a mouthful of pilchard and Mother's Pride. Eventually he went back to the telephone and dialled a number from memory. It was Remus's home number.

Stredwick came to the point straight away; he was not a man to beat about the bush when there was something on his mind. 'Edwin, that woman you saw at court during the Alexander trial, the one you recognized as having been beaten up. You said you thought her name might have been Rita Brassington. But does the name Maureen Paton ring a bell?

'No, no. It's not caused me any trouble at all,' Stredwick went on. 'There's absolutely no need to apologize, Edwin, anyone can make a mistake. But you know how I like to get these sorts of details cleared up. They can confuse people. I think this one may have confused my researcher . . .'

CHAPTER 11

Archie finally managed to speak to June that evening. At first they chatted about what he'd been doing, and she listened, not without some genuine concern, to his account of his last few days, especially his attempt at playing Captain Oates on the moors.

'What've you been up to, then?' he asked her eventually, the casualness of his tone failing to mask his anxious curiosity. In retrospect he could see this had been ill-judged; he'd been too fatigued for the question to appear anything but interrogatory. The interview with Brassington had drained him, and what energy he'd had left after it, Stredwick had soaked up in the debriefing which followed. Yes, in retrospect, it had been wrong to press June in a way that might have appeared intrusive. It had certainly been a mistake to persist with her in the same sort of tone he might have used with a resistent interviewee.

'What do you mean, "just messing about"?' he said. 'You've been totally incommunicado for almost a week. Where the hell have you been?'

'I stayed over a couple of nights with Rosie,' June said. 'I had dinner with Dave and Alice on Saturday. Hey, what have I done to deserve this? We're not married, you know—and even if we were I wouldn't feel the need to account to you for my life.'

'That's not what I mean. You could at least have rung.'

'I did ring. Two or three times. You were never there. I always seemed to finish up talking to the bloody hotel manager. When are you coming back, anyhow? There's something I want to talk to you about.'

'Talk to me about it now.'

'There are some things you can't talk about on the phone. I want to talk properly. Face to face. When are you coming home?'

Archie attempted to stifle an exhausted yawn. 'Look, it's a problem,' he said. 'Stredwick's getting uptight about the case. I think he wants to try and get it cleared up as soon as possible, or at least work out whether he wants to spend any more time on it. I just don't know . . .' He hesitated. 'Perhaps a week or two. Maybe longer.'

'What about getting away for a weekend?'

'It's difficult, really. He's got this bee in his bonnet at the moment about the student that was working at the café with Jenny Rochford. He wants to find her. I may have to go goosechasing around the country.'

June went silent. 'Have you even mentioned to him about getting away? Come on, admit it, you haven't, have you?'

'Stredwick's not that sort of person. I've told you, he's obsessed. He doesn't have normal human needs. He's just not the sort that's going to be very sympathetic to any sort of domestic responsibility . . .'

Archie pulled himself up abruptly, immediately aware that he'd said the wrong thing. 'No, no, I didn't mean that,' he said, backtracking. 'I wasn't saying *you* were a domestic responsibility . . .'

But it was too late, the damage had been done, and no amount of protestations by Archie that he was expressing things only as Stredwick would have seen them was going to repair matters. June had fired off with a salvo of righteous indignation: she was not going to stand for anyone seeing her as an appendage of his life, she was not going to put up with being seen as some dutiful wife caring for the home while he was away, she was not going to put up with him being away at all if any demands she made on his time were going to be seen just as irritating inconveniences.

'I'm not happy with this situation between us, Archie, I've told you before and I'm telling you again now,' she said at last. 'I'm not happy, and I'm not having it.'

They had parted coldly, without an endearment passing between them. A couple of days later at breakfast another of her packages had arrived for him, Webber hurling it at him like a discus as he passed the table. It struck him across the chest sharply, but its contents were to hurt him much more, leaving him feeling as if someone had delivered a blow to his solar plexus.

It contained a similarly uninspiring bundle of correspondence as the last package: a few circulars, a form from the Department of Employment and a letter from his parents. Once again, there was nothing in the way of a personal word from her, which was upsetting enough. What was more upsetting, though, was the adhesive yellow 'Post It' note which had inadvertently become fixed to the underside of one of the letters, and which had accidentally been posted much further than the writer intended. The writer, it seemed, was someone called Godfrey and the note was evidently intended for June. It was an informal note, some might have said intimate, filled as it seemed to be with 'darlings' and 'loves' on every line. It was confirmation of an arrangement to meet one night—one of the nights June had claimed to be staying with Rosie.

Archie sat staring at it for some time, aware both of a jealous turmoil gnawing at his gut, and an explosive outrage welling up inside him. It was unfortunate that at that moment he happened to glimpse Webber passing from the kitchen to a function room at the back of the hotel. Pushing his breakfast aside, Archie strode after him, through the great double door which divided the dining-room from the reception area.

Inside was a hive of activity with groups of men moving furniture, and others on ladders stringing bunting across the ceiling. Archie followed Webber as he made his way to a trestle-table at the front on which were displayed neat fans of tickets, arranged like hands in a card game.

'Do you really have to be quite so rude delivering my mail? You hardly need to hurl it at me,' Archie snapped.

Webber was dressed in an immaculate tweed suit, with a waistcoat and wide striped tie emblazoned with what appeared to be a series of crossed shotguns. He looked up at Archie in total bewilderment. 'Sorry, old man. Bit pushed, this morning. Bit busy, you know, with all the arrangements and things for tomorrow.' He spoke in a sort of formal shorthand, so clipped and abrupt that to Archie's ears it sounded completely artificial. Archie had always seen Webber as a transplanted wide boy from the city; now he seemed to have taken upon himself—in his language, and his ridiculous suit—the mantle of some latter-day squire.

'Got the Mayor coming, you know. And the local MP. Annual event. Big do for us here. You won't . . . you won't be . . . letting on, will you?'

'Letting on?' Archie exclaimed. 'What on earth are you talking about?'

Webber glanced about him surreptitiously and touched his lips with a finger. 'No . . . no, of course not,' he said.

84

'But be discreet all the same, OK? Was that all? I'll have to be getting on . . .'

It was Archie's turn to feel bewildered. He'd been spoiling for an argument as some way of venting his feelings, but Webber's disinclination to take up the challenge was totally disconcerting. It left Archie feeling even more frustrated and angry than before, as if he'd taken a swing at a punchbag only to find himself beating the air.

'Since you mention it, there is one other thing that's pissing me off,' said Archie, still disinclined to let Webber off the hook so easily. 'A friend has been trying to reach me. She's telephoned a couple of times and the messages don't seem to be getting through.'

Webber beamed a broad smile like a second-hand car salesman. 'Oh, you mean June. Yes. Lovely girl, isn't she? I'm getting to know her awfully well. We've had a couple of long chats.'

'A couple of long chats! Bloody hell, man, it's me she's been calling . . .'

'Yes, of course. But you haven't been here, have you? I told her you were busy—'

'You told her what!' exclaimed Archie, the outrage in his voice making it rise an octave so that a couple of the men around paused briefly in their work to glance at him. 'What right have you got to tell her anything? In future just take messages for me and ensure that I get them.'

Webber smiled again and got up from the trestle-table. 'Fact is, old man,' he said, trailing his arm across Archie's shoulder and leading him towards the door. 'The fact is, I *have* been taking messages, and they *have* been left for you— in your pigeonhole at reception. You're supposed to pick them up when you pick up your room key, but you haven't been leaving your room key when you leave the hotel, have you? The same goes for mail. Guests are supposed to pick that up from the desk too . . .

'Anyhow, must be getting on, you know. Nose to the grindstone, and all that.' He thrust something towards Archie. 'You better take this, while I remember.'

Webber scurried off leaving Archie staring into his hand

at a ticket he'd been given. It was a ticket for the annual dinner of the Rainsford Rod and Gun Club.

'Mr Stredwick's request,' Webber shouted as he disappeared out of sight. 'And don't ask me. I'm damned if I know the workings of his mind.'

Archie slowed down and pulled the Astra on to the pavement to allow a lorry right of way on the narrow terraced street along which he had been driving. As it passed, missing his wing mirror by a hair's breadth, Archie accelerated, and continued his slow crawl along the backstreets of Nottingham. He had never been to Nottingham before, but after today he would always feel he knew every hidden inch of it, since for most of the afternoon it seemed he'd been combing its inner areas street by street looking for an address.

For his part Archie would have preferred to have been in Yorkshire interviewing Maureen Paton who he thought represented a better bet in terms of making some progress with the case. But when he'd suggested it to Stredwick, Stredwick had pooh-poohed the idea.

'Let's walk before we run, lad,' he'd said in that condescending tone of his, as if he'd been talking to some cackhanded waiter who'd just unloaded a spring vegetable soup on to his lap. 'We'll see Maureen in due course, but first of all we want to find out a bit more about this Frampton character.'

This had been the only excuse he'd needed to take to the soap box, and for the better part of an hour Archie had been lectured on the nature of investigative journalism and how it required 'patience, perseverance and pattern'.

'It's the only way to work,' said Stredwick. 'It's not a bloody late night police series we're making, it's not a detective story we're constructing. We go about things in a routine, researched and regulated way. We don't rush into things like some angry anaconda.'

By this stage, what was getting to Archie, quite apart from the frenetic flow of the forced alliteration, was all this 'we' crap. As far as Archie could see, all that 'we' were doing was sitting in London getting in a blind panic at having fucked up the budget. 'We' weren't getting our bollocks frozen off on the moor, or getting insulted by witnesses who'd rather have seen us dead than have us in their homes. But Archie bit the metaphoric bullet. He was fast learning how many cartridges you could cram in the mouth for twenty-six grand a year.

And when Stredwick suggested the expedition to Nottingham he'd offered only the most formal of objections. 'It's a two-hundred-mile round trip,' he'd grumbled.

'It's just down the road,' said Stredwick with all the cosmopolitan confidence of one who feels the country divides into two parts, London and the rest, both as important as each other and both about the same geographical size. 'This Harry St John bloke used to be close friend of Frampton's. It'll give us a perspective on the guy.'

'I don't see why we don't just go and see Frampton in prison and make up our own minds.'

'Get your arse down to Nottingham, lad,' said Stredwick. 'You've not been given that car as a status symbol.'

And so, with the stereo blasting out Beethoven, Archie had braved the excesses of the M1 where a series of lunatic convoys of lorries seemed engaged in a conspiracy to prevent his arrival anywhere except the hospital intensive care unit. The journey took him far longer than he'd expected and, after he'd arrived, it took him far longer than he could have foreseen to find the place where Stredwick had arranged an appointment for him.

Eventually Archie screeched the Astra into the car park of a small factory tucked away on a trading estate. He was confronted by an Asian about his own age who stood apparently on guard, his arms folded and the sleeves of his white shirt rolled to the elbows like some nightclub bouncer. He was a strikingly handsome man with a wide mouth, perfect teeth and high cheekbones; beautiful almost, the more so, oddly enough, because of a long scar that meandered like an errant stream from the corner of one dark eye, across his right cheek to the edge of his jaw.

'I'm looking for a Mr Harry St John,' said Archie,

87

pronouncing the name as if it had been the gospel writer.

'It's Harry Singeon, to be accurate,' said the Asian, correcting him. 'Harbinder Singh, to be more accurate still. But there's no need to be formal, even if you are an hour and a bloody half late.' He grinned broadly and stuck out his hand. 'Alan Archibold, I presume.'

He led Archie into the factory, through a noisy gallery where rows of women sat at workbenches spooling strips of pink lace on to bobbins, and into a small room piled high with polythene sacks crammed with tangles of the same lace, like bags of candy floss. After the discordant din of the rest of the factory, this room seemed pleasantly restful.

Harbinder rearranged a couple of the sacks into a rough seat and flopped down.

'I'm sorry about your name,' said Archie 'I expected—'

'No problem,' he interrupted. 'It's a bad joke of mine. I got used to everyone calling me Harry. I thought, sod it, it's not worth the effort.'

'Where are you from, then? India? Pakistan?'

'Keighley, actually,' said Harbinder. 'But that's foreign enough for folks round here.' He came to the point immediately. 'You're looking at Terry Frampton's case again, aren't you? He's not pleased about that, you know.'

Archie raised his eyebrows.

'No, he's not pleased at all,' Harbinder went on. 'He wrote to me—what?—it must have been a couple of weeks ago now. He'd got wind of someone nosing about. He told me to have nowt to do with you, said he'd prefer to let things rest.' He gave another broad grin. 'Mind you, I never took a deal of notice of Terry when he was out of prison; I don't see why I should take much notice of him now he's locked up. I've seen your programme on t'box. It seems to me you're after helping people, not buggering them up. What can I do for you?'

'Does Terry write to you regularly?' asked Archie, taking his notebook from his pocket.

'Oh aye. He were a good mate once. You can't just desert a mate because he gets in a bit of bother, can you? Well, it were perhaps more than just a bit of bother,' he added, seeing Archie's face. 'Murder's . . . well, murder's serious, I know. It's a nasty business,' he said, shaking his head, 'a nasty business.'

'But you've still kept in touch with him?'

'Aye. And seen him a couple of times too. He got transferred to Gartree a few years back, it's not far from here. Funny, though,' he said, shifting position on the sacks. 'I doubt me and Terry'd have kept in touch if it hadn't been for the murder. We'd fell out before it all happened, you know. Hadn't spoke a word to each other in months. But you can't kick a bloke when he's down, can you? You got to stick by your mates.'

'Did you know Bill Alexander at all?' Archie asked.

Harbinder's dark eyes darkened even more. 'Oh aye, I knew that bastard well enough.' He prodded at the scar on his face. 'Bill Alexander's work,' he said. 'An original. Signed too. I owed that bastard one, and if Terry hadn't done for him first, like as not you'd have been investigating my case instead of his.

'A beer glass in me face,' he went on, seeing Archie's curiosity. 'I were in a pub wi' Terry, and Bill Alexander came in tanked up to the eyeballs, taking the piss out of me. I don't drink, you see. Nothing religious, like, I just don't enjoy the stuff. Any road, Alexander starts giving me all the Paki poofter stuff because I'm sipping an orange juice—'

'And there was a fight?'

'Was there fuck,' said Harbinder. 'You didn't fight with Bill Alexander on your own—leastways, not if you'd got any sense. He was a head case, that one. He'd have killed someone before long if someone hadn't done for him first. No, I just left. He followed me outside and wham!—suddenly there seemed to be half of Pilkingtons buried in my face.'

'But Terry was with you?'

'Aye, he was there, but he did nowt. Mind you, I wouldn't have expected it from him. He were always the first out the door if there was any aggro. But apart from that, he were shit scared of Bill Alexander. That's why we fell out. Bill and him had begun knocking about together, you see: I wasn't going to risk running into Bill Alexander again. There's only one way of handling scum like that. The next time I planned to see Bill Alexander it was going to be on my terms, and with a few of my family around me.'

Harbinder looked at Archie with another broad smile. 'You seem surprised,' he said, fingering the scar absently. 'I thought you journalists were all hard-nosed sorts. I'd have thought it'd take more than a bit of domestic like this to knock you off your stride.'

Archie shrugged his shoulders. 'I'm not a violent man, myself. I've never understood violence in others.'

'Peace, love and good vibes, man. Is that what you mean?'

Archie ignored the facetiousness. 'I get as angry as anyone about things,' he said sharply, 'angrier than most people about a lot of things. But perhaps it's because I get angry, the anger's enough in itself. I could never imagine consciously wanting to hurt someone.'

'Nobody's ever cut you up, or you might think differently,' Harbinder said, his eyes flashing. 'It's not the pain or the blood that gets to you. It's not even the shock of finding shreds of your face hanging off, or your pants wet with piss because you're so scared. It's the—the humiliation that hurts most. It's the feeling that there's nothing you can do. What's the use of anger then? Anger's just the fuel. After that you've got to do something—for your own self-respect as much as anything else.'

'You could have gone to the police.'

Harbinder looked at Archie incredulously. 'Grow up, man, this is the real world. What good would that have done? A Paki gets cut up in a bit of rough and tumble outside t'pub. Oh, I can see that'd be a big CID job; they'd probably call in the Yard on that one. No, there was only one way to get justice from a guy like Alexander. It was the only way he understood.'

CHAPTER 12

'You knew that he had a score to settle with Alexander, then?' Archie said testily. 'He told you that on the phone?'

'He was very forthcoming,' said Stredwick. 'Probably more than he was with you, face to face. He admitted that if he'd have got to Alexander before Frampton, he'd have killed him. "Stuck him like the pig he was"— those were his exact words.'

Archie fell silent. He had only been back at the hotel half an hour or so, after a reckless drive back from the Midlands. Since then he'd been on the phone trying to reach June, but it seemed she'd gone out again. He felt bitterly hurt by her, and bitterly angry at her. And he couldn't help feeling that wherever she'd gone the enigmatic Godfrey wasn't going to be far away.

Other things too were worrying him. That morning, on his way to Nottingham, he'd stopped at the building society to withdraw some cash from their joint account. He had found that more than half of it had been withdrawn.

'It seems to have been taken out on another book,' the cashier had explained to him. 'I'll check again for you, but it's on the computer.'

When Archie rang to debrief Stredwick on the meeting with Harbinder he was already emotionally frayed and short-tempered; it hadn't helped his disposition to discover that most of what he'd driven to the Midlands to learn, Stredwick already knew.

'Why didn't you tell me before I left?' he snapped. 'For God's sake, we're supposed to be working together. What bloody use is it wasting my time sending me half way across the country for nothing?'

Stredwick, who was sitting in his easy chair at home, a cup of hot, freshly ground coffee to hand and the cat nestled in his lap, sucked at one of the small cigars he infrequently allowed himself. George Stredwick, it's worth noting, was

91

at that moment in an entirely different mood from Archie's, so totally at one with the world that there was nothing, least of all the irascible outpourings of a researcher, that was going to upset his contented equilibrium.

His day had begun well with the monthly trip to the supermarket, a job he so thoroughly detested that once it was completed, he felt like someone who'd discovered he'd only got a cold after being told he had cancer. He'd loaded his trolley with four weeks' supply of Bird's Eye Menu Masters and assorted varieties of Whiskas, and returned home strengthened in his resolve to get to grips finally with the programme budget.

This had been a resolution made more in hope than in expectation of success, but in fact it hadn't taken him anything like the effort he'd anticipated, for before long he'd stumbled on an ingenious method for offsetting some of his expenditure on the Frampton case against one of the project numbers of his earlier programmes, an exercise that had so transformed his all-important bottom line that the computer, rather than showing him £21,000 over budget, now showed him a miraculous £6,000 in the black. Of course, at final accounting he knew it wouldn't wash, but he knew too it was enough to keep the Finance Department tied up for long enough for it not to make any difference, for once the money was spent there was nothing they could do.

These onerous domestic and administrative tasks completed, Stredwick spent a relaxed afternoon thinking more closely about the Alexander murder, and here too the gods seemed with him. It wasn't that the case posed any particularly intractable problems, he'd never thought that. Barring the unlikely possibility of some anonymous maniac having decided to vent his psychosis on Alexander's skull, the whole case hinged on some very simple geography that an eleven-year-old couldn't have missed. But there were some intriguing points that Stredwick wanted cleared up before he felt confident enough to start filming a programme.

And there were, of course, some critical people still to be interviewed.

Experience told him that he was unlikely ever to know

the full details surrounding the murder, but instinct told him he could know a lot more than he actually did. Archie's persistent belly-aching about the direction the case was taking was a constant reminder to Stredwick that even though he had enough theories about the case, as yet he'd actually got very little to tangibly support any of them.

The police investigation had been hurried, and fundamentally flawed, but it had at least been been meticulous—in the investigation, if not the analysis. Everyone who might have shed some light on the case seemed to have been interviewed, everyone, that is, except one person—the student who had been working at the café the morning Alexander and Frampton were supposed to have been arguing. According to what Jenny Rochford had told Archie, this student was in the back of the café when the brief scene had taken place, and so there was no question that she could have seen anything of any real relevance, let alone that she knew anything directly pertinent to the murder itself. All the same, it surprised Stredwick that the police hadn't bothered taking a statement from her. After all, they'd taken one from Bertha Greengross, the manageress at the café, and she hadn't seen anything either.

There was something about this student that—yes, Stredwick couldn't deny it—there was something about her that obsessed him. He didn't believe her role could ever be central to the case, but he felt—if one theory that was growing in his mind proved correct—that she could at least explain what the commotion in the café that morning was all about. Stredwick wanted to find her because he worked in a world of outside chances, and there was an outside chance she might be able to contribute something to the investigation; but more than that he wanted to speak to her because the police hadn't, and in Stredwick's perverse way, this was almost more of an incentive.

So instead of tearing into Archie for his impertinence—which in other circumstances he would most certainly have done—Stredwick merely puffed on his cigar, smiled to himself and urged Archie in the most moderate of tones to calm himself down and explain what was needling him.

'You'll have to excuse me,' Archie finally apologized. 'It's just been a bad day. Personal problems, you know,' he added, convinced in his own mind that Stredwick wouldn't know at all. 'And I suppose I'm feeling the strain of the case too. I can't understand why you keep sending me out to find out about things you already seem to know. How much else do you know that I don't?'

Stredwick ground his cigar butt into an ashtray. For a moment he considered lighting another, but dismissed the idea. Archie was too intelligent to be strung along like this; if he was going to be any use, he had to be played more artfully. And with a touch more honesty. The lad would catch on otherwise.

'We all have bad days,' Stredwick said. 'You'll have to take a weekend off soon, give yourself a break. Not the next few weeks, of course. But soon. I can see how this sort of investigation could be disheartening if you haven't done one before. You'll just have to trust me.'

'Trust you?'

'Trust me,' Stredwick said again. 'Perhaps I do seem to know things you don't, but I don't know enough yet. Just trust me. And believe me when I say that most of the time I'm struggling around as blindly as you.'

'But haven't you got some clear idea where we're going? To me the whole case seems to be without direction. How can I have any sort of role when things are so confused?'

'In the country of the blind . . .' Stredwick quoted, and trailed off. 'That's often the way with these things. Again, you'll have to trust me that the work you're doing is critical, as much in helping me work through my own ideas as anything you're discovering.'

'But why won't you tell me things?' Archie asked, a tone of stridency beginning to enter his voice again. 'You talk about what I'm discovering, but what *have* I discovered that you didn't know before I began working for you?'

Stredwick stretched into his chair, slipping the phone into the crook of his neck and flexing his arms above his head, like an athlete toning up for a race. He'd expected that he'd have to have this conversation at some point, but perhaps not at this point, not quite yet. But Archibold was on the ball, you had to give the lad that. You couldn't underestimate him.

'Did you go and see Bertha Greengross?' Stredwick asked, changing the subject. 'What did she say about the café windows?'

'There you go again. Am I supposed to know what relevance it has to the case whether or not the café windows had blinds, curtains or shutters? If it is relevant, why don't you tell me?'

Stredwick swept the cat off his lap and moved to his desk where he felt, if not more relaxed, then at least more efficient. 'You've not been listening to what I've been saying, son,' he snapped, a tone of impatient irritation creeping into his voice. 'There are parts of this case I'm as confused about as you are, but I'm testing theories. What I want is for you to research the theories to see if they're viable. What I don't want is you to be so involved in them it colours your objectivity. You'd be no use to me at all then. Now, get to the point, what did Bertha say about the café windows?'

Archie flicked through his notebook. 'They were boarded up. There'd been some trouble in town the previous Saturday night, and some yobbos had chucked a brick through them. They'd been waiting all week for the glaziers.'

'Interesting,' said Stredwick. 'Did she say anything about the student?'

'Jan or Janet, she thought her name was, that's all she could remember. She worked at the café over Christmas as a holiday job. Bertha seemed to think she was in her final year.'

'At a local college?'

'She couldn't remember that either. To be honest, I don't think Bertha liked her. She sacked her eventually though she couldn't for the life of her remember why. In fact, the only useful thing she could remember was the quilting . . .'

'Quilting—making bedspreads, that sort of thing,' Archie explained. 'It's a hobby for some women, isn't it? Apparently, Bertha once noticed this Jan looking at some drawings for a quilt design. Bertha remembered it particularly because her grandmother had once made quilts. It stuck in her mind.'

Stredwick slipped a disc into his computer. Down the phone Archie heard him tapping on the keyboard. Stredwick, Archie had learnt, used the computer as other journalists did a notebook.

'It's not much to go on to find her,' said Stredwick. 'But we're still going to have to try.'

Archie mused for a moment. During the conversation, he'd been constantly aware of Webber and the team of workmen on the ground floor preparing the main dining-room for the dinner the following night. There'd been noise of sawing, and of furniture being moved; there'd been intermittent hammering echoing around the corridors of the hotel, and occasionally the sound of voices shouting instructions across the reception hall. Now it had all become silent.

'Frampton and Alexander couldn't have been busting a gut to get that job at the hotel finished, could they?' Archie said eventually. 'I mean, according to Jenny Rochford they were spending quite a lot of time at the café.'

'Yes, a useful bit of information, that,' said Stredwick. 'It set my mind working. What were they doing the rest of the time when they weren't in the café and they weren't pretending to work at the hotel? I want you to see the Carringtons . . .'

'The couple that ran the hotel before Webber took the place over?'

'That's right. I've arranged with Webber for Walter Carrington to be at this Rod and Gun Club dinner tommorrow night. Find out from him as much as you can about how often he remembers seeing Frampton and Alexander working. Take him through the week in detail. It's a long time back for him to remember—but we'll never find out anything unless we ask. There might be something that sticks in his mind.'

Archie scribbled in his notebook. 'Carrington used to be something big in the local Chamber of Trade, didn't he?'

'He was a magistrate as well once, but he moved out of the district after he sold the hotel. He lives in Doncaster now. Webber's done us a favour getting him to agree to come along. He was reluctant to talk to me when I rang him a couple of months ago. You should be able to button-hole him at some stage. Just find out what you can.'

'And his wife?' Archie asked.

'Elizabeth. They've separated now. She lives in some village in the sticks. You'll have to go and see her, but there shouldn't be any problems, she seems friendly enough. While you're at it, though,' Stredwick said, almost as an afterthought, 'you might as well go and see Julie Taylor too . . .'

'Julie Taylor?' said Archie, racking his brains. 'Wasn't she working at the hotel at the time of the murder—a receptionist or something?'

'Receptionist, cleaner, bottle-washer and chief drudge, I think,' said Stredwick. 'She was off the week of the murder, so she was never called as a witness at the trial. But there's a statement from her in the files. She'll probably remember something. After all, with her job she probably had a vested interest in getting the water back on as soon as possible. When you see her, ask her if she has any idea why Alexander should have wanted to stay on at the Shornewan that night, or how he intended getting back to Leeds afterwards. I'm sure the police must have gone over the same ground with her, but it won't harm to ask again.'

Archie scribbled again in the notebook. 'Are you thinking that Alexander might have arranged to meet her?'

'I don't know,' said Stredwick drily. 'But sure as hell, he'd arranged to meet *someone*. I can't imagine Bill Alexander hitch-hiking, can you?'

'Someone that killed him, perhaps?'

'Perhaps,' said Stredwick. 'But remember—and I keep telling you this—we're not the police. The only reason I'd be interested is that it would mean that Frampton wasn't the last person to see Alexander alive.'

Archie stretched over for the Lagavulin, and poured himself a large shot. He'd had it in his mind to go and see Maureen Paton as soon as possible. With all these instructions from Stredwick, the opportunity for that seemed to be slipping away. It was as if Stredwick was determined to keep him on a tight rein.

'Just don't forget the geography of the case, that's all,' Stredwick said. 'Oh yes, and one more thing—when you see the Carringtons, if you get the chance find out—find out how much they knew about local weather conditions . . .'

He put down the phone.

Geography? Local weather conditions? Archie was pondering what on earth geography or the local weather might have to do with Alexander's murder all that evening as he attempted between glasses of Lagavulin to reach June. He was still pondering it as he drifted into drunken sleep in the early hours, and still turning it over in his dreams as he was woken in what seemed the middle of the night.

The digital clock attached to the radio at the side of his bed showed the time at 5.03. The call was from Stredwick who, if he went to bed at all, apparently didn't stay there for long.

He said: 'You can cross Julie Taylor off your list. She's dead.'

'Dead?' said Archie. He was half asleep and his head was ringing from the effects of the whisky. 'What do you mean, dead?'

'Haven't you read the papers yet?' said Stredwick who seemed totally oblivious of the time. 'She's been strangled. It seems she's the latest victim of your friendly neighbourhood rapist. Only this time it seems he's gone a bit further than he's done before.'

CHAPTER 13

Stredwick was back on the phone to the Shornewan shortly before seven.

'George,' said Webber, 'I thought it might be you.'

'You've seen the papers, then? What do you make of it?'

'It's a bad business. Of course, it could just be co-incidence . . .' He sounded doubtful.

'Any ideas?' asked Stredwick.

'Lots of ideas, not much else. You've known me long enough, George. You amateurs might work from hunches, but that was never my way. If I haven't got anything to say that I can't back with facts, then I keep my mouth shut.'

'But you can't think of anyone else who might have . . .'

'Killed her? No, why should I? I didn't know her. She worked here for a while after I first bought the place, but she left soon afterwards. She was a dowdy sort of a kid, plain-looking. Always struck me as very unhappy.'

'Family? Friends?'

'No boyfriends, if that's what you mean. Her father was around. A very protective sort, like a bloody mother hen he was, always fussing around.'

'I suppose it might be unconnected . . .'

'Like I said, George, it could be just coincidence.'

Stredwick briefly explained what he was planning and Webber provided him with a name and telephone number.

'Not that I've got that much clout with the local force,' he explained. 'They know I used to be a copper, but they leave me alone, and I don't have more to do with them than I have to. But this guy—how can I put it?—he's sound, and he owes me a drink.'

'A drink?' asked Stredwick.

Webber laughed. 'We've all got faults, George. Even you.'

Stredwick was on the verge of putting down the phone when another thought occurred to him. 'You'd better keep your eye on the lad. Just in case,' he said. 'I may be over-reacting, but I don't want him caught up in any rough-house stuff that he can't handle. It's happened before, you know.'

'That could be wise,' said Webber, 'but who's going to protect the irritating little turd from me?'

'Getting up your nose, is he?'

'He'd get up a fucking elephant's trunk, George. Does he know about me yet?'

'He may have guessed, but if he has, he hasn't mentioned it to me. But then, I wouldn't expect him to.'

'Good,' said Webber. 'Let's keep it that way. I don't want anyone knowing more about my business than they have to. I've got to make a living out of this place after your circus has moved out of town.'

'I wouldn't worry,' said Stredwick. 'The lad's discreet. Sound, you know?'

'I'll take your word for it, George,' Webber said sceptically.

Stredwick dialled the number Webber had given him. Four hours later he sat huddled over a lukewarm coffee in a Wimpy bar in Leeds talking to a man who, for all his casual slacks and sports jacket, couldn't have been anything but a police officer. He was broad-shouldered and fleshy, like a rugby prop forward gone to seed. He must have been in his early forties, Stredwick judged: old enough to be having a mid-life crisis, though too insensitive for it to worry him.

'I don't like this,' the policeman said conspiratorially, leaning over the table so far that Stredwick could smell his halitosis hanging between them.

'You don't have to,' said Stredwick. 'I only want some— some help with my inquiries.' He slipped a folded fifty-pound note under a sugar bowl.

The man looked into Stredwick's eyes, and then down at the note. He shook his head as if considering the propriety of leaving such a large sum of cash unattended in a public place. Then he picked it up.

'What do you want to know, then?'

'How did she die?'

'Strangled. Like the papers said. That's unofficial until we get the PM report, though Christ knows why we need the experts to confirm what's staring us in the face. He'd virtually decapitated her with her own tights.'

'Where did you find her?'

The policeman sipped at his coffee. 'Top end of Kirkstall Moor. At about eleven last night. She'd been left at the side of the road. Some bloke staggering home pissed from the pub found her.'

Stredwick rooted about in his briefcase for a map. 'Kirk-stall Moor? That's a bit out of the way, isn't it?'

'She wasn't killed there—just dumped from the back of a car, we think. She lived with her dad. According to him, she was in Rainsford meeting someone last night.'

'Meeting someone? I don't suppose you know who?'

'Do you think I'd be here if I did, you daft bugger. Catch him and we've got our man, I reckon.

'Well, it has to be him, doesn't it?' he said, sensing Stred-wick's scepticism. 'It's been in the papers and on the radio. If it had just been an innocent get-together, someone would have come forward by now, wouldn't they?' He broke off abruptly. 'Hey, none of this is going to get out, is it? I don't want trouble.'

Stredwick shook his head. 'Just background. Like I said on the phone. Was she knocked around?'

'Aye, a bit,' said the policeman with constrained York-shire understatement. 'Broken jaw, probably a few ribs gone, and bite marks on her tits. Her arm busted too, I reckon, judging by her position when I saw her.'

The memory of it suddenly provoked something in him, for he drew back from his huddled position over the table and jabbed at Stredwick accusingly. 'What's your interest in the case anyhow? Going to prove the murderer innocent, before we've even charged him?' He shook his head. 'You know, your programme makes me sick. Who the fuck cares if some bastard's been banged up, and there's been some technical mistake at his trial? Or if some bloody bit of irrelevant evidence has been forgotten? If you had to see half of what I do in this job, you'd have a deal less sympathy for that sort of vermin.'

Stredwick was in no mood for an argument, but he'd pored over too many sickening scene of crime and post-mortem pictures himself not to realize the implications of the investigations he did, or not to know the difference between the sanitized violence of the medium in which he worked and the messy violations of flesh and blood that happened every day in the real world. He'd seen throats cut and stomachs slashed. He'd seen faces beaten to a jelly,

101

human limbs hacked around like so many Sunday roasts, and women after rapists had used them as rubbish bins for everything from broken bottles to house bricks. And the senseless, bestial depravity to which humankind could sink affected him no less now than when he'd first started the work.

Oh yes, Stredwick knew what murder meant. But he also knew what a miscarriage of justice was. He'd sat in rooms from one end of the country to the other listening to reasons why convicted murderers were innocent. And he'd sat in countless lawyers' offices listening to the same stories. Nine times out of ten, ninety-nine out of a hundred, he'd listen politely, get up and walk away, constantly amazed how the most lumpen thug or the most gratuitously violent miscreant could sound like a community stalwart from the mouth of a devoted wife, a loving mother or even a young, idealistic solicitor just out of articles and still smarting from defeat on his first big case. To listen to some of them, you'd think the gaols of England were full of Mother Teresas.

But every now and again there'd be one that would arrest his attention, one case where a fact didn't fit, where an alibi seemed too convincing to dismiss, or an identification too unconvincing to accept. Every now and again there would be some aberration of some jury somewhere that would stop him in his tracks, and give the lie to the old cliché about the British legal system being the best in the world.

Then it was harder to walk away, because the devoted wife had tried wherever she could for help and got nowhere, the loving mother had written to everyone including the Queen and the Prime Minister but achieved nothing, and even the solicitors, young and not so young, had spent so much time poring over the letters of their law that finally they'd had to concede that there were no answers in a judicial system that so often seemed weighted against the poor and the powerless, the uneducated and the dispossessed.

He felt involved then, not just because it was his job to feel involved, but because he always felt a weighty personal responsibility for his cases. Because he knew that behind the sheaves of papers and weighty files that he assembled to understand a case, behind the experts he consulted and the television executives whose arses he licked to get the programme on air, was the desperation of ordinary people at the end of their tether. Kids without a father, sons who wouldn't be home this side of the next decade. Men and women who wrote anguished letters to their partners offering them a divorce, or encouraging them into affairs, not because they weren't loved, but because they were loved too much to be allowed to ruin their lives waiting at home with the only future anticipating some far-off release date.

Oh yes, George Stredwick knew about murder and the violence it involved, but he knew a different type of violence too, an institutionalized violence committed upon the innocent by a creaking state legal system so rigid and callous in its methods that it was sometimes as well Justice were blind, for all she might be required to witness perpetrated in her name.

Oh yes, he knew, and he wasn't having any overweight bastard with a warrant card in his pocket telling him any different.

With these thoughts in his mind Stredwick's eyes widened furiously. He wasn't easily provoked, but the policeman had touched on a subject guaranteed to get his gorge rising.

'You were involved in the Dealman case, Webber tells me,' he said eventually. 'Was that a technical mistake or some bit of irrelevant evidence that had been forgotten?'

'What if it was? What's it to you, anyway?'

'For someone who criticizes my programmes, you don't seem to watch many of them. I spent more than a year on that case.'

The policeman opposite was unimpressed. Unrepentant too. 'And the bastard was still as guilty afterwards. Everyone knew it.

'Everyone,' said Stredwick, 'except the Lord Chief Justice and the judicial system you're paid to uphold. Dealman was pardoned, you know. They let him out.'

'On a technicality. You call that innocent?'

'And you call withholding evidence a technicality? No jury in the world would have convicted him if they'd had those factory time-sheets in front of them. But that, of course,' Stredwick added, 'was why they were never made available to the defence in the first place.'

The man opposite to him smiled, not an unpleasant smile, but one that seemed to signify that he'd heard all these arguments before, and from better men than Stredwick. 'I sometimes wish you people who criticize the police could spend a month or two doing the job. You might have different ideas about things then,' he said. 'Dealman was a villain, always was, always will be. It's easy enough to sit back in some office somewhere carping at other people; it's a bloody sight harder to be out there doing the job yourself.'

He finished the dregs of his coffee. 'Do you know in this division we've had nearly an eight per cent increase in burglaries already this year? Violent crime's gone up by more than a third, and we've got so many sexual offences on our books they'd fill a second-rate porn shop. Yet you try and argue an extra few hours' overtime, or another man for an operation. Take it from me, the bosses have got no idea. When they're not at some conference or another, they're locked away in their offices working out shift patterns and bloody manning levels. I tell you, you just don't know the half of it.'

'So you cut corners,' said Stredwick coldly.

'We don't cut corners, but we have to decide priorities, we have to make decisions about what's important. OK, so sometimes things don't get done right. Do you think that makes us feel good? Do you think it makes *me* feel good? If you do a job—any job—you want to do it as well as you can, don't you?'

At another time Stredwick might have been more sympathetic to this argument, but five years after Dealman had been released, he still harboured an open wound about the case. For the year he'd worked on it, he'd got close enough to Dealman's wife Mary for it to hurt as he'd watched her turn from an optimistic and lively campaigner for her husband's freedom, to a defeated and disillusioned wreck who was downing a bottle of vodka a day without even getting drunk. And yet this was a case in which justice had triumphed, a case where a wrongly accused man had been totally exonerated.

Mary Dealman had finally got her husband back, but the woman who welcomed him home was so much a casualty of the battle for his release that afterwards the marriage never stood a chance. When he'd last heard from them, Mary Dealman was working in some seedy pub in Southampton; Dealman himself was back in prison. He'd never driven the car on the armed robbery for which he'd first been convicted, but his years inside brought him in contact with people who made him think he could, given the chance.

There were a lot of things Stredwick would like to forget about the work he did. The Dealman case wasn't one of them.

'So those factory time-sheets just went missing, did they?' he persisted.

The policeman opposite leaned across the table again. 'Look, this is going no further, is it? I mean, Dealman's water under the bridge now, and I don't want you stirring it all up again. But I'll tell you this for free, and you can take it as you like: the fact is those time-sheets weren't even examined until after the trial when his solicitor found out about them.'

'You didn't bother looking at them?'

'We looked at them, but do you think we'd have handed them over like a tube of Smarties if we'd have realized how relevant they were?'

'You mean they might have gone missing completely?'

'I don't mean anything', said the policeman. 'It would just have been a bit embarrassing, that's all. There was nothing sinister about those time-sheets not being given to the defence before the trial. It was just—just—'

'Just a cock-up?' Stredwick said. 'A bit of an administrative slip-up, eh? And I suppose it was just bad luck Dealman spent six years banged up because of it.'

The policeman shook his head. 'Dealman was a villain,' he said. 'That's the trouble with your sort. You can't see real life as it is. You walk around with your head in the clouds.'

'And the trouble with your sort,' said Stredwick venomously, 'is that you walk around with yours in the sewers. It makes you see shit everywhere.'

The policeman laughed with a friendliness that belied Stredwick's bitterness. 'Aye, happen we do, Mr Stredwick,' he said getting to his feet. 'But that's the way things are, and you're not above making use of us when it suits you, are you? I mean, when it comes down to it, we're both professionals in our different ways, aren't we? Any road, I'd best be getting off. If there's anything else I can do you for, you've got the number. Same terms, of course.'

Left alone, Stredwick ordered himself a hamburger and sat staring through the Wimpy windows for what seemed an eternity. It had begun to rain, and outside the city crowds were leaving their shops and offices for home, scurrying through the damp streets to their cars and packed buses. Stredwick glanced at his watch. It was past five and the pack of journalists that had no doubt descended on Julie Taylor's father once news of her death had broken would by now have moved on to some other squalid tragedy elsewhere. So soon after her death, Julie Taylor had been consigned to that hopeless hinterland of yesterday's news. Now it was Stredwick's turn, and though talking to the parents of murder victims wasn't a job he relished, it was a job that had to be done. He was becoming impatient of this investigation. More than this, though, it was beginning to worry him. One part of him argued that he was still wasting too much time on the peripheries; another, that things had moved too far to the centre to be safe.

And he couldn't be certain which unsettled him most.

It was the persistent paradox the journalist faced, for to stay back too far from what was being observed would mean you could never see the truth, yet in getting too close, that truth might change to accommodate you.

Stredwick wondered whether if he hadn't decided to investigate Alexander's murder, Julie Taylor might have been among the crowds going home that night. He won-

106

dered whether it might not have been better leaving sleeping dogs to lie. And whether one of them hadn't already woken up and bitten.

CHAPTER 14

In his day they used to refer to it reverentially as a death call. Stredwick's first had been as a trainee in the West Midlands when he'd been sent to see that young Walsall couple whose daughter had just died. He'd not been in journalism long and worked in a district office of a local weekly under an editor you couldn't talk to in the afternoon he was so drunk and a chief reporter you couldn't talk to in the morning he was so sober. That Wednesday had been press day, the day the office had to put together its front page before the issue went to the printers. But the day had been as uneventful as the week, and just hours from deadline there'd been nothing more exciting than a pushbike accident in the High Street to fill the blank spaces under the masthead. They'd all been phone-bashing, desperately ringing anyone they could think of for a last-minute story, but it had been Lynne, the fourth member of the small team, who had eventually come up with the goods in a call to the local police station.

Lynne was a hard-faced bitch, in those days when a woman had to be hard-faced and a bitch to get anywhere in what was still seen as primarily a man's world. All the same, her response had startled him.

'Tremendous,' she'd said, dropping back the heavy black Bakelite receiver she'd been using. 'Just what we've been looking for.' She'd stood up, unselfconsciously hitching up her skirt to adjust her suspenders. 'I'll get round there if you want, Alf. There'll be a bus in a few minutes.'

Alf, the chief reporter, had showed his teeth in a smile like a smashed bottle. 'Stroke of luck, that,' he'd said. 'You've got till eleven, luv. Get to it.'

Stredwick in his day had been as youthfully headstrong

107

as Archie and he hadn't been able to stop himself saying something. 'This is a child you're talking about,' he'd blurted indignantly. 'A five-year-old girl that's just been killed.'

'Yeah, hole in one,' said Charlie Sampson, the editor, who'd just walked into the newsroom. 'And that, son, is what makes it this week's lead. Since you seem so concerned, perhaps you should be the one to go and see her parents. And don't come back to this office without a bloody picture . . .'

The death had been an appalling accident. The child had been out for the day with her father, a lorry-driver, and had been playing outside the engineering factory where he was waiting to make a delivery. When the massive steel gates of the factory had rolled back on their castors to admit them, no one had noticed the diminutive five-year-old looking for her ball in the rebate in the wall where the gate would come to rest.

They found the ball when they eventually cleaned up the side of the gate. The child had been unrecognizable.

Knocking at the parents' door that day, Stredwick's mouth had been arid with apprehension, and his stomach churning with nervous anticipation. It surprised Stredwick then, and still surprised him, that in circumstances of such profound personal grief anyone would ever choose willingly to talk to a journalist. But talk they did, whether out of relief that their private tragedy was given a wider import by the interest of a newspaper, or out of cathartic release at having a sympathetic listener to whom they could unburden their anguish. The parents invited him in, gave him a cup of tea and made him so welcome that he went back to the office with not just a picture of the child, but a picture taken less than a month before of the girl and her father in the cab of the lorry. It had run across four columns in that week's edition, and been picked up by the national papers the next day.

Alf had been delighted, and Charlie Sampson had been pleased enough to promise him a drink at some remote time in the future should they ever find themselves propping up the same public bar together. Even Lynne, still smarting from having had her story wrested from her, had had to admit grudgingly that he'd done as well as anyone could in the circumstances.

This was the first time Stredwick discovered that he had a knack, a talent, for this sort of work. Perhaps it was his naturally lugubrious features, perhaps his sympathetic manner. Who knows? Charlie Sampson certainly had views on the matter when Stredwick reminded him of the incident many years later. This was after Charlie's retirement when his liver was playing him up so badly he couldn't even handle his own staircase let alone his whisky bottle. As it turned out, it was less than three months before he died too.

'They knew you cared, son, that's what it was,' said the ex-editor. 'I could see that, and they could see it too. It made them trust you and tell you things they never knew they were saying.'

The conversation was about as much of a compliment as he ever got, or indeed ever expected, from a hack like Charlie Sampson who was brought up in the old school. He had no doubt meant well, but all the same, what he'd said needled Stredwick. As a young journalist on his death calls, Stredwick had shared the grief he reported; it had become a part of him as it was part of the people who were closest to it.

But that intensity of feeling could never survive the rigours of day-today news reporting and the familiarity with tragedy that went with the job; it hadn't taken long for Stredwick to realize he was using his compassion crudely, for his own purposes, not as any honest expression of his feelings, but for what it might achieve. He didn't actually steal pictures of the dead off the walls as more than one journalist had been known to do, but his type of shabby barter whereby he got the picture by making the right sympathetic noises wasn't fundamentally so far removed from it.

Essentially, his sympathy was as genuine as it ever was, but at the same time it was too flawed with self-interest to sit comfortably within the ethical framework he felt was indispensable to journalism. It would have destroyed him if he hadn't been able to recognize and accept the moral contradictions of his work. If he hadn't been able to see that under certain conditions of tragedy, the compassion of an outsider became another violation of the innocent.

Stredwick was turning all this over in his mind as he drove through Rainsford, past Kirkstall Moor and up to the small, isolated cottage where Julie Taylor had lived with her father. It stood on the rise of a hill, at the side of a road snaking across the countryside between two dry stone walls.

The woman who answered the door was scarcely tall enough to reach his shoulders but she stood like a colossus barring his way. 'Are you the police?' she asked.

'My name's Stredwick. I've just been talking to them.'

This seemed enough to get him past the threshold and she led him into the living-room where Jim Taylor sat in an armchair staring blankly at a small fire flickering in the hearth. His dark eyes were red-rimmed, his face swollen and puffy.

'Inspector Stredwick, is it?' he asked, 'Detective-Inspector, I mean. I know you can offend people if you get these things wrong.'

'It's Mister, actually,' said Stredwick. 'I'm a journalist. I wondered if I might ask you a few questions?'

For a brief moment Taylor's eyes flashed in a sort of panic, and he looked accusingly at the woman who had invited Stredwick in.

'You're not going to set him off again, are you?' she piped up. 'He's had people upsetting him all day. What with the police and you people, I wonder if we're ever going to be left in peace.'

'I won't keep either of you long,' said Stredwick. 'I wrote to Julie a couple of months ago. I don't know if she mentioned it?'

The panic in Taylor's eyes became curiosity. 'Aye, happen she did,' he said thoughtfully. 'Are you the bloke from that telly programme?'

110

This connection with another past, a past before Julie had been murdered, must have given Stredwick a new credibility in Taylor's eyes, for he sat back in his chair and beckoned to Stredwick to sit down opposite.

'She never did reply to you, did she?' Taylor said absently, his eyes wandering back to the fire and filling with tears. 'It upset her, you see,' he went on. 'Being connected with—with murder.'

The word stuck in his throat, and he sank his head into his hands, twisting himself awkwardly away from Stredwick as if somehow it were possible by these means that Stredwick wouldn't notice his despair.

Stredwick, waiting silently for the moment to pass, took in the small room: the copper moquette of the 1950's three-piece on which he was sitting, the cheap but serviceable sideboard against the wall, the stuffed perch over the mantelshelf and the bank of sporting guns against the chimney breast.

'You'll have to excuse me,' Taylor said at length, rubbing at his face with a handkerchief. 'I just keep ... I keep expecting her to walk through the door, you see. It's as if all this is a nightmare.' He turned to the woman who throughout all this had been standing watching him. 'Are you going to mash, Vera? I'm sure Mr Stredwick could drink a cup of tea.'

When he was sure that she'd gone, he turned back to Stredwick, his face fixed in a determined grimace. 'You said you'd been talking to the police. Did they tell you if ... did they say if our Julie had been ... was she ...?'

'I don't think they know yet,' Stredwick said. 'It's possible, but they won't know for certain until they've done the ... the tests.'

'If I ever get hold of the bastard who did it, I'll kill him,' Taylor said quietly. 'I will, you know. I'll kill him as soon as look at him.'

His eyes were beginning to glisten with tears again, but this time he seemed to consciously take a hold of himself. He got to his feet and crouched in front of the fire, making an exaggerated display of warming his hands against the weak flames. 'No, it were me as told Julie not to answer your letter,' he said briskly to the back of the fire, as if this part of the conversation had never been interrupted. 'She were a delicate lass, you see. It upset her, that—that do. She never really got over it. She were never happy working at the hotel afterwards.'

'She was off the week it happened, wasn't she?'

'Aye, thank God. She had some days owing. She used to work weekends, you see, but she were always too busy in the summer to take them.'

'And you were in Rainsford the day of the murder, weren't you?'

Taylor swung round. 'Aye, what if I was? I told t'police everything I knew, and that weren't much. What do you mean?'

Stredwick beamed a comforting smile, far from expressive of the uncertain turmoil he was feeling inside him. 'I didn't mean anything specifically, Mr Taylor. Please excuse me if I seem rude. It's difficult. I know this must be painful for you. It's just that you were close to Julie, you used to pick her up after work, run her around a bit in the car . . . I just wondered if you'd taken her with you to Rainsford that day. For some shopping, perhaps?'

'Aye. No secret about that. I told the police that too. We usually did our shopping midweek if Julie were off.'

'And were you together all day?'

Taylor looked at him suspiciously. 'No, not all day. We went to the supermarket together, we went to the butcher's, I suppose, we always did . . . Hey, where's all this leading? What are you suggesting?'

Stredwick smiled again, more naturally this time. 'Nothing at all. Really, Mr Taylor, believe me. It's just that I was wondering if the two of you had any reason to go up to the hotel, that's all.'

'I've told you, Julie had a week off. Why should we go to the hotel? Julie saw enough of that place the rest of the year.'

'Of course,' said Stredwick, 'of course. But you were very close, weren't you. I just wondered . . .' He trailed off.

Taylor dropped back into his chair with a deep sigh. 'It were her mother dying so young, you see,' he explained. 'Our Vera's been good to us but you can't substitute a mother. It were bound to make us close. Julie were all I had, Mr Stredwick.'

'Vera's what? Your sister?'

Taylor nodded and his hands came up to his face, wiping his eyes. 'She tells me I'm a fool for thinking it, but all the same I can't help feeling I'm to blame for this. Julie had never learnt to drive, you see. I used to drive her all over. Last night, though . . . last night . . . A lass has got to have a bit of freedom, hasn't she? She can't go courting with her dad in tow, can she?'

'Last night Julie didn't want a lift,' said Stredwick.

' "I'll be all right, Dad," she said. "I'm not a kid, you know. I'll be all right. Don't you worry." I shouldn't have listened to her, Mr Stredwick, I shouldn't have listened. It wouldn't have been any bother to have run her to Rainsford. She knew she could have rung me later. I'd have picked her up too. If only I hadn't listened to her. Oh my God, if only I hadn't have listened . . .'

He broke down in tears yet again, his face twisted in anguish. And again Stredwick watched him without saying a word, wary of intruding any more than neccessary into these moments of grief which, painful though they were, and so based in futile guilt and barren regret for things past, he knew were precious too, part of the delicate healing process by which the living gradually came to terms with their dead.

Vera eventually came back into the room, her arms encumbered with a large tea-tray.

'Jim!' she said sharply. 'It's no use getting yourself worked up like this, you've got to pull yourself together. Why don't you take another of those pills the doctor gave you?'

She turned to Stredwick, handing him a teacup from a china set obviously kept for visitors. 'Drink this,' she said politely, but with an unmistakable tone of firmness in her voice too. 'Happen you'd best go then.'

113

'Yes, of course,' said Stredwick, 'I've stayed too long already.'

Before he left, however, almost as an afterthought, though it was far from that, he said, 'She came back with you then, did she?'

Taylor had been gazing into the fire again, a million miles away. It took a few moments for Stredwick's voice to register with him.

'The day of the . . . that do at the Shornewan? Did Julie come home with you after you'd been in Rainsford?'

Taylor shook his head almost uncomprehendingly.

'How did she get home, then? A bus? A lift?'

'A bus, probably,' said Taylor. 'I can't remember.'

'Are the buses regular?'

'Round here? There's one every couple of hours if you're lucky.'

'So she sometimes used to get lifts?'

'Sometimes,' said Taylor. 'With Mr Carrington. When she was working late and I couldn't pick her up.'

'But on her days off? On *that* day?'

'Perhaps,' said Taylor. 'I really can't remember. It's so long ago.'

Stredwick drove back towards the motorway, past the spot where just a little under twenty-four hours before, Julie Taylor's body had been discovered. Only a bored constable left to guard the roadside remained as testimony to her murder. It was unlikely anyone had expected the spot to reveal much of value in the way of identifying a killer, but it had doubtless been searched carefully all the same, any stray matchstick or cigarette end logged and filed, any odd tyre tread found on the verge photographed and casts made of it.

The policeman looked at him suspiciously as he pulled up the car, but Stredwick accelerated off before he could say anything.

If the policeman was doing his job right, he'd have noted Stredwick's number plate, and that too would soon be added to the growing weight of information through which, tomorrow, and the day after, and the day after that, CID would be sifting for a lead. Already the lumbering machine had started working up to speed, these due processes of the law which, stripped of their mystique, amounted to nothing more than random detail, notes on files and computer records, interviews conducted by their hundreds and occasionally the odd titbit of intelligence gleaned from a pub chat, or an anonymous phone call. Somewhere among it all there might be certainty, but there was less certainty than a public attuned to its romantic idea of policing might think, less certainty than it might be comfortable for them to accept if they only knew.

The machine was only ever the sum of its parts, and its parts, when you came down to it, were just so many blokes getting up in the morning to do a job. And whether that job were just doing a shift at a Yorkshire roadside, or presiding over an Old Bailey court, there was always the chance of a mistake being made somewhere. It was the nature of the system, and however much you tinkered with that, it always would be while the system rested on the fallibility of men who, within their own worlds, were often looked upon as gods.

Before he left Yorkshire he bought a local paper and at Leicester, the half-way stage of his journey home, he stopped for a steak at the Forest East service station where he found himself staring at a front page picture of Julie Taylor.

Her lumpish unattractiveness might have come as a surprise to anyone naïve enough to think that sexual crimes had more to do with sex than the violence and humiliation that always accompanied them. So it wasn't for that reason that Stredwick harboured doubts that her murder had actually been a sexual crime.

His suspicions seemed to be confirmed when he got home in the early hours and checked the messages on his Ansaphone. There, squeezed between one from the Controller—who'd clearly been alerted to the financial two-step that he was being sold as a substitute for a budget—and another from Archie, who sounded astonished that Stredwick had left his desk, was one from the policeman he'd met that day in the Wimpy bar.

The PM report had showed that, legally at least, Julie Taylor hadn't been raped. That is to say, she hadn't been penetrated. Ever.

'Seems she was having her period,' the policeman's recorded voice informed him. 'It looks as if that might have put off the bloke who attacked her.'

Perhaps, thought Stredwick to himself. But on the other hand, whoever it was that attacked her might never have intended to rape her. Just to kill her. And why, he pondered, posing himself the question, why is everyone so damn sure it's a man?

CHAPTER 15

Ex-Detective-Sergeant Peter Webber, late of the Metropolitan Police, was beginning to entertain some very serious doubts about having mentioned the Alexander case to anyone, let alone George Stredwick. Stredwick had been worrying away at the case off and on ever since he'd learnt about it—but at least he'd kept his distance. These last few months, however, he'd become so obsessed that Webber was beginning to curse himself for ever having opened his mouth.

For God's sake! he hadn't intended for Stredwick to launch a full-scale re-investigation; he'd only mentioned his doubts about Frampton's conviction as a conversation piece because the murder had happened at the hotel and he'd followed the court case. The last thing on earth he'd thought was that Stredwick would take it so seriously. Now the whole thing was getting out of hand, and Webber was getting drawn in to a far greater extent than he thought was wise.

In retrospect, it certainly hadn't been wise to pass on the name of his contact in the local CID. Webber knew from past experience that George Stredwick had an insidiously prickly way with not-quite-kosher coppers who happened to wander in front of his sight line. By the same token, he knew that not-quite-kosher coppers had their own insidious way with punters who made their lives difficult—especially if they happened to be licensees dependent on the local police for a touch of the Nelson's eye when it came to interpreting the finer points of the laws governing drinking hours.

It wasn't that Webber didn't trust George Stredwick. Perish the thought! Stredwick was certainly a maverick, but Webber knew that his brand of meticulous research and obsessive determination could often succeed where a more professional approach would be certain to fail. OK, he could be a bit humourless sometimes, a bit prone to sermonizing. And he had a tendency to talk shop at every possible opportunity, not to mention an almost evangelical reluctance to drink anything stronger than Coca-Cola. Even so, Stredwick was, by Webber's somewhat circumscribed method of cataloguing the world, rock solid, pure gold, twenty-four carat.

All the same, it was said you could tell a man by his friends, so how much truer was it that you could tell men by the colleagues with whom they chose to work? The appearance on the scene of the half-witted bean brain Archibold a couple of weeks before did, in Webber's mind, raise some very pertinent questions about Stredwick's relationship to reality.

Frankly, Webber wondered if he wasn't losing his marbles.

It wasn't just that Archibold was insolent, arrogant and so headstrong you could have turned him upside down and used him to drive in a fence post. Or that he was patronizing, condescending and about as subtle as a farm tractor carting pig shit. No, that sort of eccentricity Webber could have understood; God knows, he'd seen enough of it in the force.

But he was puzzled why Stredwick had bothered to bring anyone else in on the case. If he felt the need of a sidekick to do his legwork, why had he brought in Archibold who was so patently ill equipped?

Now, Webber had been a good copper, even if his standards did fall a little below those expected in the Met in the post-Mark days. And he was a good hotelier too, even if his accounting methods were a little less precise than those required by HM Inspector of Taxes. Even so, he'd never harboured any illusions about his own intelligence, which is why it struck him so forcibly that Archibold wasn't that sharp up top either. It seemed to Webber that Archibold was so totally at sea that he wouldn't have been able work out which way to go if you'd sent him a set of navigational charts and a tugboat to lead him to port. From what Stredwick had let on, it seemed Archibold hadn't yet grasped the central nub of the case, and he certainly didn't seem to suspect Webber's own part in it, even though with staying at the hotel the truth was better than on his doorstep.

Yet this was the man Stredwick was trusting himself to, the man who'd as good as been given a free hand to go clodhopping around tonight's Rod and Gun Club dinner upsetting all the county's top brass, not to mention some of Webber's closest Masonic friends who were, after all, the backbone of his weekday restaurant trade.

Webber found it very confusing. It wasn't that Archibold seemed incapable of learning from his mistakes, more that he seemed incapable even of realizing when he was making one. This morning, for instance, he'd bounced out of breakfast in a fervour of uncharacteristically good-natured bonhomie. Webber hadn't once been a detective for nothing. He noticed that Archibold was sporting his anorak and walking boots.

'For Chrissakes, you're not going out on the bloody moor again, are you?'

'And why not, Mr Webber?' Archibold had said. 'It's a crisp, clear winter's day, no clouds in the sky, no mists on the horizon. I'm well rested and well fed, thanks to your familiar episcopal ham. Altogether raring to go.'

'The last time you were out there you nearly killed yourself,' Webber reminded him. 'This dinner tonight's caused me enough problems without having to nursemaid you.'

118

Archibold had stopped in his tracks.

'Tonight,' Webber had felt obliged to explain. 'The dinner. Your meeting with Carrington. It's taken a lot of organization.'

'The dinner?' Archibold had said. 'The dinner? The meeting with Carrington? Oh shit! the dinner . . . I'd totally forgotten about it.'

He'd walked back to his room without saying another word. Half an hour later Webber had heard the hotel door slam as he'd driven off towards Leeds.

For the life of him, Webber couldn't understand how, working in television, Archibold had ever graduated from Play School. And try as he might, he couldn't understand why Stredwick had chosen him to investigate a murder.

Archie drove up the hill past the rows of junk shops and Asian grocers, into the wide tree-lined boulevard which was Parkview. The road had seen better days. Its rambling Victorian mansions must once have been home to the city's élite, its industrialists and doctors, its bankers and businessmen, with their regiments of housemaids, cooks and gardeners. Now it lay quietly crumbling, a sore on the city's sensibilities: its houses too large for any single family today, too structurally derelict for renovation.

Here was one house, boarded up; here another totally gutted after a fire. A third and a fourth had been roughly converted into cheap flats, each with a rusted fire escape tacked to its outside like some construction of a giant Meccano set.

No. 46 wasn't difficult to find. Some disconsolate tenant, no doubt peeved by the lack of anything identifying the house, had sprayed numerals a foot high on the front brickwork like a graffiti slogan.

Archie parked the Astra and climbed up the broken bank of steps that led to the front door. A gash showed where once probably had been a brass letterbox, a hole in the woodwork, stuffed with newspaper, where no doubt there had been a brightly polished knocker.

Archie hammered away with his fists for fully five minutes without getting any reply. Eventually he went back to the Astra, wound back his seat and slipped a tape into the cassette. Thomas Tallis's church music filled the car, accentuating the faded grandeur of the surroundings.

The day was proving a lousy letdown, yet when he'd got up that morning, unable to go back to sleep after Stredwick's early morning alarm call, it had promised so much. The sun had been beaming through his bedroom window, and though he hadn't slept long enough, he'd slept well, despite the sad state in which he'd left the Lagavulin bottle before turning in. The sharpness of the air after he'd showered and thrown open his window to the moor had made him lighthearted and carefree.

He'd rung Elizabeth Carrington early and, as Stredwick had intimated, she couldn't have been more polite and cooperative. She'd heard that somebody was re-investigating the Alexander murder for a television programme, and yes, she'd love to see Archie. But she had prior arrangements that day, and would Archie mind awfully coming tomorrow, perhaps sometime in the afternoon? She was looking forward to seeing him.

It was then, with a sudden ecstatic rush, it occurred to him he was as near as damn it free for the day. Even if he took time out to see Maureen Paton, there was nothing to stop him driving to Wearside in the afternoon and surprising June at work. They could go for a meal, spend the night together and, as long as he got up early enough, he could be back in Yorkshire without Stredwick ever needing to discover that he'd gone. With this plan in mind Archie had bounced down to breakfast full of *joie de vivre*, determined both to enjoy the morning's ham and to make the most of the unseasonal sunshine by clearing his head with a walk on the moor afterwards.

Then he'd run into Webber.

What was it about the man, Archie pondered, that could sour his pleasantest of moods? Webber had been all too clearly disapproving of Archie's good spirits. And rude too in that obsequious way of his that left you uncertain whether he was making a cack-handed shot at humour, or trying for a clever put-down. Sod Webber. And sod the bloody Rod and Gun Club dinner too. It had completely slipped his mind.

At this point Archie's ill-natured obloquy was interrupted by activity outside No. 46. A young black woman, her head heavy with a mass of tiny beaded braids and her arms weighed down with shopping-bags, had climbed up to the front door and was struggling about for her house key. Archie was out of the Astra in a flash.

'I'm looking for Maureen Paton,' he said. 'Do you know when she'll be back?'

He followed the woman into a large, dusty hallway where a small table stood overflowing with junk mail and out-of-date election addresses.

'She's in number six, next floor but one up,' said the woman, rooting around in one of her bags.

She handed Archie a bottle of milk. 'The old bag's probably still in bed. You'd best give her this if you're going up there. Save me the climb. Tell her that's five pints she owes me—and a bag of sugar from last week too.

'Did you hear that, Mo?' she bellowed up the dim stairwell. 'Five pints of milk and a bag of sugar. That's two pounds twenty three pee, and if I don't get it by Friday there's going to be blood spilled in this house.'

Archie waited a long time at Maureen Paton's door before he heard any movement inside. A voice he took to be hers eventually asked, 'Who is it?'

'The milkman,' said Archie, pushing the bottle at her as the door opened. 'My name's Alan Archibold. I'm hoping you can help me.'

If Maureen Paton hadn't actually been in bed when he'd knocked, then she hadn't been long out of it. Her eyes were smudged with last night's mascara, her lashes matted with sleep. She was wearing a pair of pink carpet slippers and a black nylon slip, its broken strap secured at the bust with a safety-pin.

'So you're from the telly, are you?' she said in her slow drawl of a voice as she led him through a small corridor

121

into a living-room. She swept a pile of clothes from an easy chair on to the floor to allow him to sit down.

'He's from the telly, Mam,' she shouted over her shoulder. 'He's looking into Bill Alexander's murder.'

The realization that the two of them weren't alone in the room caught Archie unawares. The place was chaotically untidy, and in the few seconds he'd been in the place he'd noticed—indeed, he couldn't fail to notice—the clothes and old newspapers littering the floor, the empty milk bottles left to gather mould in the sink, and the smell of damp and urine that seemed to hang in the air like a thick syrup. But what he hadn't noticed had been the elderly woman buried beneath a pile of bedding and coats on a couch in the corner.

He looked over to her, and her frail face peeking out from under its coverings seemed to smile at him and mouth a few soundless words.

'She's had a stroke,' Maureen explained. Then raising her voice and, addressing herself to her mother, she said, 'We're waiting for the council to find you a place in one of those nice homes, aren't we?'

She left the room and came back wearing a short black leather skirt and a creased blouse. She'd run a comb through her hair too.

'I heard you were around,' she explained from a mirror where she stood wiping her eyes with a tissue. 'You can't keep much quiet in a small town and I've still got a few friends left in Rainsford. Staying at the Shornewan, aren't you?'

She looked over at Archie and smiled knowingly. 'You reckon Terry Frampton's innocent, don't you?'

She began putting lipstick around her mouth.

Archie watched her for a moment or two, then asked, 'Do you?'

Maureen didn't answer. Instead she tossed the lipstick she'd been using on to a pile of other cosmetics on a dressing-table, and then lit a cigarette which she drew on deeply herself before holding it to her mother's mouth.

'He thinks Terry Frampton's innocent, Mam,' she said,

raising her voice again. 'You remember Terry Frampton, don't you? He was that bloke sent down for killing Bill.'

She turned to Archie abruptly. 'Me mam liked Bill Alexander. He were good to her,' she said.

'Good to her?'

Maureen dropped into a chair opposite to Archie, pulling deeply at the cigarette again.

'Oh yeah, he looked after me mam, did Bill.' She nodded her head towards an old television set against one of the walls. 'That were new when Bill got it. So were that,' she added, pointing at a battered hi-fi next to it. 'He were always bringing her presents. It upset her when she heard he'd been killed.'

'Did it upset you?' asked Archie, his second attempt at broaching directly the subject he had come to talk about.

This time the question elicited more of a response.

Maureen drew closer to him and glanced at her mother as if somehow she expected to be reproved for her attitude. 'Me? Upset? You must be bloody joking. When I heard Bill Alexander was dead it felt like I'd come up on the pools. If Terry hadn't done for him, God be my witness, I'd have knifed him myself sooner or later.' She looked at Archie, smiling. 'Mind you, I bet you've heard that from a few people by now, haven't you?'

'One or two,' said Archie. 'But I didn't expect to hear it from you. After all, weren't you . . . didn't you . . .'

'We knocked about together for a bit, if that's what you mean,' said Maureen, her bluntness making up for Archie's misplaced delicacy. 'But so what? Bill Alexander was a good-looking bloke, you know. And he could be a laugh too when the mood took him. Honest, some of the things he said could have you in stitches.'

Archie remembered the great scar across Harbinder Singh's face, and something of the distaste he felt at Maureen's inadvertent black humour must have registered with her.

'Yeah, I know he were a bad un',' she said. 'I mean, I wasn't born under a Christmas tree, was I? All that gear he got me mam didn't come from Curry's on the weekly,

123

did it? And if it hadn't been too hot to shift it wouldn't have come this way, I know that.' She shook her head. 'He were OK sometimes but he were a nutter, that was the worst thing. Violent, you know,' she explained. 'And he was getting worse too.'

She threw the cigarette she'd been holding into the hearth of a gas fire noisily hissing against one wall. Archie watched it for a few moments as it lay smouldering.

'Why did he beat you up that time?' he asked. 'He nearly blinded you, didn't he?'

'Who told you that? Rita, I suppose?'

'Nobody told me anything,' Archie lied. 'You went to the police, didn't you? You can't keep things like that quiet.'

'What's it to you, anyhow?' Maureen said belligerently. 'So Bill Alexander beat me up. So what? It was Bill's hobby beating up women, he knocked Rita about too. Mind you,' she said, 'she probably deserved it.'

'I thought she was a friend of yours?'

'She was—once. Until she got too snotty for the likes of me. She's no better than the rest of them: they all get married and move into posh houses and then they don't want to know their friends. What else did she tell you?'

Archie shrugged his shoulders, his mind moving up a gear. There was no mistaking the antagonism in Maureen's manner when she was talking about Rita, and no mistaking Rita's reluctance to talk about Maureen when he'd last visited her. A new strategy was occurring to him.

'She told me you hated Bill,' he lied. 'She told me that after he'd beaten you up, you swore you were going to get your own back.'

Maureen's reaction was curious. She became, suddenly, very thoughtful, but visibly tense too, gnawing at one of her nails which was already bitten to the quick. She searched around for her cigarettes, but failing to find them she got up from her chair, then sat down again as if she'd forgotten why she'd got up in the first place. Almost immediately she stood up again, and walked over to her mother, bending down to her until their faces almost touched.

'He thinks I murdered Bill, Mam,' she said eventually

in a high-pitched laugh that was almost a scream. 'He thinks it was me what smashed his head in. He thinks I killed him.'

Archie watched the display with some amazement. 'Did you?' he heard himself saying.

'Rita told you that too, did she?' said Maureen from her mother's couch. 'Well, of course she would, wouldn't she? But I don't suppose she told you the rest, did she? Oh no, she wouldn't have told you that. You wouldn't think butter'd melt in her mouth, that one, but take my word for it, Rita's as hard as they come. She had more reason than most for wanting Bill Alexander dead . . .'

'Because she loved Terry Frampton?'

Immediately Archie had opened his mouth he regretted it, for as suddenly as she had changed during the curious display he had just witnessed, so her attitude to him suddenly changed too.

She smiled and shook her head with a weary forbearance, as if she'd been a mother and him her son caught masturbating in the toilet. 'Bless you, you're a real innocent, aren't you?' she said. 'I don't know what Rita's told you about her and Terry. All I do know is that Bill Alexander was fucking the arse off her right up until the day he died.'

Archie fell silent.

'I think we need to talk seriously,' he said eventually.

'I think I need a drink,' said Maureen, 'and I know somewhere we should be able to get one.'

CHAPTER 16

Archie couldn't have said when it first dawned on him that Maureen was on the game. Perhaps it was after they'd left the house and, sitting next to him in the car, she'd directed him through a maze of backstreets where, even so early in the morning, and so cold, clusters of women stood around in impossibly high heels and ridiculously short skirts.

Perhaps it was when she asked him to stop the car close

125

to one of these groups and she'd got out for a few minutes to stand joking and giggling, exchanging gossip and cigarettes.

Perhaps it was later still, when she'd instructed him to park the car on a patch of waste ground beside a row of shabby shops, and led him around the back of one of them, up a metal fire escape and into a long windowless room where at one end a couple of trestle-tables and an old supermarket display refrigerator packed with cans served as a rough bar.

After the brightness of the sharp winter sunshine, the room had seemed almost pitch black. It was swathed in smoke; close and clammy with the rich smell of cannabis hanging in the air. It had taken Archie a few moments before his eyes had adjusted to the gloom. Around him desultory groups of people stood quietly drinking. In one corner two or three black youths were packing up a sound system, coiling wires and humping weighty speakers across the floor.

There was the feel of a party about the place, but the party was over and most people, it seemed, had already called it a day and gone off to their beds.

Perhaps it was then Archie began to have some inkling of how Maureen Paton lived her life. Perhaps it was when she'd ordered a can of Red Stripe for herself and a Foster's for him, explaining to the barman that Archie was OK, that he was with her and she'd vouch for him.

The barman was in his early fifties. He was lean-faced, his hair was greying at the temples. He wore an expensive suit and on his index finger was a chunky gold ring set with a garnet.

He spoke to Maureen but it was Archie he was sizing up.

'Where d'you get to then, Mo? Working?' he asked, easing the ring-pulls off the cans.

'No. I went back home at about four to get a kip and see how me mam was. I thought I might do an hour or two this morning.'

Archie had come into contact with prostitutes before. Or at least he thought he had. He knew from what June told

126

him from the Housing Department that there were certain addresses, not far from where they lived, where women entertained in the afternoons regularly enough to worry the council. Once, too, he'd done a story on a woman called Lindy Claribel, one of Bishop Auckland's most celebrated daughters, who'd spent thousands adapting an improbable suburban semi into one of the entertainment centres of the North-East. Her spare room was stocked with frillies for the transvestites, and her lounge was like a saddlery with all the equipment she'd bought for the bondage freaks.

But, from what he could make out from June, the local women were a cavalier bunch who all seemed to have husbands and jobs, and all seemed to treat what they did as a hobby. They certainly wouldn't have called themselves prostitutes any more than would Lindy Claribel who, with as fine a sense of social distinction as you'd find in Debrett, described herself in her passport as a 'professional hostess'. She owned her own house and kept well away from pimps so that, however intermittently hot under the collar the Ratepayers Association got, there was no law that allowed them to interfere with what she did in her own home.

Indeed, so safe from prosecution did Lindy feel herself that she'd virtually used Archie as her PR man, feeding stories to the nationals through him, when once, with the cheek of the devil, she'd applied for tax relief on her outlay equipping the house.

'I pay my taxes a bloody sight more regular than some of these captains of industry you're always writing about in that paper of yours,' she'd told Archie. 'Why shouldn't I get tax relief? You men can be such hypocrites sometimes.'

Yes, Archie had come into contact with prostitutes before, but the ones he'd met seemed to have about them an aura of naughtiness or smutty fun; they'd always seemed to him, in his blind way, somehow romantic, living as they did on that uncertain moral frontier between illegality and social forbearance.

He'd never before met a streetwalker like Maureen, though, who so directly challenged his comfortable sentimentality. What was more, she did it openly without any shame or embarrassment at talking about herself. She did it as work, as routinely as her weekly laundry and probably with about as much enthusiasm too.

Perhaps Archie was naïve. Even so, he felt scandalized that anyone should feel themselves reduced to it. But then he would feel that, wouldn't he? Lindy was right. Men could be such hypocrites sometimes, Archie no less than the rest of them.

'We've all got to take some shit,' Maureen said. 'It's just what type of shit you have to take. I don't have that much choice, you know. I didn't go to bloody college like you. I didn't want to spend my life sitting at some supermarket checkout or some factory production line.'

They were leaning against the bar, the barman picking his nose and half listening to their conversation. The youths clearing the sound system had finished their packing and gone home, as had the few people who'd been in the place when they'd first arrived. Even so, there seemed no pressure on them to leave. It was as if the place never closed.

They were on their third can now, and there had developed between them that intimacy of early morning drinkers that you often see between winos on park benches.

'That's all very well, Mo,' Archie said. 'But how long's it going to be before your luck runs out and the respectable punter in the suit turns out to be some raving crackbrain whose idea of a good time is knifing women in the gut? Anyway, the council'll be finding a place for your mother soon, won't they? That'll mean you could try something else if you wanted.'

Maureen tossed back her head and drained her Red Stripe. Like Archie, she was drinking out of the can.

'It'll mean I'll lose the attendance allowance, that's what it'll mean,' Maureen said. 'Besides, you're a right one to talk. You've just been telling me your mate went to see the father of that dead girl that used to be up the Shornewan. That's hardly a nice job, is it?'

'It's a job that has to be done.'

'And so's mine,' said Maureen.

Archie ordered a couple more cans, and slid one across

128

the bar to her. He looked at her quizzically. Surely she wasn't going to come out with that old chestnut about the prostitute as social worker? 'If we didn't do it, there'd be more trouble with men than there is.' Surely that one went out with Germaine Greer?

But she was. And she did.

He listened to her, fighting back the temptation to interrupt. 'But what you're doing isn't dousing the flames,' he said when she'd finished. 'It's pouring oil on them. These blokes are going to start thinking that that's all women are for.'

'They think it already,' said Maureen. 'Whatever I do's not going to change anyone's mind one way or another.'

'Somebody's got to,' said Archie. 'I mean, look at this guy on the loose at the moment. The most frightening thing about him isn't that he's a nutter, but that's he's probably just an ordinary bloke who goes to work on a Monday and visits his grandmother once a month.'

'Like I said,' she smiled. 'It's a world full of shit that we live in. I've just found a way of making money out of it. Besides, tell me when things have ever been different. Where you been hiding yourself, sunshine? You can't be an innocent all your life.'

She said almost the same thing later after she'd explained to him about Rita Brassington and Bill Alexander.

She'd shocked him and she knew it.

'You mean . . . you mean Rita actually liked being . . . she liked . . . ?'

'Rita liked the rough stuff, yeah,' said Maureen. 'As long as it didn't go too far, that is. That was the trouble with Bill Alexander, though. It got out of hand. He was getting worse and worse, and it wasn't just with women either. I mean, he'd always been a bit of thief, but just before he died he got hold of this shooter, you know. A gun,' she explained, looking around her to see that the barman hadn't overheard. 'He gave it to me to look after. If he hadn't have got himself killed, his next step, as sure as day follows night, would have been armed robbery. And probably a damn sight more, because Bill was the sort of bloke that wouldn't have been able to stop himself pulling the trigger if ever he'd got some poor bastard of a Post Office clerk lined up the wrong side of the barrel. Just for kicks, you know, just for the hell of it. He was like that. He ought to have been put away years ago. He needed help.'

Maureen lit a cigarette. 'Oh, it was OK between them for a while. Occasionally Rita used to get into work with a black eye, or a few bruises, but she used to laugh it off. You better believe it, that stuff turned her on. But, like I said, Bill got worse. He bust up a couple of her ribs one time, then he tied her up and wouldn't let her go for the best part of a weekend. Take it from me, that guy was crazy. Rita got frightened eventually, I suppose. And of course, she got involved with Terry.'

She laughed. 'He was a nice guy Terry, a gentle guy. That probably seems a strange thing to say about someone who's been sent down for murder, doesn't it? But he was OK, Terry. And he was much more Rita's sort of bloke: the respectable type, if you know what I mean. If he hadn't met Bill Alexander he'd have probably been foreman at some factory somewhere by now, and on the committee of the local snooker club. Rita wanted that sort of life herself. I suppose she got it eventually, much good it did her.'

Archie ran his finger around the top of his beer can. 'How did Rita and Terry meet?' he asked.

'Through Bill, I think. Or maybe they'd known each other before, and he brought them together again. I'm not certain.'

'And how did Bill react when they started knocking around together? Didn't it put his nose out of joint?'

Maureen smiled again and shifted position against the bar. 'All that stuff in court about an argument between Bill and Terry over her was crap, if that's what you're getting at. Bill Alexander wasn't that sort of bloke. To be honest, I don't think he'd really noticed there was anything going on between them. If he had, he wouldn't have cared anyway. He just wouldn't have taken any notice of it.'

130

She looked at Archie. 'That's what I'm saying, you see. It was never really over between them. As far as Bill Alexander saw it, he'd laid claim to Rita. As long as she was around when he wanted her, it wouldn't have mattered if she'd been screwing the massed ranks of the Queen's Household Cavalry.'

'And Rita? How did she feel?'

'Like I said, she was drawn to that sort of thing. She might have been harbouring some dream of settling down with Terry sometime. But Bill provided her with something she wanted . . .' Rita shrugged. 'Who knows, maybe it was something she needed.'

Archie tried to suppress his curiosity. But—was it his imagination?—did Maureen suddenly seem less comfortable when the conversation turned too directly to Rita? She began fidgeting with her handbag and looking around her nervously.

'What I don't understand,' he asked eventually, 'is how you got involved with Bill Alexander, realizing what he was like?'

'I *didn't* realize what he was like, did I?' Maureen snapped. 'Or if I did—I don't know—maybe I thought I could change him. He was a good-looking bloke, you know. He could be charming when he wanted to be, and like I said, he was a good laugh sometimes.' She shook her head as if her own motives were a puzzle even to herself. 'I don't know, honestly I don't. It was just that Bill had got this power over people. He had it over Terry and Rita. He had it over me.'

She gave a stark, self-mocking laugh. 'Yeah, perhaps I did think it'd be different. I just fancied him, I suppose. I were younger then, I didn't see things the same way. It were ridiculous, though. It were never going to amount to much. I mean, I wasn't into his sort of thing—you know—that,' she said with distaste. 'I'm not, even now. If any of the punters show any inclination that way, I pass them on, however much they're willing to pay.

'But he had a way of getting you involved in things, Bill. He made you want to . . . to be like him, if that makes any

131

sense. At first I just went along with him to keep him sweet. But you can't keep a rein on things like that—well, not with the likes of Bill Alexander you can't. It got out of hand with me like it had with Rita.'

She looked at Archie. 'If you went with him once he thought he owned you, you see. You couldn't say no to him. He'd just do what he wanted anyway. You've heard how it ended up. He nearly blinded me. I knew then I had to get away from him. It wasn't that easy to get away from Bill Alexander, though.'

'And Rita?' asked Archie. 'How did she react? What did she think about you and Bill?'

This time there was no mistaking Maureen's unease. Her face seemed to harden and she began chewing first at the edge of her lip, and then at the nicotine-stained skin at the side of a finger.

'Like I said, if you'd been with Bill once, he thought he owned you. When me and Bill first started knocking about together, Rita told me she was pleased to get shot of him. But then, when I found out they were still going together, her excuse was that he was forcing himself on her, and that she didn't know how to get rid of him. Honest, I didn't know what to believe . . . I don't know, even now. Rita liked that sort of thing, I've told you. And Terry was such a gentle guy, you see. He—he wouldn't have been enough for her. I just don't know . . .'

'But after Bill had nearly blinded you, you reported it to the police. You made a statement. Why did you suddenly back off from things? What stopped you taking it to court? Did Alexander put the frighteners on you? Or were you still sweet on him?'

Maureen's eyes showed her confusion. They danced from Archie's face to her drink, from there to her own hands and back to his face again.

'It wasn't like that, I hated the guy,' she said angrily. 'It just wasn't like that at all. That was nothing to do with it. You just don't understand, do you? You'll have to ask Rita, it's the only way. It's only fair. You're going to have to talk to her.'

132

'But I've already talked to her twice. I'm never going to understand unless someone tells me.'

Maureen knocked back the remains of her can and picked up her handbag. 'Look, I've got to go,' she said firmly. 'I've probably told you too much already. You'll have to talk to Rita again, that's the only way. Talk to her and then maybe you can buy me another drink.'

They left the club together and outside, in the bright sunshine again, she refused a lift. He stood and watched her as she disappeared up the street, melting facelessly into the crowds who were milling around the cheap shops and the pavement market stalls. Neither her high heels nor the drink she'd just consumed affected her steady, confident gait.

Afterwards he walked slowly back towards his car, turning over in his mind what she'd said. The interview had actually resolved little for him in terms of the facts of the case; he recognized Maureen had told him only as much as she'd wanted him to know, which was a good deal less than she could have told him. But he recognized too that with a woman like Maureen Paton there was no way he could have induced her to go further, and so he'd compromised himself to confusion, telling himself that since they'd parted on good terms he could always go back to her again to clear up the odds and ends.

The next time she might explain why she was so touchy talking about Rita. And why she was so certain that Rita was involved with Alexander 'up until the day he died'? How literally did she mean that?

Nevertheless, he felt unaccountably positive about matters, for if he'd gained anything from Maureen Paton it was an instinctive feeling that somehow she lay at the centre of events surrounding Alexander's death and that in talking to her, he'd got close to them too.

Of course, by that stage he was vaguely beginning to discern the simple geography of the case that Stredwick had seen a long time before. But as for the rest—as in so much else—Archie was sadly off beam.

Not that it would matter in the end, though. Things

would come clear without Maureen breaking ranks, and as they did, what passed for the truth would emerge with all the relentless inevitability of a row of falling dominoes.

CHAPTER 17

These early drinking sessions didn't suit Archie. He'd intended driving straight back to the Shornewan for the rest of the day, but instead, suddenly feeling the worse for wear after the half-dozen cans of strong lager he'd drunk, he repaired to a small café he'd noticed nearby where he drank a couple of mugs of thick black coffee. The effect was to compound rather than mitigate the nausea he felt. Back at the car, he was so drowsy and so bilious he abandoned himself to what was to have been a ten-minute nap. When he woke he was aware first of being chilled to the bone, then of his tongue stuck to roof of his mouth. Finally he sensed what seemed to be a dull throbbing in the faraway recesses of his skull. It was almost five o'clock and dark.

Unfortunate this, in retrospect, for had he stayed awake just a little longer, he might have noticed Rita Brassington driving by in her red Fiesta, bound for the same destination as he had been earlier.

For Rita, this decision to visit Maureen after so long hadn't been easy, and she'd thought about it long and hard. But as always with this affair, and indeed so much of her life, there didn't seem to be any other alternative open to her. It was as if having once set herself on a course of action, that course took her relentlessly forward to some conclusion beyond her control. Another woman, less loyal and weaker perhaps because of it, might have found a way of extricating herself from events before there was any threat of them overtaking her. But then, another woman would not have got drawn into events in the first place the way Rita had.

We all live with contradictions and these so underpin our actions that most times it's as well they're never probed or, like a dormant cancer which left alone might lie for years, they might, if disturbed, eventually prove too damaging and all-consuming to sustain.

The fact was that Rita could only live with the many painful inconsistencies she recognized in herself by never confronting them more than was expedient. That strength should have such a counterpart in weakness, unsettled her as much in herself as it did in others. That the respectability to which she aspired could be so much a part of the same equation as the sexual degradation which could motivate her, seemed at times inexplicable to her, as if she were not one person, but two, and not really two people either, but two separate shadows of a single personality craving for the whole.

It was obvious to Rita that these television people weren't just going to pack their bags and clear off; it was obvious too that if they kept nosing around Maureen long enough, so much was bound to come out that the two of them could only end up in serious trouble. It wasn't that Maureen was stupid, but she'd always had a big mouth. She'd already said more than she should, since why else had that prying journalist come out with those vile things about her? Maureen had obviously told him about Bill, about how he got off on violence, about how at one time or another Bill had knocked both of them about. She'd obviously told him about all that.

But how much more had she said? How much more would she say in the future? Rita couldn't trust Maureen any more, and yet she needed to be certain of her silence. Until she was, she knew she'd have to live each day on a knife edge, terrified by every knock at her door for fear it might be her past finally catching up with her, or her present closing in around her.

Unless she could force herself to take the initiative, that was. Unless she could take control of things, as she had by ringing Stredwick that day. As she had more recently with Julie Taylor.

She parked the car in almost the same position that Archie had, and like Archie she spent a long time hammering on the door until at last it was answered by the young black woman with braids from the downstairs flat.

From her, Rita learnt that Maureen wasn't at home. She left a note with her telephone number, with a request to the black woman to make sure Maureen rang her as soon as possible.

It was urgent, she said. It was important.

It was a matter of life or death.

Back at the Shornewan with an hour to spare before the Rod and Gun Club dinner was scheduled to start, Archie took the opportunity of swallowing a couple of aspirin and looking again at the two statements made to the police by Walter Carrington. He'd read them more times than he cared to recall already, but he wanted to go over them finally before they met.

The two statements had both been made in the early days following the discovery of Alexander's body, nearly a week after the murder. They were brief and terse, and so much suggested a mind accustomed to dealing with legal facts that Archie suspected they'd been dictated word for word by Carrington, rather than interpreted by a policeman from what was said during a session of interrogation, as so many of the other statements in the case clearly had.

'*On Thursday January 6, I recall making a trip into Rainsford to visit the bank,*' the earlier of the statements recorded. '*This would have been about 11.00 a.m., I can't say exactly when. Afterwards I visited my meat wholesaler. I arrived back at the hotel sometime around 3.30 p.m. I was alone, and the hotel was empty. My wife Elizabeth was out for the afternoon. My only other permanent member of staff, Julie Taylor, was off that day.*'

Archie made himself a cup of strong coffee using the sachets from the tray in his room. It probably wasn't relevant, but Carrington's account of the early part of his day had always seemed suspiciously sparse.

How long had it taken him at the bank? Ten, fifteen minutes? An hour at the absolute outside? And at his wholesaler's? Another hour? Maybe two? Even if you overestimated the travelling time for the short journey between the hotel and Rainsford, that still left an hour or two totally unaccounted for.

Any other witness wouldn't have been able to get away with it. Any lesser figure so close to a murder would have been pressed for a minute by minute account of his movements. But Carrington was a magistrate, a local dignitary, and he wouldn't have been treated the same as an ordinary witness. Even in a murder inquiry his interrogation would have been conducted with a certain deference to status and position.

Archie took his coffee over to his chair and began reading the second of the statements. It had been made a couple of days after the first when the police had already lined up Frampton as suspect number one.

'*Further to my earlier statement, I would now like to add more to my recollections of January 6th, particularly that period after I returned to the hotel following my visit to Rainsford. After further consideration, I am certain that my arrival back at the hotel was nearer 4.30 p.m. than 3.30 p.m. as I first stated. I say this because soon after getting back I recollect seeing from the window of the lounge bar the two men from the Water Board who had been working that week to repair the burst water main. They were standing near to a Water Board van which was parked under one of the car park lights, so I had a good view of it. Its back doors were open and the men were loading tools. They looked as though they had finished work for the day and were about to leave which is why I can be certain about the time. As I watched them they began arguing. I could not catch what they were saying, but the argument appeared to be heated.*

'*One of the men was taller than the other, and had dark hair. At one point he turned away from the other. I would describe this man as about 5ft 11ins tall, he had prominent eyebrows and could be described as good-looking. He was wearing a pair of blue jeans and a black donkey jacket. Immediately afterwards I saw the second man grab him by the arm from behind, and lash out with his fist. This second man was smaller, about 5ft 6ins. I did not see his face clearly but he was wearing a Water Board jacket and overalls.*

'*I could not say whether this second man made contact with his blow, or whether, after this, a fight between the two subsequently*

137

ensued. At that point I was disturbed by a telephone call and had to leave to answer it.'

Archie threw himself back in his chair and read the statement again. This second was, if anything, less satisfactory than the first, and like the first—indeed, like so many statements in the case—it seemed to confuse more than it clarified. No one could have taken it on face value, but surprisingly, Stredwick, who was normally sceptical of most things, seemed totally to accept everything Carrington had said.

'How come he didn't remember this fight the first time he spoke to the police, then?' Archie had asked when they'd discussed it.

'He was being interviewed more than a week afterwards,' Stredwick had replied. 'People do forget what they did very easily. Try and remember exactly what you were doing yourself a week ago. You can't read too much into that.'

'But he's claiming Frampton took a swing at Alexander,' Archie had protested. 'There was nearly a fight between them. That's not the sort of thing you forget in a hurry. Surely that would have stuck in his mind?'

'Come on, son,' said Stredwick. 'A couple of blokes having an argument together? You only think it's significant because you know with hindsight that one of them was subsequently murdered. But if you'd seen what Carrington did, at the time he did, you'd have probably taken no more notice than him.'

'OK, perhaps not. But I'm damn certain I'd have been more specific than he was about the time I got home. Come on! First he says he got back to the hotel at three-thirty and then it suddenly becomes four-thirty! At that time of the year that hour is the difference between light and dark. Surely he'd have remembered that much, wouldn't he? He remembered eventually, didn't he? That's why he made a point in the second statement of saying the Water Board van was close to the car park light. He wouldn't have been able to see anything otherwise.'

Stredwick hadn't been totally convinced, but eventually he'd admitted with some reluctance that there were inconsistencies in Carrington's statement which were unusual. Unusual, but not particularly relevant.

'Take my word for it, son,' he'd said. 'I've had more experience than you in this sort of work. Sometimes you just have to accept the fallibility of human recollection. It's not important here. Forget it.'

But reading Carrington's statements again, Archie wasn't able to forget it. Looked at one way, there was too much that was convenient about the statements. That telephone call, for instance. Such a critical moment for it to come through. And how promptly Carrington had answered it. Archie knew that if he'd been in Carrington's place the telephone would have been left ringing. Nothing would have dragged him away from watching how the scene developed. It was just too opportune, that telephone call. It had prevented Carrington having to give more details about the argument than was necessary. If it had been Carrington who for some unknown reason had smashed in Alexander's skull, then the expedient of inventing that call would have allowed him to incriminate Frampton without saying too much that later might possibly incriminate himself.

But perhaps Stredwick was right. Perhaps sometimes you just had to accept the inconsistencies. Real life wasn't a tidy construction. In real life, the loose ends never did get tied up. In real life, people were as liable to forget the most obvious things as they were to remember the most inconsequential detail. You couldn't account for the workings of the human mind; it wasn't a machine, after all.

Archie threw the statements to one side, changed, and made his way down for dinner. The normally empty Shornewan car park was packed with cars, the normally sedate Shornewan bar milling with well-cut suits and out-of-season sun tans. Everyone seemed to be clutching drinks and laughing heartily.

Webber caught sight of Archie immediately and pushed his way to him through the noisy crush. 'I expected you down earlier.'

'Is Carrington here yet?' Archie asked.

139

'He got here half an hour ago and he's in a lousy mood. I'm afraid I let it slip that you were seeing his wife tomorrow and that seemed to niggle him. Here, cop this,' Webber said, handing Archie a large whisky as they passed the bar. 'He's in the lounge. It'll be a bloody miracle if he says anything to you. Just take it easy, though, or he's likely to walk out . . .'

Carrington was sitting in a small window recess overlooking the car park and he rose unsteadily to his feet as Archie and Webber approached. He was a small frail man, shrunken even, with thinning swept-back hair and a grey sickly pallor to his face. Webber was right. Carrington was in a lousy mood. It showed.

'Walter, this is the young man Alan Archibold I was telling you about,' Webber said by way of an introduction. 'He's been reinvestigating the Alexander murder. Been staying at the hotel. A week now, is it? Two? It's been good for business anyway.'

Webber laughed, but this appeal to the camaraderie of an ex-hotelier seemed not to wash with Carrington, who, unsmiling, offered Archie a flaccid and unwelcoming hand. 'I don't altogether approve of your programme,' he said before Archie had even sat down.

His voice was like his handshake, cold and measured.

'It seems to me,' he went on, 'that although the personal distress of an unjust conviction for a serious crime is immeasurable, and represents a damning indictment of our legal system, more serious damage can often be caused by highlighting what is, after all, only an aberration in a system that for the most part works perfectly efficiently.'

It was like a set speech, and Archie was thrown by it, uncertain how he should reply. Webber was no help either. He sat staring absently out of the window, apparently uninterested in proceedings.

Archie gave a polite nod which Carrington seemed to take as some form of acquiescence, for he continued unabated in the same vein.

'You see, those of us who have lived through a war know better than most that only a thin line separates civilization

140

from savagery. That line is the law, Mr Archibold, the institution much more than the process. Take away respect for the law and little separates us from the abyss. I have always found that when a journalist interests himself in the law, for whatever reason, however laudable, the result at best may be some minor improvement to the processes, but almost without exception this is achieved at the cost of respect for the institution.'

'You don't believe journalists have any role in investigating miscarriages of justice, then?' Archie asked, rather lamely.

'We live in a free society, Mr Archibold. Within the broad parameters set by the law, neither I nor any other person has the right to decide what journalists investigate.'

'But all the same, you'd prefer we kept away from the law? Left it to the professionals?'

'I believe power implies responsibility, Mr Archibold. I believe that before journalists begin to investigate any topic they should at least understand the broader implications of their work.'

'The broader implications?' said Archie. 'I'm not sure I know what you mean by that.'

'We all have a responsibility to preserve the order on which society depends, the journalist no less than any other citizen,' Carrington said. 'Increasingly, though, I see that order threatened by crime. I read of murder, I read of rape. Burglary and vandalism are now commonplace. It seems that with every year that passes we sink increasingly into an anarchic mire.'

He picked up a glass of sherry and sipped at it carefully before replacing it on the table. 'Unfortunately, I find the current social role of journalists so often in conflict with the responsibilities I would expect of them. You look sceptical Mr Archibold, but I wonder why that should be? As a journalist you must recognize, if you'd care to face it, what an awesome influence lies in your hands—an influence totally out of proportion to either your training or your education. This is why I have such grave reservations about your intentions, Mr Archibold. You broadcast a

141

programme saying that so-and-so is innocent of a crime for which they have been duly convicted, and millions believe you. What is more, they believe in the failure of the legal system, and moving from the specific to the general, they begin to believe that all judicial convictions are fundamentally flawed.'

'I only wanted to ask you a few simple questions,' Archie protested, looking vainly at Webber for rescue.

Webber remained silent, his face impassive. Carrington broke into a sardonic shadow of a smile. 'A few simple questions, Mr Archibold? A few simple questions? How innocent you make it all sound. No doubt you intend to ask my wife Elizabeth a few simple questions too, even though, as you know perfectly well, she was away visiting a friend the day of the murder, and wasn't even at the Shornewan.'

He shook his head. 'I, at least, was a magistrate for twenty-three years, Mr Archibold. I know the implications of talking to journalists. My wife, regrettably, does not, though I will say she harbours an intuitive antipathy to those involved in your trade, which may make any discussion you have with her more personally distressing than you anticipate. All the same, what worries me on her account, Mr Archibold, is not your few simple questions, but what you might make of her few sadly inadequate answers recalled from half-remembered events a decade ago. You will doubtless attempt to construct from them an edifice of innocence. And she might unwittingly get drawn into complicity, and become a part of your artifice. Isn't that a danger?'

'You sound as if you'd prefer I didn't see her?'

'I have no feelings about the matter one way or another, I can assure you, Mr Archibold,' Carrington said, the merest hint of irritation in his voice. 'My wife is a totally independent agent and she will no doubt deal with you as she thinks fit. I merely mention to you in passing that she shares my antipathy to journalists. We had more than enough to do with the media at the time of this unfortunate death.'

Mercifully, at that moment, before the discussion could continue, they were disturbed by a sudden high-pitched wailing scream from the car park.

Carrington, despite his frailty, was on his feet in a flash.

Archie was only a little slower in getting out to the car park, where a cursory search showed the rumpus to be emanating from the burglar alarm of a large BMW. Next to it, bumper to bumper, another car stood with its engine still running, its owner behind the wheel looking uncomfortably sheepish.

'I was backing up,' he explained. 'Must have just touched and set it off.'

In the adjacent bar a crowd had gathered against the window, alerted by the commotion. In the window recess of the lounge, Webber stood surveying the scene, curious but unconcerned. 'Is it OK?' he shouted to Archie. 'Much damage?'

'Just a bit of a nudge,' Archie shouted back. 'No problem.'

'None at all,' said Carrington, who had suddenly appeared at his side. 'It's my car. I'll just reset it before dinner. We are dining soon, aren't we?'

Archie walked back to the hotel foyer where he met Webber crossing to the dining-room.

'Queer old stick, isn't he?' Webber said.

'A very odd man,' Archie had to agree. 'But fascinating in his own way.'

Webber looked doubtful. Anyone who could find Carrington fascinating had to be mentally defective. 'I've put you next to him at the table, anyhow,' he said. 'But I doubt you'll get much more out of him than you already have. I told George it was a waste of time, but he will have things his way. As far as I'm concerned, Carrington's a long-winded old fart. I'd have left you to him if Reg had been a bit sharper finding the car.'

'Finding the car?'

'There are a hell of a lot of BMWs around tonight. And then when he found Carrington's, he had the devil of a job manoeuvring his car to make any knock seem credible.'

'Credible?' said Archie, the penny gradually beginning to drop. 'You mean that—that was all set up?'

'Of course. Didn't you know? Didn't George tell you?'

Webber smiled thinly in a way that did nothing to assuage Archie's growing indignation as it dawned on him just how little he was party to any of Stredwick's plans. He hadn't known a thing about the car, though it wasn't difficult to see what Stredwick was trying to get at, however theatrically he'd chosen to make his point.

'How did Stredwick know Carrington's car was fitted with a burglar alarm?' Archie asked eventually.

Webber shrugged his shoulders. 'I thought you'd told him. Search me how George Stredwick knows half of what he does. But it would figure, wouldn't it?'

'Yes . . . yes, I suppose it would,' Archie said thoughtfully. 'Is that how you see things too?'

But the question was never answered, for Webber had slipped away into the impatient crowd which was moving to the dining-room in anticipation of dinner.

Webber was keen to get the meal under way.

And in any event, he seemed to have made up *his* mind, that much was clear enough.

CHAPTER 18

The Rainsford Rod and Gun Club had been formed in 1834 as a loose association of landowners and squires with a common interest in country sports. Barring statutory breaks for occasional wars, and a brief period at the end of the last century when its membership dwindled virtually to extinction, the club—and the quaint custom of its annual dinner—had survived to the present day, albeit changing as the social cachet of its membership changed too, so that nowadays you'd have been hard pressed to find anyone associated with it owning more than a large garden, though if you'd been looking for an estate agent, a surveyor or an accountant, you'd have been spoilt for choice.

144

Similarly, the club continued to maintain the anachronism of its name, even though for the past forty years its activities had had absolutely nothing to do with hunting and fishing. Most of the current membership wouldn't have known a twelve-bore from an Armalite, and the closest most of them got to fishing was driving across the Leeds and Liverpool Canal. Nowadays it was a cross between a golf club without the golf, and a Rotary Club without the charity work.

Most of the guests that night were half cut before they sat down to eat, which Archie thought was perhaps a wise precaution considering the quality of the food. The first course of pâté had the curious texture of window putty, and the soup which followed tasted as if it was so fresh from a supermarket shelf that to have got it any fresher you'd have needed to serve it unopened in the packet.

Not that it seemed to matter to anyone. Before the main course had appeared on the table a series of bread rolls had begun to sail across the room, and at least one guest had had his flies opened and a bottle of Australian Chardonnay emptied into his trousers.

'I said you'd enjoy it,' Webber observed as he passed Archie at one stage in the proceedings, shepherding a harassed flock of temporary waitresses. 'It's like this every year. It gets better too.'

It struck Archie that a disreputable bear garden of this sort was a curious place to find a pillar of society like Carrington—until he remembered that the assembled company included the local MP, the Mayor, and the best part of the local council too. The Rod and Gun Club annual dinner was apparently a traditional date in the Rainsford social calendar, and the sort of function at which you were likely to be considered a poor sport unless you entered into the schoolboy spirit of things.

Even the churlish Carrington had managed an austere smile after he'd been hit on the shoulder by a deflating condom which had zipped across the room with all the aeronautic grace of a burst balloon.

Archie had tried to engage him in conversation when

145

they'd first sat down, but all he'd got for his trouble had been a tedious catalogue of crime statistics, and an interminable lecture on the declining moral standards of twentieth-century life. At times he'd sounded like Stredwick, but whereas Stredwick at least peddled his views with an involved passion, and a sense of the fundamental absurdity of existence, Carrington recited his lines in a monotone as if he'd been reading from the *The Times* law reports or the proceedings of some Parliamentary Select Committee.

Archie couldn't have said what he'd lost first, his patience or his interest. Eventually he'd begun talking to the person on the other side of him, a man about his own age who'd started a plastics company and had been invited to join the club after he'd featured on a radio documentary on young entrepreneurs. He seemed as uncomfortable as Archie at the riotous beanfeast that was developing around them.

The revels continued unabated during the speech of the MP who was guest of honour, and they reached a crescendo when the club chairman got to his feet and, familiar with the prevailing tenor of these dinners, attempted to enliven a speech on local conservation issues with so much suggestive innuendo he sounded like a third-rate club comic.

It was too much for Archie, who made his excuses and left with the guests from the top table, which was being cleared to form a stage where eventually a real comic, and strippers too, would entertain the club hard-liners long into the early hours. In the lobby, Archie watched Carrington as he collected his coat from the cloakroom and made his formal goodbyes. The Rod and Gun Club dinner may have been a traditional facet of Rainsford life, but judging from those departing, it was equally traditional for anyone with pretensions to respectability to leave early.

'You're not copping out on us now, are you?' Webber challenged Archie. 'It's just beginning to liven up.' He was carrying a trayful of brandy bottles, meandering in an uncertain line back to the dining-room, as drunk as most of his remaining guests.

'I promised to ring Stredwick. I'll be down later,' Archie lied.

But Stredwick, unusually, wasn't at home. Archie left a message for him on his Ansaphone, irrationally irate that he wasn't available and hadn't said where he was going. Once again, it seemed to Archie, he'd been excluded from Stredwick's scheme of things, left in the wings like some supporting actor at a play with no script. Somehow, surely, there had to be a role for him? Why else had he been employed? Why then, whenever he felt he might be finding that role, did the dominating shadow of Stredwick fall across the stage like the lead player in a totally different drama?

Damn it, why did he feel so much in awe of Stredwick? Why did he feel so cowed and intimidated by him?

From downstairs, raucous laughter and cheering filtered through to his room. Archie felt suddenly very lonely. It was so often the way that after a long day he'd be taken with this awful sense of isolation, feeling so little involved in events about him that they appeared to be happening in a different world to his, a world in which he had no real part. Tonight the feeling seemed more intense than usual. Perhaps it was Stredwick, or perhaps the depressive effects of drinking too much too early. Perhaps it was just simple tiredness. Or then again, perhaps this sense of alienation was in the nature of the work he did.

He was missing June, that was probably all it was: June kept his feet on the ground. At least with her, he could be true to himself, for he'd realized long ago that it was impossible to be totally true to himself in his professional life. Not when the job was such a compromise to truth, when every question he ever posed had so much an ulterior motive it verged on deception. Not when it made him see people as sources of information rather than human beings in their own right.

He rang Rosemary, expecting June would be with her.

'Archie, do you have any idea what time it is? I was asleep. I haven't seen June since we left work. Isn't she at home? You have tried ringing her at home, haven't you?'

He was half way through dialling before he made his decision. It might be late, and he might be tired, but with

147

the noise from downstairs he'd have difficulty sleeping even if he wanted to. And the fact was, he didn't want to. All day he'd wanted to be with June, but in this mood he needed to be with her. In this mood he needed to be at home.

As Archie left the hotel Carrington was leaving too. He must have been delayed talking while Archie had been in his room.

The two of them drove away from the hotel at the same time, both taking the moorland road leading away from Rainsford. Carrington was behind Archie as they left the car park, and he was still behind him some two or three miles later when Archie, dazzled by the glare of his head-lights, reduced speed to allow him to pass.

But Carrington, the selfish bastard, slowed down too. It was a pitch black, moonless night, and the moorland road was totally unlit.

Archie accelerated the Astra to get away from him.

Curiously, Carrington increased speed too. Of course, it could have been that Archie was simply being used to lead the way along the treacherously winding road. If Carrington was selfish enough not to care too much about his headlights, he'd be selfish enough to do that.

But somehow Archie didn't believe it. Silly perhaps, but he was beginning to suspect that he was being tailed.

Again he slowed down, and again the BMW slowed down too.

Archie, God knows, was quick enough to get angry at anything; he was certainly getting angry at this childish game. At the next junction, instead of turning right as his route to the North-East dictated, he swung a sharp left to nowhere.

The BMW turned in the same direction and it stayed with him as Archie turned another left, and a third, bring-ing them back in a wide arc to the junction from which they'd first started the detour. Now there was now no doubt in Archie's mind. He *was* being tailed, though for what reason it was difficult to conceive. Perhaps Carrington was just lost, and hoping that Archie would lead him to a main road? But Carrington knew this area better than any out-sider. It didn't make sense.

Eventually Archie joined the road to Ripon, and not long afterwards Carrington seemed to lose interest in the chase. He turned off at some small village along the way, leaving Archie with the road to himself until he met the overnight commercial traffic on the A1.

After Carrington had gone Archie found that he'd been more unsettled by the incident than he cared to admit. It had been a disconcerting experience to be inexplicably followed along deserted country lanes in the early hours of a dark night. The more so, to be followed by a man like Carrington in whom such apparently illogical behaviour seemed peculiarly chilling—a man who, after all, might have been involved in a murder. Perhaps two murders.

What on earth could he have been thinking of?

Archie's exhaustion was beginning to catch up with him and he briefly considered abandoning the trip completely and going back to the Shornewan.

It might have been better if he had.

It was almost morning by the time he got to Wearside, the night paling slightly over the familiar streets of home.

He'd hoped to surprise June in bed, perhaps wake her with a kiss. But the door was bolted and he was reduced to hammering on it to get her to let him in.

When, eventually, it was opened, it was not by June, but by a man. It was a man he didn't know, a man wearing the dressing-gown June had bought him as a present the previous Christmas.

'Hello,' the man said, obscenely chirpy considering he'd evidently just got out of bed. 'Who are you?'

'Who am I?' said Archie. 'Who am I? I'm just the person who lives here, that's who I am. More to the point, who the fuck are you?'

CHAPTER 19

It was his own fault, he knew that. Try as he might, he couldn't blame the cat. All the same, with its disabilities, Stredwick wouldn't for the life of him have believed Squiffy was agile enough to get up to the table, let alone stupid enough to polish off the remnants of last night's vindaloo. But the cat was used to scavenging anything it could, and over the years Stredwick had developed such a partiality for takeaway curry that it was predictable that eventually the cat would too.

The bloody creature had been enough of a waste disposal unit when he'd inherited it. Recently, though, it seemed to have become totally indiscriminate in its culinary inclinations, and had developed a taste for the contents of ashtrays, not to mention a predilection for chewing old newspapers. God knows what was going through its mind—though what had been through its stomach had, that morning, been a matter of more public demonstration.

Stredwick had woken to a pool of cat vomit on the kitchen floor, a cheerless enough way to start any day. Worse was to come though. The cat was naturally over-affectionate, a symptom of its congenital brain damage; that morning, though, its stomach gripe seemed to have inclined it towards even greater displays of devotion than usual.

No sooner had Stredwick cleared up the mess and sat down to his breakfast than the cat launched itself from its maimed back legs like an uncoordinated Exocet, upsetting a cup of scalding coffee over his lap. It was at this precise moment the Controller rang, unsympathetic to all Stredwick's protestations at the inconvenience of his timing.

'It's always inconvenient when I ring, George. Frankly, I couldn't care less if your balls were dropping off. I've had complaints about these two researchers from Current Affairs that you've set to work. You can't just commandeer staff off the corridors, George.'

'They weren't in the corridors. They were sitting in the canteen. They'd been sitting in the canteen for days, months for all I know. Christ, Malcolm! They'd been there so long any decent accountant would have had them down as fixed assets.'

'Perhaps, George, but you can't just conscript people. They've got to be paid for. They've got to be budgeted to a programme.'

With his genitals poaching under his sodden trousers, George Stredwick was in no mood to argue the finer points of broadcasting costing policy. 'They *are* budgeted to a programme, Malcolm,' he snapped. 'It's just they weren't doing anything for that programme. They weren't doing anything for *any* programme. I need to trace this student quickly, the one working in the café that day. I've told you, it could be important. What am I supposed to do? Come on! Get off my back.'

He finished by slamming down the phone. It was bad politics, he knew that: there weren't that many people in the company he could depend on half as much as Malcolm. But really! Malcolm should have known better than to pester him about details—not at a time like this. Not when he was anguishing so much about the coffee and the case.

Later, Stredwick rang the Shornewan.

'Any progress on that criminal check on Alexander?' he asked Webber.

'As we thought, George. As long as your arm. Mainly GBH and petty theft.'

'Nothing sexual, though?'

'Nothing on the record. But that doesn't mean much, does it? If what we've found out from Paton is true, then it's hardly likely to have been reported. That stuff isn't. Not unless it gets out of hand.'

Stredwick toyed idly with the keyboard of his computer, lost in thought. 'I went to see de Groot again,' he said eventually. 'Just as I thought: all manner of dire warnings about the weather.'

'Well, that sounds innocent enough to me, George. It can be atrocious, you know that.'

151

'Of course I know that,' Stredwick barked. 'There's always an innocent explanation if you try hard enough to find one. But I still can't help thinking it's significant. I think someone was trying to frighten him off the moor. OK, so it didn't work, but it *might* have worked, and the body wouldn't have been discovered for months then.'

The two men fell silent. At the Shornewan a wind from the moors rattled through the lobby; from the dining-room came the sound of plates clattering as the staff prepared breakfast. In Stredwick's small flat in Kennington, the cat was settling itself into its tray for the umpteenth time that morning, sending showers of the litter across the newly cleaned floor.

Eventually it was Webber who voiced what was going through both their minds.

'What are we going to do now, then, George? You're in the driving seat. We don't seem to have come any further than when we first started, though, do we? And yet, looked at one way, the case seems so simple.'

'Too bloody simple, that's always been the trouble,' said Stredwick. 'But we've only ever worked on suspicion, haven't we? We still haven't got anything reliable to go on, let alone tangible proof. Sometimes I wonder if we've been on the right track all this time. Who knows, maybe Archibold is on to something new? The way we've been working, I'd have expected something to have crawled out of the undergrowth before now.'

'Perhaps it will, when the beaters have been crashing around,' said Webber optimistically. 'Isn't Archibold supposed to be seeing Elizabeth Carrington today? Maybe something will come of that?'

Stredwick wasn't convinced. 'If everyone just keeps their mouths shut, there's no reason anything should come out. It's like a heap of old bricks that's been left after some demolition. No one's arranged the pile, but it's perfectly stable. If we could only force some movement . . . We're going to have to take a few more risks, Peter,' he broke off suddenly. 'It's the only way. And I'll have to give the lad a bit more encouragement, take his ideas more seriously.'

'Archibold?'

'It's not fair on him,' said Stredwick. 'What if we *have* been barking up the wrong tree? I'm being pressured to make a decision down here: the money's ticking away like a taxi-meter. Worse than that, I still haven't decided whether I want to go ahead on this one. Even if we're proved right, the way things are shaping up there might even be a certain balance of justice about the whole case— at least as far as Frampton's concerned.'

'And if we're wrong?'

'Exactly!' said Stredwick. 'If we're wrong then we're up shit creek anyhow. At least the lad might stumble across something.'

'There's been a second murder, though,' Webber reminded him.

'I can't forget it,' said Stredwick. 'And I can't understand it: it has such a totally different stamp on it. But at least no one's blaming Frampton for that one, are they? Not unless he's supposed to have done an overnight bunk from Gartree.'

'Or unless someone's been doing his dirty work for him,' said Webber, more seriously.

'Get Archibold to ring me when he surfaces,' Stredwick said. 'Tell him I need to talk to him. Urgently.'

After he'd put down the phone Stredwick sat staring at the wall for a while, uncertain of his next move. Eventually he called the office and spoke to his two new researchers. He was encouraged to discover that at least they were both at their desks glued to the phones, though they didn't seem to be making much progress on the work in hand. But what else could he have expected? They were searching for a woman called Jan who, ten years before, had had a holiday job in a café in Yorkshire. She had been a student interested in making quilts. That was the sum total of their knowledge of her.

The national secretary of the Quilters' Guild had provided a series of addresses; now one of the researchers was phoning round the Guild's regional branches, compiling, as far as was possible, a list of every member called Jan or Janet who, ten years ago, might have been the age of the young woman who'd once worked in Rainsford. The other researcher was ringing every Polytechnic, University and College of Further Education in the country, attempting to discover through the Students' Unions whether there'd ever been a craft club or handicraft association in which members made quilts, and whether any membership lists were still likely to exist for them.

It was a thankless task. Without a surname to go on, they were searching for a needle in a haystack. Even if they found the woman, Stredwick couldn't be certain she'd be able to tell him anything. After all, she was at the back of the café the morning of the murder when Alexander and Frampton had come in. She couldn't have seen anything of the alleged fight, he knew that.

If Stredwick was honest with himself, the evangelical zeal with which he was searching for her was a sign of his desperation. He wasn't even allowing himself to consider the possibility of the search failing, let alone succeeding but failing to be useful. It seemed to him, as it seemed to Webber, that they hadn't really come much further than when they'd started. Stredwick couldn't countenance the prospect that when he found her, this ex-student Jan would be unable to help him. When he found her she *had* to help him. He had to believe that. It was the only way he could do the job. It was the faith of the religion he practised.

Later in the day, Stredwick dialled a number in Yorkshire. He didn't bother disguising his voice. The chances were the recipient wouldn't recognize it. But what if she did? It might not be such a bad thing if he could sow a seed or two of doubt in her mind, unsettle her a little even though she was probably unsettled enough already.

'Mrs Archery, Mrs Rita Archery? Do excuse me for calling you like this. I hope I haven't caught you at an inconvenient moment. My name is James Turner from Nationwide Opinion Polls . . . We're doing a telephone survey on attitudes to car ownership. May I ask you, do you have a car?'

He fired a series of questions at her about the make, the year, the mileage. He asked her how often she drove. And where to.

'Journeys longer than twelve miles? Six? Three? How many times a week? Is that local trips? Within the county? Outside?'

He was practised at this technique, though he was never comfortable with deception, which—looked at one way—was odd, given that his working life was so often built on deceit, and the medium in which he worked was geared to it with so many of its electric shadows pretending to be real. It was a paradox, but it was a paradox too that even the most untrustworthy people were themselves invariably trusting, the former Rita Brassington no less than anyone else. She answered his questions without any suspicion. And why not? She believed Stredwick because when he lied Stredwick believed himself. It was the only way to lie credibly.

'And so how many years have you had a licence, Mrs Archery? And a car?'

This information about the car had been all he'd wanted to know, but he kept the deception going until the receiver was safely replaced.

Afterwards he tapped a line or two into his computer, made himself a cup of tea, and took a taxi into town. It was raining as usual, and he sat staring absently at the streets through the distorting droplets on the window. Did it ever stop raining in this bloody town? Were things ever what they seemed to be, or would they always fracture into caricature through one screen or another?

Stredwick knew he wouldn't be long at St Catherine's House. It had been observant of Archie on his first visit to Rita's to notice the birthday cards on the mantelshelf. It made the job no more than a mechanical task.

He pushed his way through the crowd of people who were sheltering in the doorway waiting for the rain to ease. Inside, it took him only a few minutes to trace the volume he wanted, and only a few minutes more to leaf through its dog-eared pages to the information he was seeking. As with so much of this case, it was no more than he expected.

Rita had registered the father of her son Gary as Terry Frampton.

Of course, it explained a few things. Stredwick knew about the parole system and it explained why Rita was so obstructive in getting Frampton's case raised again. But it didn't take the case much further, did it? It was actually rather predictable.

More unpredictable—a total bolt out of the blue, in fact—was the telephone call Stredwick received when he got back home. It was from the policeman he'd met the day before in the Wimpy bar.

Apparently a letter had arrived that morning for Julie Taylor; it had been delayed in the post. Her father had opened it, realized its possible implications and immediately contacted the authorities.

The letter was from a woman, and was most intriguing, Stredwick's policeman said. The writer seemed to be suggesting that she and Julie Taylor had something very important in common and that it might be useful for them to talk.

The letter, it seemed, was from Rita Brassington. In it Rita had suggested meeting Julie in Rainsford one evening, the very evening Julie had been murdered.

'You'll understand that this is an official call, Mr Stredwick,' said the policeman, reverting in his language to the formalities of a courtroom. 'I understand from information received that in your own inquiries you've been showing some interest in Rita Brassington?'

'Mmm,' said Stredwick, with some understatement. 'You might say that.'

CHAPTER 20

Yes, it explained a lot. It explained the note from Godfrey and the money missing from the building society account. It explained her absences from home and her declining interest in him. It even explained why she was so keen for him to come home, since even June wasn't going to be such a shit as to ditch him over the telephone. Presumably, this was the something she'd wanted to talk to him about.

What was it she'd said that day? That there were things you couldn't talk about on the phone? It had been dishonest of her, that. A relationship didn't just self-destruct; it decayed slowly, imperceptibly, as much for lack of growth as for any conscious lack of care. For her to have gone so far, there must have been a lot over the past few months that she couldn't talk to him about at all. The phone had nothing to do with it.

But when had it started? And how long had it been going on? Surely long before he'd taken this job? June wasn't one to rush into things, she wasn't one to let her heart rule her head in any unconsidered way. It wasn't that she was a callous person, but she'd never made any secret of the responsibility she felt she owed herself. It was part of the independence she so jealously guarded, part of her self-confidence that he'd once thought selfish until he'd come to understand it, and love it as part of the strength he loved in her.

A woman like June evolved into decisions rather than ever make them. For her to have taken such a decisive step she must have been dissatisfied for months, unhappy for much longer. Why in God's name, though, hadn't she said something? Why hadn't she let him know what she was feeling, at least allowed him to play the doctor rather than just dump him in the mortuary like this? Why had she withdrawn into herself when if she'd shared what she was feeling they might have worked things out together?

He ought not to have reacted the way he did, he knew that. This Godfrey bloke looked a nice enough fellow—a bit staid, maybe, not the sort he'd have thought June would go for. But he'd got a sensitive sort of face. Archie ought to have stayed and perhaps the three of them could have talked things over like intelligent people, calmly and rationally. Yes, he ought to have stayed; even at this eleventh

157

hour it surely couldn't be over with her, not after so long when they'd been so close?

Yet as he'd stood there on the doorstep, it wasn't logic or sense that had governed his actions, but blind hatred and raw anguish.

He didn't know whether he'd hit Godfrey, but he'd certainly swung at him, and the pain in his knuckles told him that he'd hit something. It might have been the door; it might have been Godfrey's face that had jarred so satisfyingly under his fist. Either way, surprised so that he stumbled, or struck so that he fell, Godfrey had crumpled to the floor, and Archie had kicked at him wildly, seized with such a livid rage that if he could have managed to get near his face he'd have reduced it to a bloody and lifeless pulp. But Godfrey had curled himself on the floor clutching his head in his arms protectively, screaming for all he was worth, and June had suddenly appeared at the door in her nightdress screaming too, trying to get herself between them, so that to have gone on, he'd have had to kick his way through her as well.

Archie had stormed off back to the car but it wasn't until he was on the A1 again that he'd realized how far he'd driven, or how fast he was driving. It wasn't until past Scotch Corner that he noticed his hands were trembling on the steering-wheel, and that he seemed to be crying, but crying without tears, sobbing with a sort of choked passion as if he'd been the one who'd been hit, not Godfrey.

He needed time to think, time to adjust. He needed to clear June from his mind, and ideally he needed his mind clear from Stredwick and the demands of the job too. That wouldn't be possible, of course, not immediately anyhow. Without June, without even a home now, the job represented his only future, his only hope of a new life separate from her. Without June, the job *was* his life. He'd have to get a place of his own now, that had to be a priority. Maybe he'd move to London, maybe even buy a place. June had talked often enough about that. Perhaps without her he could find the impetus to organize a mortgage for himself. He would need to do something to make a clean break, something to restore his confidence and re-establish his self-esteem. He had to have time to think, that was the most important thing. It was futile making any decisions until he'd come to terms with life without her.

Of one thing he was determined, though, and that was that he wouldn't be crushed by what had happened. Perhaps he had been too dependent, perhaps too cloying in his love, and too comfortably selfish in it too so that it became restrictive and negative, not a part of the real world at all, but a first line of defence against it. In this way what he'd had with June had excluded even her, for even in his lowest moments after he'd been sacked by the paper she'd never shared his sense of despair at the world. She'd seen things more positively. Less self-indulgently. She'd wanted him to go freelance, to write a book, even start a newspaper of his own. They'd been different that way, and perhaps eventually she'd come to realize it, and realize too that being such different people they would always be pulling against each other.

Perhaps a break-up had been bound to happen at some stage; perhaps what had happened might eventually all prove to have been for the best. Curiously, despite his long day, and his night without sleep, despite the hours he'd spent driving and the emotional exhaustion that dogged him after events in Wearside, he felt somehow liberated by what had happened. He had wanted to see June so much last night; now he wondered if he ever wanted to see her again.

Yet even as he wondered, he knew that he did, that he was already missing her hopelessly, and that the pain of losing her was already becoming so intense he didn't know how he was going to be able to bear it.

The Rod and Gun Club dinner was long over by the time he arrived back at the Shornewan. Webber was on duty behind the reception desk, chirpier than anyone who'd been on the tiles most of the night had a right to be.

'George has been trying to reach you urgently,' he said as soon as he saw Archie. 'Oh, and June's been ringing all morning too. She wants you to call her at home. She's taken the day off work. It's none of my business, I know . . . but she seems very upset.'

Archie had no intention of ringing June, but he called Stredwick immediately. Archie's news seemed to animate him.

'Following you? Are you sure?'

'As sure as I can be about anything,' said Archie. 'I can't think of any other reason why he'd be wandering around the countryside that time of night.'

'Strange. Perhaps he was lost?'

'I thought of that too, but it doesn't really figure, does it?'

Stredwick grunted. 'Did you talk much to him over dinner?'

'You must be joking,' said Archie. 'He wouldn't talk about anything except the rising crime rate. He's obsessed with it. He believes criminals are only one stage removed from reducing society to total anarchy. I suppose that's what twenty-three years on the bench does for you.'

Stredwick laughed flatly. 'There are a couple of things I want you to do for me as soon as you can. I'm still intrigued why Frampton and Alexander left the café in such a hurry that morning. I want you to send me a verbatim transcript of your interview with Jenny Rochford.'

'Jenny who was working at the café? Whatever for?'

'Don't ask questions,' snapped Stredwick. 'Just get it to me. Webber's got a fax, hasn't he? I also want you to go and see that woman Bertha again, the one who was manageress at the café. I know you've seen her already but I just want you to be certain there's nothing else she can tell us about this student. Anything. Any small detail, however insignificant. By the way, I'm sending you a tape of my conversation with Julie Taylor's father,' he said. 'You should get it in the post tomorrow. I'd be interested in what you make of it.'

He gave Archie a rundown on what to expect. Afterwards Archie fell silent.

'But why on earth did you ask Julie's father *that*?' he

160

asked eventually. 'You seem to be suggesting . . . that Julie Taylor and Carrington . . .'

'I was suggesting nothing,' said Stredwick. 'I was just asking questions. Trying to find out anything I could.'

Archie couldn't hide his scepticism. 'But Julie Taylor? And Carrington? It seems incredible.'

'Almost certainly it is,' said Stredwick. 'After all, there was a perfectly innocent explanation. He was her employer, after all. It's natural he'd run her back home from time to time if she was working late and her father couldn't pick her up.'

'But that day? The day of the murder? We've no evidence that she was anywhere near the Shornewan. And even if she was, are you implying that she and Carrington . . . ? No, that's even more incredible. She was a virgin anyhow, wasn't she?'

'I'm just flying kites,' explained Stredwick. 'Maybe it hadn't got that far. Truth doesn't always follow logical paths, son. It's just one intriguing possibility among many. You mustn't jump on every hypothesis as a certainty.'

Again Archie fell silent. He was troubled by this new perspective and its implications; even to consider it seemed a violation of the dead.

'OK,' he said eventually, 'I take your point as far as it relates to Julie Taylor and Carrington. But what you seem to be suggesting now is that there might have been two people involved in Alexander's murder.'

Stredwick gave another of his impersonations of a laugh. 'Perhaps. Who knows? We've evidence for it, haven't we? Not conclusive evidence, I agree, but it has to be a possibility. Alexander weighed more than fourteen stone, after all. It would have been the devil of a job for one person to shift his body without leaving any sort of drag mark, and there were no drag marks in the mud anywhere near to where his body was found—you can see that on the crime photographs. More to the point, though, is that if two people were involved in the crime, it would go a long way to explaining why there appear to have been two totally different attacks made on Alexander, the first which killed him, and the second which caused the lacerations on his face.'

'But where does that leave our contention that Frampton's innocent of the murder because of his fingernails?'

Stredwick's mood changed abruptly the way it was always prone to do. Suddenly he became very agitated. '*Our* contention? Ours?' he snapped, his voice rising as he spoke until he was all but screaming down the phone. 'That might have been your view, but I've always been much more circumspect about what I've thought. I've never said that Frampton's innocent. All I've said is that the truth of this murder's never fully come out. Until we get firm evidence to the contrary, Frampton's guilty. Understand? Guilty. Convicted by a court of law.'

Perhaps at a different time Archie might have waited for Stredwick's outburst to blow itself out, and for calm to be restored. His hysterics never lasted long, and they never signified much except, maybe, Stredwick's frustration at the obdurate workings of his own mind. Another time Archie might have let it ride, the way he'd let things ride before. Today, though, despite what had happened with June—or maybe because of it—he felt furious at Stredwick's tortuous vacillation.

Either Frampton was innocent and they ought to work on that, or he wasn't and they ought to have junked the case long ago. Stredwick was playing around with him. All these theories of his weren't real theories at all, but jumbled irrelevancies thrown in to confuse him.

Archie found himself shouting back down the phone, screaming in the same way Stredwick was screaming at him. What were they doing wasting their time, then, if they didn't fundamentally believe there'd been a miscarriage of justice? And what was all this crap about truth? Truth didn't exist in a vacuum. The search for a truth had to have some limitations to it. There had to be some certainties or else you couldn't function. You couldn't just open up every possibility and expect order to emerge from chaos, like throwing a fucking jigsaw on the table and expecting it miraculously to fall into place.

At one point Stredwick seemed about to hang up, but he seemed to get distracted and eventually seemed to decide that a costive silence was more in order, and that it was best to allow Archie's animosity to burn itself out. It was a curious reversal of their roles.

More curious still was afterwards when, as if nothing had happened, he said, 'You're not going to quit on me now, are you? Not at this stage?'

There was almost a tone of pleading in his voice.

It stopped Archie in his tracks. He'd really not considered how Stredwick would react to a haranguing of the sort he was so accustomed to mete out to others. Not like this, though. Never in a month of Sundays would Archie have thought it possible.

'Quit? No . . . no . . . It hadn't . . . it hadn't crossed my mind. I've arranged to see Elizabeth Carrington this afternoon anyhow,' Archie stammered, as if this were some sort of explanation.

'I mean, I don't know if it'll be worth the effort,' he went on. 'Carrington says she's hostile to journalists. That she just invites them round to insult them. But you did say to see her? You did say to interview her?'

'Yes. Of course,' said Stredwick absently. 'Elizabeth Carrington. Yes. Of course. I think she could be useful.'

Later, it was to occur to Archie that Stredwick suspected the significance Elizabeth Carrington was going to have for the investigation. Later, he began to believe he might even have suspected it himself too.

After all, you can only push so hard on a door before it begins to open. Or before the frame starts cracking.

CHAPTER 21

'You seem to be suggesting that my husband might have been having some sort of affair with Julie Taylor. Have I understood you correctly, Mr Archibold?' she asked, an unmistakable and mischievous incredulity in her voice.

163

Archie felt extremely discomfited. It was enough that he too thought the suggestion crass, without Elizabeth Carrington's remorseless amusement at his all too evident embarrassment at mentioning it. Was this, he wondered, Elizabeth Carrington's way with journalists? Was this what Carrington had been getting at when he'd warned Archie about his wife at the dinner? Carrington's terminology might have been tortuous and the tone patronizing, but there was no mistaking his meaning: 'Mr Archibold, go and see my wife if you want,' he was saying, 'but she'll eat you for breakfast.'

Thankfully, Archie had arrived too late for breakfast. Even so, given the likely state of play, he'd come to the conclusion it might be wise with Elizabeth Carrington not to be within biting distance too close to any mealtime.

'You say you met my husband last night,' she went on, 'Well, he's hardly a Byronic philanderer, do you think? Hardly a West Riding Lothario?' She threw Archie a winning smile. 'Still, to the arrogant everything seems possible, and sexually you men are so arrogant. Because you all believe yourselves capable of so much, you deceive yourselves into thinking other men capable of it too.'

She shook her head like an admonishing traffic warden who'd caught him parked on a yellow line. 'Be serious, Mr Archibold: he was thirty years older than her. Julie Taylor, I grant you, was unworldly beyond belief, but she'd been brought up according to a rigid regime, the way Yorkshire girls used to be. She'd learnt to keep her hand on her purse and her legs together outside wedlock. Actually, in my day there wasn't much more a woman really needed to know. Now, of course, it's different . . . there's so much violence everywhere.' She shook her head again. 'Poor Julie, poor unfortunate girl . . .'

They were sitting in the drawing-room of Elizabeth Carrington's low-ceilinged house near Bingley, looking out over the patio and the lawn to a canal and the pale outline of hills beyond. It had been a sharp, frosty day, and the late

164

winter sunshine streaming through the french windows imparted to the room the deceptive feel of an August afternoon.

Just as deceptive was Elizabeth Carrington herself, who, since his arrival, had been unrelentingly rude while at the same time being faultlessly polite. Like her husband, she was physically very frail, almost skeletal. But she was meticulously dressed and presented—in a way that Archie always found intimidating in women, as if their penetrating eye for the detail of their own appearance could suddenly be turned upon him and his very perceptions. Her hair was intricately coiffured, her nails a demonstration of the manicurist's art. She wore a simple cashmere sweater and a skirt so sharply pleated he could have shaved with it. What was more, her mind seemed just as sharp. She'd picked up on his intimations of an affair before he'd even realized he'd made them.

'We have to investigate every possibility, however outlandish, Mrs Carrington,' he explained by way of an apology.

'Of course,' she smiled. 'But I'd be more comfortable while you're doing it if you'd call me Liz. Formality does so hamper conversation, don't you think? You're . . . Alan, did you say?'

'Archie, actually,' said Archie. 'Or at least that's what everyone calls me.'

'Then I'll call you that too, Archie,' she said, reaching over to pat him on the hand. 'Shall we have something to drink?'

The drinks when she brought them turned out not to be contained, as he'd anticipated, in the ubiquitous Yorkshire teapot, but in tall plastic glasses, from the bases of which, integral to their construction, plastic straws spiralled uninvitingly outwards and upwards like petrified sections of the colon. They seemed to contain some unseasonal concoction of fruit juices. Elizabeth Carrington had made him nervous and his nervousness had made him dry. Archie gulped at the liquid greedily.

It was only after it hit his stomach that he recognized

165

what he'd drunk as alcohol. Virtually undiluted too, judging by the state of his throat.

Elizabeth Carrington's lips remained frozen but for some reason Archie got the impression she might almost have been laughing at him. 'My, my,' she said. 'Isn't this cosy? Now, Archie, you must tell me exactly what I can do to help you. Would you like to ask me if I stoved in Mr Alexander's head, or whether perhaps Walter might have killed him? I can't, of course, speak for my husband, but having lived with him for nearly forty years I'd have to concede there was something murderous about him—though whether this qualified him as assailant or victim, I really couldn't say. But you've met him, of course. You know what I'm talking about. However,' she went on, 'as for myself . . .'

'You left to visit a friend on the day of the murder.'

'Indeed. You are clever, Archie. I was with Amanda Parsons, an old school chum of mine who lives in York. I left the Shornewan around two or three o'clock on the Thursday afternoon, and I didn't arrive back until after the weekend. But of course, you must know all this from the police statements. And you must know too that the police checked my movements thoroughly. I'd give you Amanda's address to check yourself, except that the poor dear passed away last year. Knowing her penchant for other people's business, though, she's no doubt looking down on us at this very moment. The idea of her old dorm mate Liz as a murder suspect would amuse her mightily.'

'A murder suspect?'

She took a sip of her drink and glanced at him over the rim provocatively. 'But of course! Archie, please don't feel you have to be delicate on my account. You said yourself you had to examine every possibility, however outlandish.'

'All I was hoping is that you might be able to tell me something about Frampton and Alexander. About what they were doing the day of the murder?'

Elizabeth Carrington arched her eyebrows. 'What do you think they were doing?' she exclaimed. 'They weren't a

166

couple of interior designers, you know. They worked for the Water Board; we had a burst water main. I presume they were repairing it.'

'All through the day?'

She took another sip of her drink and fixed him in her gaze again, becoming visibly irritated at the interrogation. 'Archie, you are a most extraordinary young man. How on earth should I know? I wasn't monitoring them. For all I know they might have been having a cocktail-party in that hole of theirs. I really wasn't that interested. Whatever are you suggesting?'

It was at times like this Archie wished he smoked. It might at least have provided him with some oral distraction, some way of softening the edge of those difficult things that sometimes had to be said and which otherwise might emerge too boldly as scornful disbelief. It was obvious that Elizabeth Carrington was not being totally honest with him. It was inconceivable that she wouldn't have been interested in the work Frampton and Alexander were doing. Until they'd finished there was no water at the hotel. She couldn't have taken a bath for a week. For such a meticulous woman it must have been an ordeal verging on the unbearable.

Again though, she picked up what was going through his mind before he could even voice it. 'I'd had enough, Archie, that's what it was, you see. Those men had been pretending to work on that water main for a week, and we'd all but been reduced to washing in Perrier. Frankly, as far as I was concerned at that stage, I didn't care if they strung the job out until Easter. By then it was of no concern to me whatsoever. I told Walter, "I will not endure these conditions one day longer, Walter," that's what I said to him. There were cross words spoken between us, believe me. Voices were raised. Passions ran high. That was the only reason I went to stay with Amanda. I mean — I know one shouldn't speak unkindly of the dead — but take my word for it, Archie, Amanda Parsons was not the sort of woman with whom one would choose to spend four days except in the direst of emergencies. Under normal circumstances she had very little to offer anyone. At least with the Shornewan as dry as a sand dune she could put her bathroom facilities to some useful social purpose.'

Despite the worry that Elizabeth Carrington's tongue might just as easily be turned on him as a dead friend, Archie couldn't help finding her engaging, though her cheerful amorality troubled him.

'Didn't you think it odd, Mrs—uh, Liz—that they were working so hard that Thursday?' he went on, 'after doing so little the rest of the week, I mean? I'm surprised you didn't mention it to the police.'

This idea seemed to scandalize her. 'Mention it to the police? My dear boy, why ever should I have done that? I'm sure there was some perfectly lucrative explanation for it. Don't they have overtime, bonuses, that sort of thing?' She broke off abruptly. 'Archie, I'm beginning to find this conversation painfully tedious. For God's sake drink up your grog and I'll mix you another. Let me at least show you the garden before it gets too dark.'

Archie allowed himself to be led outside where, to his urban eyes, the garden seemed remarkably uninteresting. Around the lawn lay a series of bare flowerbeds containing the stumps of well-pruned roses. A winding path of crazy paving led to the canal's edge where, as they approached, some curious black bird with an orange beak strutted into the water, its tiny head vibrating out of turn with its legs in some ornithological silly walk.

'Of course, in the summer when the hire fleets are out, it is a little like living on the edge of a motorway,' Elizabeth Carrington said. 'Still, one can only withdraw so far from the modern world. One can't, regrettably, retire from it completely.'

'Would you want to if it were possible?' Archie asked. 'Retire completely from the world, I mean?'

'I find it fundamentally too venial, its concerns too materialistic and trivial if I'm honest, Archie. Not that one's immune oneself, but there's far too much self-satisfied smugness in the air for my liking—even among those who have least to be smug about. All the same, I probably wouldn't want it any differently. Why should I? As I get older I find I care less about what the world thinks, which allows me to be more honest in saying what I think of the world. It's a valuable freedom. It's been worth waiting for.'

She took his arm and led him along the water's edge. 'Of course, my husband believes the whole edifice is about to crumble and, who knows? he may be right. There's certainly enough evidence to support his view. Riots. Civil unrest. And crime, of course. The hotel was burgled while we were there, did you know that? We were in bed and they got in through a downstairs window. It was all very efficiently done, mind you. No mess, no damage apart from a single broken pane of glass. And we were insured, of course. But Walter took it so very badly, almost as a personal affront. He felt himself under siege, as if he were the final enclave of civilization at the onset of a new Dark Age.'

Archie smiled. 'The hotel seems immensely well secured against intruders now,' he said, remembering the palaver Webber had gone through to open the front door the night he'd arrived.

'You might wonder what it's all for,' she said, stooping down to remove the stray skeleton of a leftover autumn leaf. 'I know that eventually I did. I could understand the burglar alarm, of course. I mean, one might harbour a deep fascination for one's fellow creatures, but it doesn't do to have them wandering around one's home in the dead of night. Walter was terribly angry. I've never seen him so livid—' she hesitated—'and so obsessed too. He began putting locks on everything. I was surprised he didn't padlock the lavatory seats.'

She turned back towards the house. 'Frankly, Archie, it became a bit much both for me and our guests. I live on my own here and I observe the necessary proprieties in terms of security. I keep my windows locked when I go out, and my jewellery well hidden. It's true too that I keep a gun, and though it is only one of my grandfather's war souvenirs, it affords me a certain confidence at nights. I find this is more than enough to make me feel secure. Even so, were I ever to become a victim of crime again, I don't think I'd see it as anything more than bad luck. You see, Archie, Walter has never adjusted to the modern world. As a magistrate, he sat on the bench like Canute confronting the tide. I think he considered every case he ever heard as a personal violation.'

'Hardly the best person for the job, I'd have thought.'

'He wasn't much of a hotelier either, if the truth were told,' she said acidly. 'Between you and me, he wasn't up to it and I didn't like it. Frankly, I was pleased to leave the Shornewan. We were there fourteen years, and I never felt comfortable in the place.'

'Was that . . . was that because of the weather by any chance?'

Elizabeth Carrington stopped in her tracks and turned to face him. 'Goodness gracious, Archie! You are a most peculiar young man! What on earth has the weather got to do with it? No, it was the clientele I found most disconcerting. The rocks regularly attracted as extraordinary an assortment of curiosities as you'd find outside of an institution. There was always somebody exposing himself, or interfering with little boys. It's the world we live in, I suppose,' she sighed. 'I know such behaviour is hardly condoned, but nevertheless, it seems to shock people a good deal less than it once did.'

She screwed up her face distastefully. 'At the time of the murder the police asked me if I'd seen anyone suspicious around the rocks that day. Well! what was I supposed to say? The only time there *weren't* odd people around the Shornewan rocks is when the weather was so bad they risked killing themselves by being there. Even then, it didn't stop some of them. God knows what it was that attracted them to the place.'

'And did you see anyone?' asked Archie.

She shrugged her shoulders. 'I can't remember. There was one businessman in a car who regularly used to read his dirty magazines there. But I think the police checked him out. And yes, there was a carful of coloured people who'd been spending a lot of time up there that week—'

'Coloured people?'

'Yes—you know—Indians, Pakistanis. They just seemed to be waiting for something or other. The police didn't seem to think them very important.'

'What did they look like?'

'What did they look like? Really, Archie, what do you expect them to look like? I didn't examine them, you know. I only saw them from a distance. One of them seemed to have a scar on his face. Or I think it was a scar, but really, I went over all this with the police . . . . Archie, are you all right?'

'A carful of Asian men, you say? One of them with a scar on his face?'

'Yes, that's right. But, Archie, whatever is the matter? Perhaps you ought to come inside and sit down for a while. You look very pale. Aren't you feeling well?'

He'd been staring over the countryside, his eyes totally blank but his mind racing in overdrive. Now he turned to her, and making an effort to suppress what he felt, he said, 'Yes, I'm perfectly all right, I've never felt better. But I think I must go now. I think I must go straightaway. Perhaps I could see you again? Perhaps ring you?'

'Of course,' she said. 'I think you might find you'll want to talk to me again. I think you might find this whole thing coming back to me,' she added enigmatically.

But he didn't hear her. By that time he'd already rushed off and she was left alone in the garden as the afternoon sun began to sink behind the hills.

CHAPTER 22

'So you were up there, then? At the Shornewan? On the day of the murder? Why didn't you say anything?'

'You didn't ask,' said Harbinder Singh. 'Mind you, I wouldn't have said even if you had.' He gave Archie one of his wide, handsome smiles. 'Now it's come out, though, I don't see there's owt to be gained by denying it. But I will

171

if you're planning to say owt on t'telly. I'll swear blind then that I didn't say a word to you, and there'll be a dozen witnesses who'll say the same in court.'

They were sitting in the small front room of Harbinder's house in one of the network of Nottingham terraced streets near the factory where he worked. The room was dominated by a three-piece suite covered with freshly laundered antimacassars. It was meticulously tidy and smelt of Pledge furniture polish, a room for special occasions, for weddings, wakes or anniversaries.

It seemed fitting that they should be talking in such a room. Since leaving Elizabeth Carrington, Archie had a sense of something momentous in the air. He couldn't help feeling the case was close to falling into place. He couldn't help feeling Harbinder might have the key to some truth about events, that Harbinder might actually be the key himself. Archie had little conception of a murderer, but listening to Harbinder he found he was auditioning him for the role. Did murderers smile as much as Harbinder smiled? Were they as relaxed and comfortable with themselves as Harbinder seemed to be?

'So who was with you that day?' Archie asked eventually.

Harbinder gave another of his wide grins. 'Now, you wouldn't expect me to tell you that, would you? Let's just say it was a few friends.'

'Friends that didn't mind helping you rough up someone? Friends a bit handy with a knife, perhaps? Even friends that wouldn't have minded helping you kill someone?'

'Maybe. But what's that to you? Alexander got what was coming to him, and I haven't heard of many tears being shed on his account. I certainly haven't lost sleep over him. I hated the man, I made no secret about that. His sort of scum is better off dead. In any other country it'd have been done legal, not left to decent people to settle their own scores. In any other country the law would deal with people like him, and leave the rest of us in peace.'

He ran his finger ends lightly over the scar on his face.

172

'We're too soft on his sort,' he went on. 'But this whole bloody country's gone soft. A bloke like Alexander smashes a glass in someone's face, and if the police are bothered enough to investigate and manage to catch someone, they're lucky to get a jury willing to convict. And what happens then? Some judge doles out a few hours' community service, or a year on probation. Somebody smacks the back of his hand and tells him he's been a naughty boy. Does it surprise you some of us feel our own ways are the best?'

'Your own ways? To set yourself up as police, judge, jury and executioner? What sort of law is that?'

'At least it's a just law, a law that people understand. The Sikh holy book teaches us not to bow before injustice: in this country people cower before it.' He sat forward in his chair and prodded an admonishing finger at Archie. 'Do you know, I wonder sometimes if that's why people in this country dislike us so much. I mean, us—people from other backgrounds, other cultures. Sometimes I wonder if it's because we've got something they've lost. They say we're cliquey, that we don't mix. Well, does it bloody surprise you? You see kids out on t'streets round here until gone midnight, and their parents have got no idea where they are, or what they're doing. Why should I want my kids to mix with theirs, getting into bad ways? Why should I want to have anything to do with them? They've no respect for owt, some people. In my community we've still got standards: honesty, respect for the old—respect for justice. Funny, that, you know, because when you look at them, they're just the old values this country was built on. Yet we're classed as outsiders—'

They were disturbed by a woman who came into the room carrying a tray. Harbinder's wife, perhaps? She was dressed in a traditional sari and she kept her eyes averted from them as she unloaded a plate of small pastries on to a side table, and poured them some bitter tea from a saucepan.

'I don't understand you,' Archie said, after the woman had left. 'You claim that Terry Frampton's your mate. You visit him in prison. How can you do that knowing the injustice of his conviction? How can you live with that responsibility?'

For a moment or two Harbinder looked at him, bewildered. Then that characteristic, wide-mouthed smile of his began to crease his face again. 'Hang about a bit. I think you've got your lines crossed here,' he said. 'You don't think I killed him, do you? You don't think it was me smashed his head in?'

'What else am I supposed to think? Why else were you at the Shornewan? And why were you so cagey about saying you were there that day?'

'Hey, slow down,' said Harbinder. 'Just because I was at the Shornewan doesn't mean I killed him. Not that I wouldn't have done, given half a chance, mind you. But I never got that chance, did I? Do you expect me to go telling the police that? Come on! Grow up! This is the real world we live in. My face is a different colour from yours: it wouldn't have taken them long to find out I had a grudge against Alexander, and if I'd have so much as hinted I was at the Shornewan I'd have been behind bars faster than it takes to say "guilty".'

'Then I don't understand what you were doing there.'

Harbinder shook his head in disbelief. 'Are you simple, or just a bit slow?' he said. 'Do you need it spelling out? A, I was up there with me mates. B, We were after Alexander. C, I was going to kill him. You better believe it, this was no spur of the moment thing; we'd been watching him on and off for months. I'm not going to apologize for it either. I told you before, sooner or later I fully intended to have justice for what he did to me—'

'So why didn't you, then? What stopped you?' Archie asked.

Harbinder picked up his tea and ruminated on the question for a while as if considering his options. 'Look,' he said, 'I don't want this going any further; leastways, I don't want to get involved if it does. So mind! this hasn't come from me. Understand? But it was . . .' He hesitated. 'It was that woman of his . . .'

'His? Alexander's?'

174

'Aye. I'd have had him that day otherwise. Believe me, I'd decided I was going to kill him. But she turned up. Drove up in a car. What was her name now? Maureen, wasn't it?'

'Maureen Paton.'

'Aye, that's right,' said Harbinder. 'Maureen Paton. She was as common as muck, I remember. I wonder what's happened to her after all these years?'

It had been after 4.0 when Archie left Elizabeth Carrington, after 8.0 by the time he got to Harbinder Singh's in Nottingham, and nearly midnight before he got back to Leeds again. He drove straight to Maureen's. Parkview was in gloom when he arrived, most of the street lights out and even those that were functioning so dim they scarcely penetrated the dispiriting murkiness that hung over the area. The place looked different at night and he'd driven past Maureen's house before he realized.

He was in the middle of a three-point turn when he noticed a figure hurry from one of the houses, and screech off into the night in a crescendo of burning tyres and a cloud of exhaust fumes. This in itself would have been enough to alert Archie's suspicions, but by that time he'd got his bearings. By that time he knew that it had been from Maureen's house the figure had come.

He was out of the car and at the house in an instant.

The front door had been left open by whoever had rushed out. Archie went inside and stood for a moment in the foreboding hallway, listening to the echoing of a television set somewhere in the bowels of the building. Something alerted him to a danger, something chill and instinctive which, though he couldn't understand, he could at least recognize. He had felt this way some years ago, in that terrifying moment at that road junction outside Newcastle when he realized with horror that he'd turned against the traffic and there was nothing he could do to prevent the accident that would smash his leg in four places and put him in hospital for the summer.

His mouth had begun tingling, as if it were filled with dry

175

sherbet. His heart had begun beating against his ribcage so hard it surprised him not to hear it echoing in the vaulted dustiness around him.

It crossed his mind to seek help, to call for the police perhaps, or at least to alert someone else in the house to his suspicions. But what suspicions? What could he say that could be credible? That he'd seen a figure rushing from the building and that his instincts told him it was something to do with Maureen? That he felt like he had once when he'd had a road accident? Archie could almost laugh at his own cowardice. Even if the person he'd seen rushing away had come from this house, then why should it have anything to do with Maureen? There must have been at least a dozen flats in the rambling Victorian pile. And even if his fears were justified, then what was it likely to signify? Most probably one of Maureen's punters had done a bunk without paying, no more than that.

Archie felt his way up the wide staircase to the landing of the first floor, his eyes straining in the darkness for anything that would point his way. Eventually he made out the dim glow of a luminous switch. He pressed it and by the tenebrous light of a forty-watt bulb he made his way to the top of the building where Maureen's flat was located.

The door there had been left swinging open too.

Archie went inside, into the small corridor from which four internal doors radiated. From behind one of them, open too, came the sound of another television set, and the deadened hush of a late-night snooker commentary. By now Archie was convinced that something was amiss and convinced too that he wouldn't stand a chance if, for any reason, someone was still in the flat, someone connected to the shadowy figure he'd seen leaving: another burglar perhaps, maybe a second rapist.

His best bet if anyone appeared would just be to turn tail and run. His best bet would be to scream blue murder and hope to rouse the house. It might not be what you'd do in a film, and it might not be the macho thing to do anywhere. But in the circumstances it seemed the safest contingency.

He pushed the living-room door timidly, half expecting to be attacked. Instead he was greeted by a round of sympathetic applause from the television for the break he'd just ended on a missed blue. The room looked scarcely different from when he'd been in it the previous morning. There were the milk bottles still gathering mould in the sink, the heap of clothes carelessly strewn on the floor. The place still felt damp despite the gas fire hissing in the hearth; the air still smelt of stale, sour urine.

He almost relaxed.

Until he heard a strangled voice behind him.

He swung round expecting a knife in his gut or a boot between his legs, expecting to be confronted by a gang of hooligans or at least a couple of local mobsters.

Instead, there was nothing.

'Hello,' the voice said again.

It came from a pile of clothes on a couch in the corner. It came from Maureen's mother whose existence had completely slipped his mind.

'Hello, Mrs Paton,' he said, in a voice radiating a deceptive confidence. 'I'm just looking for Maureen.'

She gave him an uncomprehending grin, and turned her attention back to the television set and the difficult red he'd left her with.

Archie returned to the corridor and tried another door in the flat. He found himself in what at first seemed to be a junk room, piled with cardboard boxes and broken furniture. From the rancid smell and the stained mattress in the corner, an enduring testimony to Mrs Paton's micturitions, he could work out it had once been her room before she'd abandoned herself finally to a lifetime of late nights at the Crucible.

He moved next door to the bathroom where once again nothing seemed out of place, in that everything was: cosmetics and old magazines littered the floor, and a thick dust of talcum and face powders hung in the air.

There only remained the final room, Maureen's bedroom. He'd pushed open the door before he realized its handle was covered in blood.

Frankly, after this build-up, he'd have been disappointed not to have found a body inside.

He wasn't disappointed.

CHAPTER 23

The two researchers had their noses to the grindstone. Infected by Stredwick's urgency to find the quilter called Jan who had worked at the café in Rainsford, they'd spent their day without even a lunch-break, hammering the phones so hard it was a miracle they hadn't corns on their ears. The woman was especially assiduous; a winsome slip of a thing just down from Oxford, she was clearly ambitious to impress and she'd been ringing Kennington throughout the day, virtually every hour on the hour, with a progress report.

'It's better than a treasure hunt,' she said. 'We're assembling a list of names and telephone numbers. We're hoping to be able to contact most of them by the end of the day. Is it OK if we stay on late?'

Midway through the evening Stredwick was fixed in front of his computer when she rang him for what was to be the last time. She was scarcely able to contain her excitement. 'I think we may have found something, Mr Stredwick,' she said. 'At least, it looks promising. I thought you'd like to know about it straight away.'

She had found a quilter named Janine Linney, whose mother had confirmed that she'd been at college in Yorkshire. It was a long time ago—but yes, her daughter had worked on holiday jobs up there, and yes, her mother did seem to recall that once Jan worked in some café.

The researcher gave Stredwick Janine Linney's current telephone number. Janine Linney was now Janine Murray. She lived in Esher in Surrey.

Her phone was a long time ringing. The male voice which eventually answered sounded harassed. Stredwick could hear a baby crying in the background, and a young child, a boy, kept interrupting their call by picking up an extension phone and shouting 'bum, belly-button, willy' at the top of his voice.

'Where did you say you're ringing from?' the voice asked. Stredwick told him again.

'Well, you of all people ought to bloody well know where she is,' he snapped. 'Listen, if you see her, do you think you could do me a favour? Do you think you could tell her that Tanya's got the colic again? Ask her to give me a ring. Tell her I can't find the sodding Dentinox.'

Stredwick called the Controller at home. 'No crap, no criticism,' he said. 'Most of all, no complaints. Not now, Malcolm, please. I'm on to something. I want to know if the name Janine Murray—Janine Linney—means anything to you?'

Stredwick could sense the slowly turning cogs of the Controller's mind grinding into movement. He'd probably be into his third G&T by now. He was probably settled into his carpet slippers, with his legs up on the sofa, listening to some Radio Four drama, because the truth was that despite his job he really didn't like television.

'No, I don't think so,' Malcolm said hesitantly. 'Not unless she's something to do with Linney Productions Ltd. They're an independent outfit we're using at the moment; they're doing a programme on women's cinema with us for Channel Four—George! George, are you OK?'

'Yes, yes. Sorry,' said Stredwick. 'Are we bed-and-breakfasting them?'

'They've got their own office in Covent Garden some-where, but they're using our editing rooms. Just down the corridor from you, as it happens—hold on a minute.' Stredwick heard him shuffling through some papers. 'Yes, Room 2143. Main building. George! George, are you there . . . ?'

Stredwick found her without any trouble. She was hunched over a Steenbeck, viewing footage with a woman film editor, the two of them ankle-deep in offcuts. She wore low-heeled court shoes, a grey suit and a colourful hand-printed silk scarf worn like a tie. It was as impressive a

179

piece of power dressing as Stredwick had seen in a long time.

'Hello,' he said. 'You're Janine Murray. You used to be Janine Linney. You're married, live in Esher and have a son who tends towards the foul-mouthed and a baby daughter named Tanya with a delicate stomach. I'm George Stredwick. And by the way, your husband's having trouble with the medicine cabinet.'

He stuck out his hand.

'Believe it or not, I didn't hear about the murder until long after the trial,' she told Stredwick later as they sat in a wine bar close to the office. 'You see, I finished working at the café that Friday—the day after it happened—before the body was even discovered. It was only a holiday job. I went home that weekend, and on the Monday I went back to college in York for the new term. I've got some vague memory of seeing a couple of stories about some murder near Rainsford in the papers—but it didn't register with me. I mean, it wouldn't, would it? You never think your life can touch on murder, however indirectly. No, I found out about it—what?—it must have been two or three years afterwards. I'd not long been working and I was doing a programme in Yorkshire; I was passing Rainsford and decided to stop for lunch. As it happened, I ran into someone I'd got friendly with while I was working at the café. She told me all about it.'

'And you found out that the murderer and his victim had both been at the café the morning it had happened?'

'No, I didn't know that until you mentioned it. I find it a bit creepy.'

Stredwick took a handful of peanuts from a bag and chewed on them carefully to avoid them getting under his dentures. He wasn't drinking, he rarely did, and never at times like these when he needed his head to be absolutely clear.

'So there was never any attempt by the police to interview you?' he asked.

'No, but why should they have wanted to? I mean, I

didn't see or hear any argument. I'd done an early shift serving at the counter, I remember that. But most of the morning I was in the back, peeling potatoes.'

'You remember things remarkably clearly given that it's nearly ten years ago,' Stredwick said.

Janine Linney smiled confidently. 'Yes, I suppose I do. It's not because I've got a brilliant memory, though, don't get that idea.' The smile became awkward and she coloured slightly. 'No, I remember that morning very well indeed, too well: the afternoon's a bit of a blur, though . . . You see, that day, because I was leaving at the end of the week, I'd arranged to see some friends in the pub for a farewell drink. You know the sort of thing. Well, at the café we only got a half-hour lunch-break; I took mine early that day so I'd be back for one o'clock, which was always the busiest time of the day. The trouble was the few drinks turned into a few drinks too many . . .'

'You got plastered?'

Janine coloured again. 'Absolutely blotto. Out of my head. Anyway, I pulled myself together enough to go back to work, but it must have been gone three by that time. Bertha—that's Big Bertha, she used to run the place—she was furious. She sacked me on the spot. Sacked me! I was really shocked; I hadn't expected that. Anyway, I had to go back the next day for my outstanding wages, and we had a set-to about the hours I'd worked. She claimed I'd left for the pub earlier than I had because she hadn't seen me around. She wouldn't believe I'd been out the back making bloody chips most of the morning.'

Janine picked up the Scotch and soda Stredwick had bought her. She positioned her carefully made-up mouth on the edge of the glass and sipped at it delicately so as not to disturb the careful construction of her lips. 'So you see, Mr Stredwick,' she said with a peremptory decisiveness, 'unfortunately, it doesn't look as if I'm going to be able to help you.'

If Stredwick was disappointed that his search which had ended so preposterously close to him was now to end so inconclusively, then it didn't show. He took another handful of peanuts, absently tossed them into his mouth, and then took what was for him the uncharacteristic step of taking someone into his confidence.

'Between ourselves, I've been working on a theory,' he explained, leaning over the table and lowering his voice. 'You see, I'm absolutely certain in my mind that there never was an argument that morning between Frampton and Alexander. I don't think the evidence warrants that view. On the other hand, what's indisputable is that for some reason they were rushing to get outside. Now I may be barking up the wrong tree here, but I think the most likely reason to explain that is that they were rushing to avoid somebody—somebody who they were worried might recognize them. I know that on their way out they almost knocked down a girl—a young woman—who was on the pavement. But I know too that the person who told me that couldn't have seen this girl if she had been on the pavement. You see, I think this girl was seen as she was coming *into* the café, and I've a suspicion that it was her Frampton and Alexander were trying to avoid. I know it's a long shot, but I was hoping you might have some idea who this young woman might have been.'

Janine was about to take another sip of her drink, but she stopped abruptly, the glass half way to her mouth, and put it down on the table again. 'Look, I don't want to prevaricate here, but . . . but I'm not certain I should be talking to you about this.'

'Because this is a murder? Because you know who that young woman was?'

'I know exactly who that woman was,' Janine said. 'She was one of my friends who'd come in to . . . to talk to me about something. Something personal. She came into the back and was with me until went to the pub. But look—' She broke off. 'Why is this important to you? Is it . . . is it likely to be relevant after all these years? Is it likely to have anything to do with the murder?'

'Almost certainly it has,' said Stredwick placatingly. 'That's why I must know who she was.'

For a moment or two Janine sat considering her options.

182

Then, appearing suddenly to make up her mind, she said: 'It was a woman called Julie Taylor. You probably won't have run across her, but she used to work up at the Shornewan when I was at the café. As a matter of fact, she was the person I was talking about—the person who told me about the murder. It upset her a lot. I don't know where she's working now, but I can give you her address, I doubt she's moved. I really ought to have dropped her a line myself before now, but I've been so busy . . .'

Stredwick screwed up his empty bag of peanuts and deposited it in an ashtray on the table. 'You don't read the papers very much for a journalist, do you, Janine? Listen, let me get you another drink, a brandy perhaps . . . ?'

After Stredwick had told her, as gently as he could, about Julie Taylor's murder, Janine, visibly shaken, said to him, 'Do you think we could go back to the office? Somewhere more quiet? I think in the circumstances there's something else you ought to know . . .'

If Stredwick had appalled Janine Linney by his revelation of Julie Taylor's murder, then it was nothing to the shock she dealt *him* after she'd divulged the confidence she'd been harbouring for almost a decade. Stredwick hadn't led a sheltered life, but after he'd listened to her story he felt nauseated.

He tried to tell himself it was something about the cities and rugged landscape of Yorkshire that seemed to engender a particularly squalid sort of male bestiality. But it wasn't just Yorkshire, he knew that. It was the same everywhere in this cesspit of a world, in which violence in all its manifestations was becoming such a way of life it seemed to be contaminating more and more people, either as victims or assailants.

The case was beginning to fall into clear shape, like a picture on a camera viewfinder being brought into focus. But all the same, it made him sick.

Back at home in Kennington he got another call from his Wimpy bar policeman.

'We took Rita Brassington in for questioning,' he told

183

Stredwick, 'but we didn't keep her for long, there wasn't any need, as it happened. You see we arrested someone for the rapes, and he put his hand up to Julie Taylor's murder too. I thought you'd like to know before it got in the papers. He's an insurance salesman by the name of Duncan Parker—I can't imagine you've ever heard of him. Regular sort of chap: wife, company car, own home in Harrogate, and two lovely girls at private school. Just seems he had a penchant for terrorizing women. Like so much of the scum we have to deal with.'

'Duncan Parker,' Stredwick repeated. 'I don't suppose there's any chance of—'

'A mistake, Mr Stredwick? No, not this time. It seems the bastard fancied himself as a bit of a photographer, and some of the lads here have seen his albums. There's a picture in it of Julie after he'd finished with her . . . Christ! And you wonder why some of us want to bring back hanging . . .'

Stredwick rang Webber immediately.

'So Julie Taylor's murder had nothing at all to do with it?' Webber said. 'Just a coincidence?'

'If you want to call it that,' said Stredwick, 'but I'd call it a social attitude. Anyway, it looks as if we might have been on the right track all along. I'll drive up straightaway. Reserve me a room. I can't see any reason for not confronting things now; it's the only way we're going to get anywhere. Where's the lad, by the way? You better tell him I'm coming.'

'Archibold? He rang a few hours back from some motorway service station. Said if you rang I had to tell you he'd gone to Nottingham. He seemed very excited, he said he was on to something.'

'Christ Almighty!' said Stredwick. 'That's all I need at the moment. Look, Peter, find out where the hell he is. I don't care how you do it. Find out where he is and tell him to lay off the whole thing. Tell him to do nothing until I arrive. Understand, NOTHING. If he goes poking his nose about any more it's going to turn very nasty . . .'

184

CHAPTER 24

Archie had never seen a body before. When his father had died he had been thought too young to be allowed to assuage his grief at the deathbed like the rest of his family. He'd been born of a generation for which death was awkward, and the dead so much carrion which had to be disposed of furtively, in much the same way as you might dispose of a dog turd that you inconveniently discovered under the table just as you sat down to dinner.

So this was what all the fuss was about, this was what inspired the poets, and what the philosophers puzzled to understand. So this—give or take a hospital room, a graveside or a few grieving relatives—this was how it all ended?

It all seemed mundanely unimpressive. Maureen Paton lay on her bed in a parody of the fetal position, her knees almost touching her chin. Her right hand trailed above her head across a pillow; her left was twisted awkwardly under her chest. Across her temple was a streak of coagulated blood which reached to her neck. Her tights, he noticed irrelevantly, were ripped at one knee. They had laddered downward towards her heel, but were curiously unflawed above the tear.

No doubt, had he stopped to think about a thousand lessons taught from detective novels and TV films, he would have left the room untouched and phoned the police immediately. But some grotesque curiosity impelled him towards the bed, and once there, constrained him to burrow to where her left hand was trapped by her breast, seeking out her pulse.

The shock of her moving almost put him in the grave he'd earmarked for her.

'Here, you don't get any of that without there's money on the table first,' she said, her voice cracked and shaking, and a good deal less forceful that the virulence of her black

185

humour. 'If you've got nothing better to do, chuck over me fags.'

After he'd propped her up, cleaned her up, and brewed up, he sat at the foot of the bed awaiting an explanation. He knew sooner or later one would have to be forthcoming since he'd threatened otherwise to ring the police, the last thing she wanted in these or any other circumstances.

'And I'm not going to be palmed off by any story that it was one of your blokes,' he said. 'I saw her leaving. It was Rita, wasn't it?'

'It was nowt.'

'It looks a bit more than that,' said Archie, eyeing the gash down her neck which he'd attempted to clean up but which was still oozing blood. 'Another half-inch and she'd have sliced straight through your jugular. You've taken a bit of a clout on you lip, too. You could do with some stitches. Drink up and I'll run you to hospital.'

'And have them prying into my business . . .'

'You can tell them it was an accident.'

'What? That I cut myself shaving?'

'Something like that,' said Archie. 'Here, put your arm around my neck. I'll carry you downstairs.'

Before he'd got her into the car she'd started retching with shock; inside, even with the heating up full, she began trembling violently. Archie slipped off his jacket at a set of traffic lights and tucked it around her.

'You'll be OK, luv,' he said, as gently as he could. 'They'll patch you up in no time.'

She'd been sitting with the side of her face pressed against the window, weeping with a childlike intensity, but as he accelerated away on the green light she threw the jacket on to the floor angrily.

'Don't patronize me,' she flared at him. 'I don't want your sympathy. You're as much a bastard as the rest of them despite your posh voice and your posh bloody job. You're always after something, aren't you? At least the punters are honest—they know what they want and they're willing to pay for it. You—' she spat out the word—'you're

186

like a fucking parasite living on other people's blood. You lied to me. You told me Rita had said things about me. Rita told you nothing, did she? But you wormed out everything you wanted to know from me eventually, didn't you?'

'I've got a job to do,' said Archie.

She began crying again, wailing in breathless bursts that shook her whole body. 'Why didn't you just let it alone? Why did you have to rake up the past after all these years? Why couldn't you just have let it rest? All for a television programme . . . all for the sake of a fucking television programme . . .'

Archie pulled up outside the casualty department. He switched off the engine of the car. 'So Rita wanted to shut you up, did she? Is that why she went for you?'

'She was frightened,' Maureen said, her shoulders heaving uncontrollably as she spoke. 'But you wanted her to be frightened, didn't you?'

Archie shook his head. 'I don't know. Honestly, I just don't know,' he said. 'I've not really known what I've been doing since I started working on this case. I still don't know why you were at the Shornewan that day.'

Maureen eyed him mistrustfully. When she spoke again she'd stopped crying and her voice was edged with heavy cynicism and an unconcealed bitterness. 'You're such a barefaced liar, you bastard. You don't know what I was doing at the Shornewan? You mean to tell me you and your crony have been nosing about on this case all this time and haven't even worked that out. Don't you even know Bill Alexander's form?'

'His form? You mean his record for petty theft and—'

Suddenly a part of things fell into place for Archie. 'Oh, I see,' he said. 'Yes, of course. It's obvious really, isn't it? Alexander was going to turn the place over, wasn't he?'

Maureen threw back her head and laughed hysterically. 'You make him sound big league, like the bloody Brinks-Mat gang or something. Bill might have had ambitions for bigger things, but he was never more than a thug and a piddling thief at heart. Wherever he was working he used to steal gear. Him and Terry had been lifting stuff ever

since they'd worked together—they'd been lifting stuff all
that week. He was just going to pick up a few bits and bobs
from the hotel, that was all, stuff that wouldn't be noticed
straightaway. Bill had a key, didn't he?' she explained.
'Because of having to get in and see to the taps . . .'

'And you came to help take the stuff away—just in case
anyone found it in the van and it incriminated the pair of
them? You must have driven up there, then—you must
have had a car?'

Maureen glared at him. 'You think you're so sodding
clever, don't you? Well, Terry wasn't involved at all, he left
in the van, didn't he? He didn't want to have anything to
do with that job. Rita wouldn't let him. She wanted him
out of Bill's clutches. That's why she was—'

'That's why she was up there too that day, is that what
you were going to say? To make sure Terry didn't get into
trouble, to make sure he came home like a good little boy?
Then did it occur to her there was a more efficient way of
making sure Terry never had anything to do with Bill? Or
was that your idea? A way of settling your own score with
him? Or maybe the three of you together thought
that . . . ?'

'You bastard!'

Before he could finish she'd lunged at him, screaming,
her nails flailing at his face. He grabbed for her wrists, but
she twisted out of his grip, and in the confined space somehow managed to scramble on top of him so that to get her
off he had to dig his own nails into her eyes, and pull at
her hair so violently tufts of it came out by the roots. In the
struggle the wounds on her neck and lip opened. By the
time he'd got her back into her own seat and she'd calmed
down, the car was like an abattoir and Archie's shirt might
have passed for a butcher's apron.

Maureen slumped against the window again, burying her
face in her hands and whimpering like a child. 'Why didn't
you just leave things alone? Why didn't you just let the
dead lie?' she seemed to be sobbing. 'All for a story, all for
half an hour of bloody telly . . .'

She glared at Archie accusingly. 'And why us?' she asked.

'Why not that girl who was a waitress up there? Why not that hard-faced bitch who owned the place? They were up there too that afternoon, they were there when I left, I saw them. But that didn't come out in court, did it? Why don't you go fucking up their lives instead? Why does it just have to be us?'

Archie heard what she was telling him, but his mind only gradually absorbed what she'd let slip in her anger. So Julie Taylor *had* been at the hotel that day. And Elizabeth Carrington had been there too, much later than she'd let on. And Maureen herself had been there. And, of course, Rita Brassington.

But not one of them had said anything for fear of implicating themselves.

'Come on, luv,' said Archie eventually. 'Let's get you inside. You'll bleed to death if we don't do something about those cuts.'

She waited compliantly while Archie got out of the car and walked round to open the door for her. She allowed him to drape his jacket across her shoulders again, and allowed him to help her from her seat. But then, as he leaned supporting himself against the door frame, easing her out by her arm, she jumped aside smartly and sent the door crashing shut against his hand.

He stood for a moment or two staring at his fingers, scarcely comprehending what had happened until the agonizing pain registered fully on his nervous system.

Maureen tossed his jacket back at him.

'Bugger off,' she shouted triumphantly.

Archie ought to have followed her into casualty. She'd broken at least two of his fingers, maybe three. But what she'd said to him had set his mind racing so that despite the pain, and despite the exhaustion he felt from the previous night's trip to Wearside and the long day that had followed it, he couldn't have done anything other than he did. He found himself driving towards Rita Brassington's house in the suburbs. It was an ice-cold night, the stars like glinting sugar in a sky of midnight blue, a frost already settling on the city. He scarcely noticed it, though, his mind in turmoil, fixed for the moment on a single objective.

Rita's lights were on when he drove up. Her door was answered by a woman he didn't know. She looked him up and down suspiciously: such a strange visitor, so late, his shirt splattered with Maureen's blood, his hand held awkwardly like a stroke victim.

'She's gone to . . . to help the police with their inquiries,' the woman said, relieved to have fixed on some popular cliché to avoid having to explain more. 'She's not back yet. I'm just looking after the kids.'

Archie went back to the car. He slipped his Tallis tape into the cassette and listened, calmed only slightly as the wave of resonant sound flooded over him. Then he slipped the car into gear and drove out of the town towards the moors and the dales and Elizabeth Carrington's canalside cottage.

The lights in her house were on too when he arrived.

'Goodness gracious, Archie,' she said. 'You do look a sight. Can I get you a plaster?'

'I wanted to ask you a few questions,' he said.

She opened the door a little wider but showed no inclination to invite him in. 'Yes, I thought you might want to eventually,' she said. 'In fact, you could even say I was expecting you. I thought I saw a little glint in your eye when I mentioned the—the Asian gentleman. Did it take you all that time to drive to Leeds and back? Or did you stop off for a bloodbath somewhere?'

Archie didn't smile at her caustic joke. 'He lives in Nottingham now.'

'Really? How interesting!'

'Yes, I found it interesting,' said Archie. 'You see, he saw someone he recognized at the Shornewan that day, and that person recognized you. You were seen much later in the day than you told the police, after you were supposed to have left for York.'

'How fascinating,' she said. 'Now I suppose you're terribly curious about everything?' She smiled. 'Well, unfortunately, Archie, I really don't think at this juncture I can

190

help you any more than I already have. If you have any more questions you'd like me to answer I think perhaps they might most properly be addressed through my solicitor. Would you like me to get his telephone number for you?'

Archie went back to the car. The pain in his hand was intense, though somehow in his agitated excitement he wasn't feeling it as pain, but as nausea. He had scarcely eaten all day, that was part of it, but now everything was catching up with him: his lack of sleep, his tension, his emotional turmoil. Even the frost seemed so much colder now after his brief time on Elizabeth Carrington's doorstep. He felt like vomiting.

He headed back through the countryside to the Shornewan, shivering uncontrollably, his mind turning over the rapid developments of the day. What on earth would Stredwick make of it all? Would he be able to arrive at any conclusions from out of the confusion?

So Maureen and Rita had been at the Shornewan that day? But then so had Harbinder Singh, Elizabeth Carrington and Julie Taylor too. What did it all signify? Harbinder Singh had been honest to a fault in admitting he wanted to kill Alexander. What capital could there be for him in denying he'd actually done it? And what on earth could Elizabeth Carrington have had to do with Alexander's death? Surely that one was beyond even the bounds of conjecture?

Julie Taylor was different, perhaps. Stredwick had always suspected her for some reason. Why else would he have wanted to speak to her father at such a tragic time? But where she fitted in Archie couldn't for the life of him say.

He pulled into the Shornewan car park.

No, it surely had to be something to do with Maureen and Rita. That would at least explain Rita's reluctance to help him, it would at least explain Maureen's reluctance to break ranks with her former friend. It *had* to be something to do with the two of them—and maybe, after all, with Terry Frampton too. Unless . . .

'Oh my God,' Archie muttered to himself.

What was it Stredwick had been saying all through about the geography of the case? The bastard must have known all along!

Archie screeched the car out of the car park and accelerated across the moorland road. He flicked over the Tallis tape and turned it up to full volume, deriving some strength at least from the vigour of the choir.

The bastard *had* known all along, Archie decided. He *must* have known. Why the hell, though, had he kept him on a string like this?

He swung the car left at the first small village he passed, and then right to emerge on to the moor again. It was the same route he'd taken the previous night on his way to Wearside—though that seemed like another age ago, another era. The same road as the previous night, the same road and—Archie noticed suddenly in his rear-view mirror—a driver behind him as there had been yesterday.

Archie was travelling faster than was safe, but the car behind him was travelling faster still. No sooner had he noticed it than it seemed on his tail, its headlights glaring full beam, blinding him.

He slowed down to allow it to pass. But as on the previous night, the car slowed down too.

And when he accelerated, the car behind him accelerated.

Archie felt suddenly very frightened.

It's Carrington, the bastard, it *has* to be him, he thought ambiguously.

Archie drove on for a short while and then suddenly without warning swung the car off the road on to a farm track. From what he could make out in the brief moment as the other car passed, the driver seemed, illogically, to be a woman. Archie reversed quickly into the road, and turned tail back towards the Shornewan again.

But when he checked, he realized the other car must have turned too for it was still behind him.

Once again he slowed down. Once again he accelerated.

The car behind mirrored his movements. It was as if the two cars were connected by some invisible cord.

192

'Sod this,' Archie said to himself. He slammed on his brakes and brought the Astra to a halt.

The car following pulled up too.

Outside the night air was so raw that it took Archie's breath away. He stood for a moment adjusting to the temperature, and then walked purposefully towards his pursuer. As he did its driver got out. She—for it surely was a woman—stood in the centre of the road, obscuring part of the radiance of the headlights behind her so that as she moved it was if she was on a stage, the star doing her final number, casting long shadows across the world.

Archie squinted his eyes, but there was no identifying who she was.

There was no mistaking what she was doing, though. A dim shadow she might have been, but she seemed to be nestling something into the crook of her shoulder.

She couldn't have missed with the first shot. He was almost on top of her when it ripped into his arm.

The second was unlucky to hit him and tore into his back as he scurried on to the moor.

There was nowhere else to go, it was his only escape. But already the night mists were beginning to thicken.

CHAPTER 25

He lurched across the moor, reeling through patches of dry, tangled bracken that tore at his ankles, and over rocks that cut his legs as he stumbled. He had no idea which direction he was taking, or why; he knew only that he had to get away from her, that he had to escape from her.

At first there was no pain, no feeling of any sort, except blind panic. He had no sense of the chilling cold, or the damp mist-filled air around him; even his wounds seemed part of the bewildering emptiness of the moor, as if they were not his wounds, and this not his body at all.

He clambered into a dry stream bed, slipped—fell—picked himself up and clambered onwards again, scrambling up the loose stones of the valley which led to the summit of the moor. Only when he reached it did he pause briefly, wondering whether he was still being pursued.

Higher up the mists were thicker, the darkness and stillness more consuming. He strained his ears for any sound around him, but all seemed silent, except for the gentle murmur of the wind and the irregular rhythm of his own congested breathing, bubbling like a water pipe in the recesses of his lungs.

He became aware of a leaden heaviness in his limbs, a tiredness beginning to overwhelm him and dog his movements. To go back to the car was too much of a risk. The only alternative was to press on in the hopes of reaching the road as it skirted the moor at another point. But his strength was ebbing away. At every step he could feel his sense of direction failing, and the pain from his back, arm and hand gradually beginning to insinuate itself into his consciousness.

This body he found himself burdened with seemed not to function any more, this arm attached to it seemed not to move as he wanted it, or not move at all until the mood took it, and only then in brief jarring spasms over which he could exercise no control. It was bizarre. Bizarre too how he seemed to be bleeding, not bleeding in any way he'd ever done before, but pumping thick blood like a glutinous jelly. Was he dying? Was that what was happening? The idea amused him in a detached way, and had he not become aware of his chest tightening and his breathing becoming more laboured, he might have been inclined to laugh at the absurdity of the whole incongruous farce.

Somehow the whole process seemed much less conclusive than he'd have imagined it would be, less significant and less troubling. He'd certainly have preferred to finish things on a better note with June, and he'd have liked to satisfy his curiosity about Alexander's murder too. But on the whole, if this was dying, then he wasn't plagued by any guilt or regret for his life, or disquieted by any great sense of a destiny he might be leaving unfulfilled.

In fact, this drift into eternity seemed a relatively serene process, more like slipping into a dream than a momentous leap into the unknown.

Ahead of him was a dry stone wall. He staggered towards it as best he could, collapsing in a heap against its base. Every movement now was debilitating, every breath arduous and exhausting.

There was no way he had strength to go on further, and the wall seemed as good a place as any for it to end. He leaned against it, suddenly shaken by a fit of congested coughing. Then, with a beguiling irony that even in his present condition he couldn't fail to appreciate, it occurred to him where he was.

This, surely, was the wall against which Alexander's body had been discovered? Yes, there was no mistaking it. He remembered the patterns of the stones from the police photographs and—yes, there it was still—the rock with Alexander's blood fresh upon it. The blood had seemed so unusual to him when he'd been here last, almost supernatural. Now it seemed so much an indigenous part of the order of things, part of this moor and part of the strange mythology of this county and its ghosts of sacrificed innocents.

The rock felt oddly soft when he touched it, as if it were coated in velvet. But the blood was still wet and sticky to the touch. Archie wiped his fingers on his trousers and ran them over the rock again to confirm to himself that it wasn't his own blood he was feeling.

And he smiled to himself.

Such a paradox, so close to the end, to know where he was, and know too that if he only had energy enough he might be able to work out some route to the Shornewan. Such a paradox to know that he was so close, if only he could have summoned up the will.

To make any move at all now seemed futile, though. The cold had become so much a part of him that any choice he might have he'd abandoned to its chilling grasp. He felt too peaceful in himself to fret, far too comfortable to care any longer. It was as if he were lying in his own bed at the end of a draining day, waiting calmly for sleep to overtake him.

Even the pain in his arm and hand, and across his torn back, didn't seem discomfiting enough to be disturbing now.

The moorland mist closed around him like a reassuring blanket, yet strangely, it was if he could see through it to the lights of Rainsford flickering in the far distance. Everything around him was silent, yet it seemed too he could hear a voice calling to him, June's voice . . .

Curious.

Curious that he should think of June at such a moment when she'd so betrayed him. Curious that he should almost be able to see her in front of him, and touch her, and feel her touching him.

'He's over here. Thank God, he's here,' she seemed to be saying.

But where else should he be when he was dying?

More curious still, though, was why Webber should be there too. Webber. Webber? Why should he have thought of Webber at such a time? Why Webber of all people? And why from his imagination should he be summoning up a third figure, a lean, cadaverous figure with a voice like George Stredwick's?

'Lift him under the arms, Peter. As gently as you can. I'll take his feet. Come on. Quick! He's lost a lot of blood,' he seemed to be saying.

'Blood. Blood,' Archie heard himself repeating. 'Alexander's blood . . . On the rock . . . still fresh . . . still wet . . .'

'Moss,' said the man who talked like Stredwick. 'A lichen. It's fed on the stain. Forget it, I'll explain it sometime. First, let's get you to hospital. Just forget it for the moment . . .'

Archie suddenly became conscious of the throbbing in his back and arm again, a relentless agony, like an acid burning through his flesh.

As they moved him he stiffened in pain. 'Forget it? What do you mean, forget it?' he cried. 'Some bastard's just shot me, for Christ's sake, I'm dying, can't you see? Can't you help me? *I'm dying* . . .'

196

And he screamed deliriously, his voice echoing away to nothing in the blackness into which he seemed to be drifting.

CHAPTER 26

It was more than three months later and life had attained a certain familiar routine, punctuated by June's telephone calls.

She left the house as she'd always done at 8.15 a.m., only now, if he were asleep, she'd creep out without disturbing him. She'd ring him at 11.0 a.m. on the dot, and again at lunch-time. In the afternoon, she'd disturb whatever she was doing and call at 3.0 p.m., and again at 5.30 p.m. just before she left. While he was convalescing the department kept her off evening work; they'd never spent so much time together in their lives.

Since he'd been allowed up, if only for short periods, Archie had taken to preparing the evening meal. It exhausted him, but now he was feeling better it provided some focus to his life, most of which he was still having to spend in bed. But he was on doctor's orders to rest as much as possible, warned he'd be weak for many months yet.

In films, gunshot injuries were always flesh wounds, repaired by a sticking plaster and a splash of Dettol. Archie's wounds had been altogether more serious, but though he was still in some pain, the worst of his convalescence was over. Youth had been on his side, they'd told him, youth and a natural stubborn resilience of constitution.

Tonight it was a simple pasta. He worked slowly and purposefully, but long before he had begun to peel the onions he was crying, as he seemed to be so often and so unpredictably in recent weeks. The doctor had said it was delayed shock, and that given time it would be less of a problem. But if anything, as he got physically stronger, the memory of that last horrific half-hour on the moor had become more psychologically vivid. The doctors said that

197

in time the trauma of it all would fade, but somehow Archie doubted it. Three months had gone by and although he'd already had to relive what had happened in statements the police had taken from him, still the thought of Yorkshire made him nauseous. Three months had gone by, and though the salary cheques kept appearing in his account, he couldn't bring himself to speak to Stredwick.

He heard June's key in the door and dropped the spaghetti into the boiling water he'd prepared for it.

Sitting at the table, he was taken with another of his tearful fits.

'I'm sorry . . . I really am . . .' he said, sobbing unselfconsciously.

'Archie, don't be silly, I've told you: we can always buy another house. It's not important. I shouldn't have taken a step like that on my own, I should have consulted you.'

'But you'd set your heart on that place.'

'Oh, Godfrey's sure to be able to find something else for us; estate agents see hundreds of houses every year. It'll take more than a knock on the nose to put him off if he scents a commission.'

June smiled. 'Oh come on, Archie, cheer up. Even you must be able to see the funny side of it. I mean, really . . . me and Godfrey! How many times do I have to tell you? Apart from the fact that he's Rosie's cousin, he's as gay as a golfing umbrella; he was only staying over because she'd talked me into doing him a favour while his own place was being done up. You know she lives in a rabbit hutch, she hasn't got enough space. Besides, she can't stand him . . .'

'I feel so—so stupid though, so absolutely dumb. The money you withdrew from the building society . . .'

'Just the deposit for the house.'

'I know that now,' said Archie. 'But at the time . . . I just thought . . .'

She leaned across the table and took his hand in hers, squeezing it tenderly. 'I know what you thought, love,' she said. 'That's why I rushed to the Shornewan after you that day; I wanted to explain. You were wrong, though, weren't you? You've been wrong a lot recently.'

In bed that night she woke to find Archie sobbing into his pillow. She switched on the bedside lamp and rested on her elbow, lightly stroking the nape of his neck and that part of the top of his back where a small raw scar and the marks of two lines of stitches showed where a bullet had entered him, and where they'd operated to remove it.

'Don't you think it's about time you talked to George,' she said quietly. 'You're going to have to lay the ghost sometime. It's going to be preying on your mind forever otherwise . . .'

But even so, it was more than a week later before Archie felt able to make contact. It wasn't that Archie blamed Stredwick, but during his stay in hospital and the lonely hours he'd spent at home recuperating, he'd ruminated too much on Alexander's murder to believe that anyone could ever have any comprehensive answer, least of all Stredwick. An order had been fractured, a symmetry destroyed; it would take more than just a solution to restore harmony, if harmony had ever existed. That was too much to expect from any one man.

Stredwick sounded pleased to hear from him; if he didn't ask after Archie's health it wasn't out of any lack of compassion. Unbeknown to Archie, he'd been in touch with June regularly and kept himself informed at every stage about his researcher's recovery.

'It was Carrington, of course, wasn't it?' Archie said immediately. 'You knew all along, didn't you? But why him, of all people? And why didn't you tell me? For God's sake, how did it all happen . . . ?'

Over the telephone Archie heard Stredwick move from his desk and heard the scratch of a match as he lit a cigar. 'Love. Revenge. Survival. These are very powerful emotions,' he said. 'Perhaps I'd better explain . . .'

'You see,' Stredwick said later, 'from the moment that Webber first put me on to the case, I was struck by a sense of the simple geography of events. Frampton and Alexander were working at the Shornewan that week; Alexander's body was discovered close to it. The murder was clearly connected to the hotel, that much was obvious, but it was so obvious·that it was easy to miss the significance of it. You see, the Shornewan's an isolated place. According to the evidence that came out in court, there were only three people at the Shornewan most of that day. One was Alexander who was murdered, one was Frampton, and the other—'

'Carrington.'

'Of course. And if we weren't happy with the conviction against Frampton, then it followed—at least from the evidence in court—that the only person who could have murdered Alexander was him. That made things difficult, because as I've told you before, our job isn't fingering guilty people: that's in the hands of the police and the courts, thank God. You, though, being the sort of person you are, immediately began to want to find a murderer, and nothing I could say could stop you. Can you see now why I didn't want to let you know the way my mind was working? If you'd have so much as suspected Carrington, you'd have been after him like a steam train. It would have prejudiced you far too much. I wanted you to be open-minded, you see, I wanted you to look at the case dispassionately. Frankly, I didn't care how many people had a grudge against Alexander and how many people would have liked to see him dead, or even killed him themselves. I wasn't interested. What was much more important was how many of these people could have geographically been in a position to kill him.'

Archie listened to all this in silence. Stredwick was telling him nothing more than he'd come to know himself, nothing more than had struck him the night of the shooting after he'd driven back from seeing Elizabeth Carrington. But it irked him he hadn't seen things sooner. Or as clearly.

'I suppose Carrington's statement was the giveaway,' he said eventually.

'Well, it *was* dreadful,' said Stredwick. 'If Carrington hadn't been the pillar of society he was, it might have been probed more. But it didn't prove anything. That's why I wanted you to look at the case, that's why I employed you.

I wanted you to pick holes in what seemed obvious. You see, ignoring the possibility of some passing motorist having just taken it into his head to kill, everything—absolutely everything—implicated Carrington in that murder. It was all just too apparent. I wanted someone intelligent, but with no experience of this sort of work, to nose about a bit to see if there was something equally obvious which Webber and I might have missed. I wanted someone naïve enough to ask questions about things we might just have overlooked in our sophistication.

'That was the main reason Carrington's statement worried me: because of you! It occurred to me that if the case was so obvious to us, then sooner or later it would become obvious to you. You'd have been useless to me then, do you see that? I needed you to keep an open mind as long as possible. I could ensure it for so long by keeping things from you, confusing you sometimes as to the possibilities, even advising you that things weren't important when they obviously were—I tried to do that as soon as I realized you were becoming too suspicious of the statement. But I couldn't keep doing it. Not indefinitely.

'Forgive me for sounding patronizing, Archie, but you've got a sharp mind. Sooner or later, regardless of what I said to you, if the case was as simple as Webber and I thought, you were *bound* to arrive at the truth; indeed, it was crucial that in due course you *did* arrive at it. It was the only way I could ensure that we'd got things right. It was our guarantee, you see, our way of checking.

'I thought you might have rumbled things too soon, though—after you'd first spoken to Jenny Rochford. Rationally, after you'd made up your mind talking to her that there wasn't any argument worth speaking of that morning between Frampton and Alexander, you really ought to have become more suspicious of Carrington. With more experience you probably would have been. It was logical, really: if there wasn't an argument in the café that morning, then either they must have started arguing later in the day, or they didn't argue at all and Carrington was lying. And come on! that had to be the most likely possibility, didn't it? You know how fundamentally frightened Frampton was of Alexander, how deferential and compliant Frampton was. The fact is, Frampton wasn't the sort of person who would argue with Alexander at any time, morning or afternoon.'

'So Carrington's account of them shouting at each other—?'

'They may have had words together. After all, Alexander had been planning all week to rob the Shornewan before he left, and he wanted Frampton along with him as usual. But Carrington didn't see anything, and besides, this time—'

'This time Rita put her foot down,' said Archie.

'That's why she was at the Shornewan: to make sure Frampton didn't get involved,' Stredwick agreed. 'Rita's a determined woman. She realized thieving from the hotel was just too risky, that Frampton was bound to get into trouble. Besides, she wanted him out of Alexander's clutches. It was the first stage in getting out of his clutches herself.'

'So Carrington's statements were—?'

'A total fabrication—for the most part,' said Stredwick. 'In the first one there was no mention at all of any argument, but I suspect he got to hear from the police what was supposed to have happened in the café. He realized how useful if could be to him, and embroidered his second statement accordingly.'

'So why the theatricals with Carrington's car at the dinner?' Archie asked. 'It was almost like pointing the finger at him.'

Stredwick chuckled. 'That wasn't for your benefit, believe me. It was just that in his statement Carrington said he'd been standing in the window recess of the hotel when Alexander and Frampton had been shouting at each other. Yet he said he hadn't been able to hear what they were saying. That was patently untrue. After Carrington's car alarm had gone off you virtually had a conversation with Webber who was standing in the same window recess, and you both heard each other perfectly well.

'No, that little scene was all arranged for Carrington's benefit. It was a bit crude, I grant you, but I'm not a man of great imagination, I couldn't run to anything more subtle,' he said self-effacingly. 'You see, at that stage I wanted to let him know that we were on to him. I was curious how he'd react. Our investigations weren't throwing up any evidence; in the absence of anything tangible his reaction might have proved the only thing we'd got to go on. I suspected he was likely to panic in some way, but I didn't for the life of me anticipate he'd follow you like he did that night. I don't know what he was thinking of; I doubt that at that stage he was thinking clearly enough to know himself. I suspect maybe he was considering . . . well, killing you. But really, he's too intelligent for that, he knew it wouldn't have solved anything. Besides, Carrington's just not that cold-blooded.'

'But what I don't understand, though,' said Archie, 'is that if his involvement was so obvious to you and Webber when you first read through the statements, why wasn't it obvious to the police at the time? Were they just stupid?'

Stredwick suddenly became indignant, his voice rising a pitch or two. 'Look, son, are you ever going to learn? I said this was a simple case—I didn't say it was an easy one. If anything, it was difficult precisely because it was so simple. I've told you before, the police aren't stupid. Neither, on the whole, are they corrupt. Or inefficient for that matter— or at least, no more inefficient than any other large organization. It's all to do with perspective; I'm not saying it's satisfactory, but at least you can understand it. Their perspective at the time, close up, put Frampton in the frame. OK, so maybe it wasn't an award-winning bit of detective work. Perhaps a few odds and ends didn't tie up. But why should they spend a lot of time on this sort of low-key rough-house stuff? They've got other more important things to do with their time, and besides, they knew Alexander. He was a thief, a bit of a thug. They probably thought he got what was coming to him like a lot of people did. And Frampton? Well, Frampton was one of his associates, wasn't he? He got tarred with the same brush. He was another bruiser, like his mate. The two of them had an argument. So one of them got killed? It happens every day in every town in the country. It doesn't warrant the Sherlock Holmes approach.'

Stredwick broke off for a moment. 'You see, re-examining cases after a long time can often be a disadvantage,' he said meditatively. 'Evidence has often disappeared, people's memories have faded, and time distorts what they do recall. But in a paradoxical way the passage of time can be an advantage too because it provides an objectivity on events; it can give you a different perspective, often a more accurate one.'

'But why Carrington?' Archie asked. 'Why him of all people? I just can't see it. It seems so totally improbable.'

Stredwick laughed. 'Why not Carrington? Any of us are capable of killing, given the right circumstances. It's in the nature of things; violence is a part of our make-up and it's just a comforting fallacy that most murders are committed by sick psychopaths. Most are committed by people like you and me, or that bastard who strangled Julie Taylor: ordinary people harbouring darknesses that are only half understood.'

He looked over towards Squiffy, who, replete from a recent meal, lay stretched against the fire, purring to himself contentedly. 'On the surface we're reassuringly domestic,' he said, 'but only touch some raw instinct that's lying dormant, and the basic animal in us takes over. It's like Carrington said to you himself—there's only a thin line between civilization and savagery.

'He caught Alexander thieving, that was all; it wasn't premeditated. Carrington just arrived back from Rainsford and found somebody—an outsider—stealing from him. It was his worst fear encapsulated—a violation of his territory, another example of the social degeneracy he saw day to day on the bench. I'm not condoning it—you can't condone it—but I've been burgled myself, I know what it's like. I felt very angry—furious. I suspect Carrington felt the same way and just hit out blindly with the nearest thing to hand. That just happened to be the water key which Alexander had taken into the hotel with him.'

'What, to protect himself?' Archie sounded sceptical.

'In a way,' said Stredwick. 'You see, after a day I spent at the British Library what I think happened was that although the water main was repaired by the end of that day, Alexander turned off the supply so that if he was disturbed in the hotel he had some sort of explanation for being there. He could have said he was checking the flow to the taps, or something like that. Only I don't think he got much of a chance to say anything . . .'

Archie took all this in without saying a word. Part of the picture was clear, but by no means all of it, yet he could sense an impatience in Stredwick, as if Stredwick was losing interest in the story.

'Look, I have to go,' Stredwick confessed eventually. 'I'm a bit busy. But listen, we can't keep always talking on the phone: when you feel up to it, why don't you come down to London for a few days? Bring June. I could check you both into a hotel and you could make a weekend of it.'

'Yes, I'd like that,' Archie said. 'I'll suggest it to her. But before you go, there's just one thing—one thing that's been troubling me. It's just that I can't see why Elizabeth Carrington should have told me about Harbinder Singh. It doesn't make sense. It was almost as if she knew she was starting me off on a trail that would lead back to her. It was tantamount to implicating herself. Sooner or later she must have known she'd have to stop me . . .'

Stredwick laughed, a fuller laugh than normal, this. He was genuinely amused. 'Elizabeth Carrington! Stop you? Good God, son, you surely don't think she had anything to do with Alexander's murder, do you? You don't—you don't think it was *her* that shot you, do you? Wherever do you pick up these extraordinary ideas?'

CHAPTER 27

June steered the car around the small roundabout opposite Lord's cricket ground, managing at her second attempt to negotiate the correct exit. It was Friday night and the traffic had been so frenetic she hadn't said a word since leaving the motorway. Now she found her voice again, resuming the conversation they'd been having as if the break between hadn't happened.

'So Carrington was the source of all the warnings to de Groot about the moor, was he?' she asked.

'Apparently,' Archie said, 'but Stredwick didn't let on to me about it. He just kept going on in his mysterious way about the weather. Honest, I thought he'd cracked up . . .'

June pulled up at traffic lights and glanced over her shoulder to the back seat where Archie was draped on a mound of cushions doing an impression of an invalid. She'd been worried that he was up to this trip, that it would tire him. But exactly the reverse had proved the case. Since leaving Wearside he seemed to have discovered a new energy and enthusiasm that belied her concern. At home, he'd not wanted to talk about the case at all; now, he could scarcely be stopped, and his face looked more animated than it had since she'd caught sight of him briefly driving in and out of the Shornewan car park the night he was shot.

That night, he'd looked deranged, almost insane. He'd been intending to confront Carrington, it transpired. June had been sitting with Stredwick and Webber at the Shornewan waiting for him, and they had all seen the crazed look in his eyes, but it was Stredwick alone who had sensed an impending danger and insisted they should follow him along the winding country lanes. Eventually they'd come across his abandoned Astra. They'd been too slow to prevent the shooting, but Stredwick's prescience had undoubtedly saved Archie's life.

'Of course, the weather on the moors can be dangerous, I know that better than anyone,' Archie continued, as they made their way down the Euston Road, 'but Stredwick was suspicious of Carrington's warnings—he felt there might have been some ulterior motive to them.'

'To keep de Groot off the moors?'

'Exactly. Stredwick reckons it must have been a bit of a shock for Carrington to find that de Groot was intending

206

doing a bit of out-of-season walking. He hadn't thought there was much chance of anyone finding Alexander's body until the spring.'

June weaved through the West End in no time, and cruised the car over Westminster Bridge. 'What about the rest of it, though? Rita and Maureen? Where do they fit in?'

Archie strained his eyes, trying to work out their bearings from a map Stredwick had sent him. 'Search me,' he said. 'I've thought about it until my mind goes round in circles. No doubt we'll be told everything eventually. Turn left at that phone-box over there. This is the street. I think he lives in that block—the one over there.'

'My God, what a slum,' said June.

Stredwick had been intending to entertain them at home, but he'd got involved in work and lost track of time. At the last minute he had booked a table at an indifferent kebab house in Peckham.

'You see, Janine Linney was critical to the case,' he explained, as they all sat over the debris of a meal later that night. 'It was all to do with that curious incident at the café the morning of the murder. After I'd come to the conclusion there hadn't been an argument between Frampton and Alexander, there still remained the intriguing question of why they were in such a rush to get out of the place. At that stage I really didn't believe that the incident could have had anything directly to do with Alexander's death, but even so, I was curious about it. In the end I was proved right, of course: what happened had absolutely nothing to do with Alexander's murder. But finding Janine Linney did help to put the case in context.'

June and Archie looked at each other blankly.

'You see, after Webber got one of his mates to do a check through the police computer for me and I'd found out about Alexander's form for thieving, it occurred to me that while he was supposed to be working that week he might have been turning over houses with Frampton,' Stredwick explained. 'One explanation of why they were rushing to get out of the café was they they might have been trying to avoid being recognized by someone.

'I thought at first it was probably someone they'd burgled. But of course, if you're burgling houses you try and make sure no one does see you. That's when it first struck me that the two of them might have been involved in something more serious. It was all these recent assaults on women, and eventually Julie Taylor's murder, that set my mind thinking along this track. Apart from anything else, it seemed to fit in with Alexander's character: he was an abhorrent man who obviously got turned on by sexual violence. As a theory it seemed to be worth at least considering. I knew that there was a student working in the back of the café; maybe there'd been an assault, maybe they'd assaulted her? Maybe they'd seen their victim and it was her they were rushing to get away from . . . ?

'It was only a theory, I grant you,' said Stredwick, seeing the scepticism on Archie and June's faces. 'But theories were all I had to go on. Even assuming I was correct, I still couldn't see how it might be relevant to Alexander's murder.'

He suddenly brought his hand crashing down on the table. 'It was really stupid of me not to have seen the truth a lot earlier. Stupid! It was staring me in the face! Jenny Rochford had told you about this girl that Frampton and Alexander had nearly knocked over as they'd been leaving the café. And do you remember, I asked you to check on the café windows? Bertha who'd been the manageress told you that they were boarded up, that there'd been some trouble in town a few nights before and that they were waiting for the glaziers . . .'

Again his hand came crashing down on the table. 'I didn't take it into account,' he shouted. 'I didn't even consider it!'

'What, the windows?'

'No, the fact that Jenny Rochford might be unreliable. Can't you see?' Stredwick said. 'She maintained Frampton and Alexander had nearly knocked this girl over on the pavement, in other words what had happened, happened *outside* the café. It followed then that Frampton and Alexander's rush to get out of the café couldn't have been anything to do with her because the windows were boarded up, and they couldn't have seen her until they got outside.'

'Seems logical enough,' said Archie.

'Only it wasn't,' snapped Stredwick, 'and I should have seen that. How did Jenny *know* it was a girl? She must have seen her, right? But she couldn't have seen her through the boarded-up windows any more than Frampton and Alexander could—'

'You mean the girl was *inside* the café?' said June.

'Exactly,' said Stredwick.

'Julie Taylor . . .' said Archie.

'Precisely,' said Stredwick. 'It was her they were rushing to get away from. That's why they went straight back to the Shornewan and sweated to get that job finished Thursday instead of stretching it out the week. Running into her once was enough; they weren't going to risk it again.'

'I always thought it was odd that Julie was as upset as she was by the murder,' said Stredwick. 'She may have been a particularly sensitive girl; I think she probably was. Even so, it seemed a bit of an over-reaction to give up her job because of it, and she did that so soon after the murder that they were clearly connected. She'd lived such a sheltered life, though. Her father cosseted her. I don't think he could ever see her as anything but a child, right up until the day she died. All the same, it would have taken a lot to make Julie give up her job—more, I always felt, than just a body being discovered on the moors.'

'You're not saying that—that Julie was involved in murdering Alexander?' asked June.

'Good God, no,' said Stredwick. 'Carrington was able to manage that all by himself. She was involved in the aftermath, though, I'm sure of it. She probably helped Carrington carry Alexander on to the moors, which would explain the absence of any drag marks near the body. What I think happened, you see, is that she bumped into Carrington in Rainsford after she'd left Janine Linney's farewell party at the pub. I fancy she was a bit drunk and because the buses weren't very regular Carrington offered to run her home. For some reason, though, he wanted to drop into the Shornewan first. In his statement to the police he said he'd been to his meat wholesalers, do you remember? That was probably true. Even Carrington wouldn't have been so stupid to have lied about something that was so easily checked. He'd probably picked up some stock and wanted to drop it back at the hotel. That's when he discovered Alexander . . .

'I think Julie must have stumbled in just after Carrington had hit him,' Stredwick went on. 'It all happened very quickly. Don't get the idea Carrington stood about wrestling with his conscience. He just saw Alexander, realized he was being robbed and struck out. But Julie recognized Alexander, you see, even with his head smashed in . . .'

A look of horror passed over June's face. 'You mean . . . ?'

'Yes,' said Stredwick. 'What I suspected turned out true, I'm afraid. Only it wasn't the student, Janine Linney, whom Alexander had assaulted, it was Julie Taylor. Janine confirmed it for me. You see, she and Julie were close friends: Julie confided in her.'

Stredwick moistened his lips with the tip of his tongue. In the work he did he had lived so long with the degradation of crime that you'd have thought he was inured to it. Except that watching him as he spoke, June could see the distaste he was feeling at the story he was compelled to recount. He seemed uneasy at having to continue, almost embarrassed at the repugnance of what he had discovered. It made him vulnerable, she thought, almost childlike.

'It had happened earlier that week,' he went on, eventually. 'Julie had been at home on her own and they got into the house. Maybe they were going to turn it over and thought the place was empty; maybe Alexander was after her.'

Stredwick shook his head sadly. 'Julie had a lot of old-fashioned attitudes. She was humiliated about what had happened, she was ashamed about it, as if she'd done something wrong. Janine tried to get her to report it to the police, but Julie just wanted to forget the whole thing. And who can blame her? When she saw Alexander, though, even dead, something must have snapped inside her . . .'

'The fingernails. The scratches on his face,' said June, so quietly she could have been talking to herself.

For a long time they were all silent. Outside, the sounds of a London Friday filtered to the restaurant, a Friday night in the city, any city. A group of drunken men were shouting, a bottle was smashed, a car tyre screeched. Someone laughed hysterically, half way to a scream.

Archie was the first to speak. 'I thought you said that she was a . . . you know . . . I thought the post-mortem report said . . .'

'That she was a virgin, is that what you mean?' said Stredwick bitterly. 'Oh, Alexander didn't rape her. Or at least not technically, the way the law defines rape. There are worse things, though, much worse . . .'

'Oh my God,' said June. 'Both . . . both of them?'

'No. Terry Frampton didn't actually get involved, according to what Julie told Janine,' Stredwick said. 'But he was there all right, no doubt about it—and the bastard did nothing to stop what was happening. He just watched as if it was a bloody floor show.'

'Oh my God,' said June again.

Later, back at Stredwick's flat, they sat drinking coffee. Stredwick was on the floor, lounging in front of a gas fire, idly toying with the cat. In one way, sprawled there, he looked much younger than he was. His hair, though streaked with grey, was still thick and cut short enough to be fashionable. His figure was modishly meagre, almost skeletal. It was only his face which looked old: very old and, for once, very tired.

'What fascinated me—a point I think you missed, Archie,' he said, 'was that whatever the true nature of Rita's relationship with Frampton, and however it was

211

complicated by her sexual infatuation with Alexander, what seemed to be undisputed was that Rita and Terry were very close. Exactly how close I discovered when I went to St Catherine's House. Rita's elder child—the boy—'

'Gary?'

'Yes. Frampton's down in the records as being his father, though how Rita can be so certain he's not Alexander's, I don't know. Perhaps that's why her relationship to the kid is so ambiguous. Anyway, what I couldn't understand was why the hell Rita wasn't more helpful to us. We were only trying to help Frampton, after all.'

'The assault on Julie?'

'It all seems so obvious now, doesn't it? Rita knew all about the attack on Julie—Frampton had told her about it, I'm sure. Once he was away from Alexander, what he'd been involved in sickened him. Terry Frampton's not a totally despicable man in the same way as Alexander was, but he's timorous—and impressionable—and he was too terrified of Alexander to think of stopping him. At the beginning Rita never believed that Terry Frampton would get convicted of murder—she thought the evidence of the fingernails would clear him. What she was trying to do was protect him from any charges he might face as an accessory to a serious sexual assault. That's why, at the time of the trial, she never told the police what she knew. After he was convicted, though, she became more worried about her own position and the fact she'd withheld evidence. That's why she was so uncooperative with us.'

Archie had been sipping at his coffee, listening to Stredwick in silence. Now he put down his cup and leaned forward protesting. 'I just don't see it,' he said. 'Rita wasn't uncooperative when I first saw her. The first time I went round to her house she was on the verge of telling me that she'd seen Julie Taylor at the hotel. That could have been a real breakthrough. It could have saved us no end of trouble.'

Stredwick laughed sceptically. 'Do you really think so?'

'She as good as came out with the name.'

'You're kidding yourself, son. What she said to you—

correct me if I'm wrong—was that she had a pretty shrewd idea of who'd killed Alexander.'

'And who else could she have meant but Julie Taylor?' said Archie. 'She must have seen Julie Taylor going into the hotel. She must have suspected that Julie Taylor had been involved in the murder.'

'Perhaps,' said Stredwick, 'but do you think in a month of Sundays she'd have said anything to you about it? Rita Brassington's been terrified all through this investigation that she's been breaking the law by withholding evidence about serious crimes. Do you think she'd have said anything to you if there was a chance of it rebounding on her? She hadn't said a word to anyone for nearly ten years, why would she come out with it to a journalist she's only just met? No, I may be wrong, but I think what she was doing that day was preparing the ground to implicate Maureen Paton if Maureen implicated her.

'You see, that's where that confusing information from old Remus was so critical. Remus had never met either Rita Brassington or Maureen Paton, he'd just been given a file by the local police on a nasty assault and asked whether there was any possibility of a forensic case if the main witness refused to testify. He remembered that witness from a photograph when he saw her at Frampton's trial. But what he didn't remember clearly was her name. He thought it was Rita who'd been nearly blinded by Alexander, whereas in fact it was Maureen.'

'I know all that now, Maureen admitted it to me,' said Archie. 'But how is it relevant?'

'Just look at it from Rita's point of view,' said Stredwick. 'When you first went to see her, because of the mistake Remus had made, you thought that it was *her* that had been nearly blinded by Alexander. You asked her about the beating up, didn't you? Well, she *had* been beaten up by Alexander—but that was a totally separate attack. Now, from her point of view, how could you have known about that? As far as Rita could see, the only person who might have told you was Maureen. And if Maureen had told you that, how much else might she have told you? How much more might she tell you in the future? It worried Rita that it might come out she was at the hotel that day. If that had happened, it could have put her in the frame for something a good deal worse than withholding evidence.'

'You mean, that the police might have come to the conclusion she'd been involved in the murder,' said Archie.

'Well, that was the conclusion you reached, wasn't it? And I suspect that's what was at the back of Maureen's mind as well. You see, Maureen had driven to the hotel to collect Alexander and the stuff he was intending stealing. She'd seen Rita leave with Frampton, and she'd seen Carrington arrive with Julie Taylor soon afterwards. That's when she probably left too, thinking Alexander was bound to get caught. Instead, she learns later that he's been murdered. Now who would you have thought most likely to have killed him in those circumstances?

'No, I'm almost certain that that's why her friendship with Rita ended so abruptly. OK, Maureen isn't the sort to lose any sleep over Alexander's death, but I think even she'd draw the line at continuing a friendship with a woman involved in killing him.'

Archie poured himself another cup of coffee. 'But what I don't understand, though, is why Rita Brassington wrote to Julie Taylor. What on earth did she want to see her for? What was in her mind?'

'You've got to understand that all along Rita's been terrified about getting involved in this affair. What most worried her—what was in her mind writing to Julie—was the possibility of getting implicated. You see, I think that as she was leaving the Shornewan with Terry Frampton, she saw Julie arriving with Carrington. But if she'd seen Julie, then presumably there was always the risk Julie might have seen *her* too. Let's say the police had started nosing around the case again because of the interest we were showing, then who knows? Julie might have said something. Rita Brassington's not an idiot, you know. She saw the danger. She had to ensure that Julie Taylor kept her mouth shut.'

'So what on earth was Rita intending to do?' June asked. 'Kill Julie?'

214

Stredwick shifted position on the floor. 'I just don't know,' he said, 'I really don't know. Rita Brassington's certainly got it in her to do violence to anyone she thinks threatens her. She attacked Maureen and of course—' he looked up at Archie—'she shot you too. But all the same, she's a shrewd woman; her problem is that there seems to come a point with her when she feels so trapped, her actions fly in the face of logic.'

He fixed Archie in his gaze. 'That attack on you was totally senseless, absurd. And it was absurd the way she went for Maureen too. She could never have got away with killing either of you. If she'd have thought about it she'd have known that what she was doing would land her in prison, and then the whole sordid story which she was going to such lengths to suppress would come out anyhow. But, you see, after she'd been taken in for questioning by the police, I don't think she *was* thinking—or at least not thinking in any clear or rational way. I don't believe she really had any intention of killing either of you; she was just acting instinctively—like an animal might act. She thought Maureen threatened her, so she struck out; she thought it was your fault she was taken in by the police, so she went for you too.'

'With the gun that she'd stolen from Maureen,' said Archie.

Stredwick laughed. 'Alexander's gun. Ironic, isn't it?'

He looked up at June. 'Rita Brassington's the sort of woman who craves respectability. All she really wants is to put the past behind her, and to settle down with Terry Frampton in some suburban semi somewhere.' He shook his head. 'No, I can't believe she'd have killed Julie Taylor; it would have been ridiculous sending her a letter in those circumstances. No, I think Rita had just worked out that since she'd seen Julie Taylor at the Shornewan on the day of the murder, and Julie hadn't appeared in court as a witness, then Julie probably hadn't told the police she was there either. I think Rita had probably worked out for herself that Julie Taylor was somehow implicated in the murder. I think that she was just going to let Julie know her suspicions. That way Rita could ensure that if Julie had seen anything, then at least she'd keep her mouth shut.'

'So who did Julie meet in Rainsford the day she was killed?' Archie asked, puzzled. 'She was dead before Rita's letter arrived for her, so what was she doing there?'

Stredwick smiled. 'You know, son, you expect too much certainty from the world; you expect too many answers. The simple explanation is that I don't know. Perhaps she was going to meet a boyfriend? Perhaps he was married? I don't know, I just don't know. The police haven't managed to discover anyone who'll admit to a tryst. My opinion, for what it's worth, is that she met Carrington. I think because we were nosing about, Carrington was getting edgy in case she cracked and told us anything; he was another one who wanted to ensure her silence. I'll confess to you, right up until the police made their arrest, Webber and I both thought Carrington had killed her. It seemed the only logical explanation. Otherwise we'd have had to admit the coincidence of a woman who'd got assaulted ten years before, getting assaulted again.

'Mind you,' he said, an unmistakable note of anger in his voice, 'perhaps that isn't so much of a coincidence as it seems. Look at the statistics: violence against women is like child abuse—there's far more of it taking place than gets reported, far more than society likes to accept.'

Stredwick went silent. Outside another car screeched around a corner; another group of men made their way noisily along the street. In the distance the wail of a police siren pierced the night.

'So Elizabeth Carrington wasn't involved at all?' Archie asked. 'But she must have been at the hotel sometime that day to have seen Harbinder Singh. Why didn't she tell the police she'd been there?'

Stredwick got to his feet. 'My God, you want spoonfeeding, don't you? You want all the odds and ends neatly tied up like a Christmas parcel. How the hell am I supposed to know? You're the one who's been in Yorkshire doing the research. Besides, I don't look for the clear solutions like you. I've done too many of these cases ever to believe you can know every detail about what happened, even if you wanted to. And remember, I've never wanted to. I've only ever wanted to know if Terry Frampton committed that murder . . .'

'You're avoiding the question.'

'Not at all,' said Stredwick. 'But I just want you to understand that though real murders can sometimes be as complicated as detective stories, most of them, when you strip away the dross, are basically as simple as this one. Murder's a simple response to a problem; that means most of the time the solution to a murder is simple too. The way people respond to murder though?—well, that's a different matter altogether, that can be as complicated as their response to life itself. Believe me, the complexity of that is difficult to exaggerate.

'I really don't know what Elizabeth Carrington was doing at the hotel that day. Perhaps she'd forgotten something, left something behind. Perhaps she'd seen her husband pick up Julie in Rainsford, and perhaps despite her acidic comments about him, there was some suspicion in the back of her mind that the two of them might have been having an affair. But really . . . I just don't know, this is all conjecture. I don't think we'll ever know what she saw, only that she saw something that clearly implicated her husband in a murder.

'It played on her conscience, though,' said Stredwick. 'I think that's why their marriage broke up and they sold the hotel. It was almost certainly the reason she told you she'd seen Harbinder Singh—even though she knew that by doing that it would eventually come back to her. For a while I thought telling you about Harbinder was a way of deflecting suspicion from her husband; now I'm more inclined to think it was a way of shopping him. But who knows? As I say, it's difficult to predict the way people react to murder. That's why murder is a difficult crime to fathom.'

CHAPTER 28

'So you won't be making a programme, after all?' June asked as they drove to their hotel. It wasn't late, just a little after one o' clock, but London wasn't New York and though the roads were busy with cars, the pavements were all but deserted. From time to time they'd pass a group leaving a restaurant, or two or three young people on their way to a party somewhere. Here and there they'd go by a small crowd huddled around a bus stop waiting grimly for some night service, or pass a club where they'd hear the faint bass throb of a disco beat, and, through a guarded doorway, glimpse the flickering of lights inside.

It had begun to rain and a pall seemed to have descended on the city.

Archie shook his head. 'No, there's no evidence worth speaking of. And even if there was . . . Christ, Frampton's a rapist. There might not technically have been a rape, and he might not even have been actively involved with what happened. But he's as guilty as if he had.'

'Not guilty of murder, though,' said June.

Archie stared out of the window, tracing the gathering raindrops with his finger as they ran down the glass. 'I know, it worries me,' he said eventually. 'And I wonder, was it all worth it? I mean, I go to Yorkshire, I upset people's lives, I nearly lose you and nearly lose my life in the process—and what for? Stredwick maintains he's after the truth investigating cases, but when he arrives at the truth, he sits on it. Truth can't exist in a vacuum. It's like justice. Justice is only justice when it's publicly acknowledged. Surely the truth needs confirmation somewhere?'

'Stredwick says that court cases don't take place to establish truth,' said June. 'I was talking to him about it at the hotel the night you got shot. He said that court cases are about the innocence or guilt of the person in the dock and that truth hasn't got a lot to do with it. I can see what he means now. Strictly speaking, what happened to Julie Taylor wasn't anything to do with Alexander's murder, was it? But it was part of the truth of it, all the same.'

'Surely, if it's worth anything, justice has got to be indivisible,' said Archie. 'It has to apply to the dishonest as well as the honest. It's no use saying that just because a man's a thief he shouldn't be judged fairly if he's accused of a robbery . . .'

'Or because he's a rapist, he should be judged guilty of a murder he didn't commit?'

Archie shrugged his shoulders. 'I just don't know,' he said. 'It's difficult. Truth and justice are so entangled in this case. The truth is that Frampton didn't commit that murder but if he'd have been charged with his part in the assault on Julie Taylor he might have received a sentence just as long. So I suppose there's been a sort of justice done, even I couldn't deny that.'

'Then why are you so unhappy?' asked June. 'What do you want to do? Make a programme saying that a woman killed by a rapist had been abused once before in her life; that a man who'd had his face viciously slashed wanted revenge on the person who did it to him? Do you really want to make a programme that pries into Rita and Maureen's sex lives and brings the tabloids camping on their doorsteps again? God knows, more than enough's likely to come out anyhow. George has had to bend over backwards already to keep the shooting out of the papers, but now you're well enough to give evidence there's no way he could stop the police charging Rita, even if he wanted to.'

'I just don't know,' said Archie again. 'Murder—any murder—even of a man like Alexander—is such an absolute crime. It seems wrong that someone isn't punished for it. It seems wrong that Carrington should just get away with it. I realize it's absurd, but now I know what happened, I feel I ought to be somehow comforted by the truth. Yet I'm not. Rather than feel there's any order in the world I feel—I don't know—as if I've edged open some window and seen the awful chaos outside. Ridiculous, isn't it?'

June pulled the car into the hotel car park. She manœuvred into a free space, switched off the engine and reached over and hugged him. 'You're tired,' she said. 'You need to sleep. I don't know if it makes you feel better, but Carrington hasn't got away with it. According to George, he's got cancer. He's dying, Archie, and he's going to die alone and embittered. Isn't there a sort of justice in that?'

At that moment there was a knock at the window, a hotel commissionaire, dressed in a purple uniform with military epaulettes. 'Mr Archibold? Do excuse me, but a Mr Stredwick sent this around by motorbike messenger. He asked particularly that you were given it tonight, the moment you arrived. Apparently he'd intended to give it to you himself this evening but it slipped his mind.'

He handed Archie a canvas hold-all. In it were half a dozen black lever-arch files.

'I was asked to tell you that it was another case,' the commissionaire said. 'A murder case, you know,' he explained, as if he were called upon daily to deliver files of murder cases to hotel guests.

After he'd gone June and Archie stood against the car staring at each other speechlessly.

'Is he mad?' asked June eventually.

'I think so,' said Archie, 'I'm really beginning to think so.'

But as he picked up the bag he noticed something lying at the bottom.

It was a bottle of Lagavulin.